Janice Sims

Constant Craving

ARABESQUE®

ISBN-13: 978-1-58314-806-8
ISBN-10:   1-58314-806-X

CONSTANT CRAVING

www.kimanipress.com

Printed in U.S.A.

I am my dear one's, and toward me is his craving.

—*The Song of Solomon* 7:10

This craving is constant, not something
that comes and goes like the tide.
A fearless kind of yearning that knows
no boundaries, and does not hide.
There is no doubt that you are desired
and valued. Love does no harm.
It lifts up, accepts flaws, has faith, and
seduces with heart-pounding charm.
Yet, it embraces truth because lies cloud
judgment and renders you weak.
Strength lies in having your eyes wide open.
It's *true* happiness you seek.

—*The Book of Counted Joys*

Chapter 1

The scream of frustration was shrill but short-lived. It came from the bride's room. It was Saturday, December 10th. Elise Gilbert, who was not a member of the wedding party but the date of the bride's brother Franklyn, heard the shriek as she walked past the door on the way back from the bathroom. She stopped and listened.

No more screams. She was concerned, but didn't want to barge in if there was nothing seriously wrong. But then another, longer, scream came from the other side of the door.

Elise immediately turned the doorknob, found the door unlocked and strode into the room.

Erica Bryant, the bride, was standing in front of a full-length mirror in her wedding dress and holding her side, where a long rip revealed the skin of her midriff. Her short black hair was freshly washed but not yet styled.

She looked at Elise with a panicked expression. "I don't

know how this happened. The seam ripped open like tissue paper. What am I going to do!"

Elise closed the door behind her and walked farther into the room. She and Erica were both in their late twenties. Elise was taller by a couple of inches and also weighed more than Erica. They didn't seem to have much in common. Elise had just started dating Erica's brother, and she and Erica had met on only two occasions, so she was a little reluctant to offer advice on Erica's wedding day; she might not take it well.

Elise gently clasped the torn sides of the dress, assessing the damage.

Thankfully, it was just a matter of the stitches coming undone. It wasn't the first time a seamstress had had her sewing machine malfunction and not perform its job adequately. The length of the stitches was, she noticed, too long, and when Erica had put on the dress, putting stress on the seams, they had naturally split.

Elise smiled. "It's not as bad as it appears. Do you have a sewing machine?"

They were in Glen Ellen, California, at the hacienda-style home of Eric and Simone Bryant, Erica's parents. The Bryants were winemakers, proprietors of one of the few African-American-owned wineries in the country.

Erica shook her head. "No, that's not a skill Mom or I ever had an interest in learning."

"Needle and thread?" Elise asked. She could repair the dress by hand. It would just take longer.

"Yes," Erica said, brightening. "Oh, Elise, if you can fix this mess I'd be eternally grateful. You've already come through with that beautiful cake!"

"It was my pleasure," Elise assured her with a smile. "If

you'll take the dress off and go get the needle and thread, I'll check out the damage while you're gone."

She placed her purse on the canopied bed and sat down.

"I can't believe this is happening to me," Erica said, her voice muffled due to the dress covering her head. "I should have known some disaster would strike me. Things have been going *way* too smoothly."

She handed the dress to Elise, then looked at her reflection in the mirror. "Maybe I've gained weight since my last fitting."

"That's not it," Elise said. She told her about the faulty stitches. "My mom does a lot of sewing. She taught my sisters and me. This is not your doing."

Erica breathed a sigh of relief and fairly beamed at Elise. She liked Elise. She didn't want to be too demonstrative, though, because she didn't want to chase the poor girl off. She tried not to grin too widely when she saw Elise and Franklyn together. The sight of Franklyn in love made her so happy, she felt like doing triple somersaults. It had been a long time coming.

According to Lettie Burrows, Franklyn's sous chef and a close friend of the family, Franklyn had been head over heels in love with Elise for nearly three years. If not for Lettie's keen observations, Erica and her mother, Simone, might not have known about Franklyn's attraction to Elise. Franklyn was painfully shy.

Erica had thought it was a minor miracle when he'd had the nerve to ask Elise to the harvest celebration here at the winery a few months ago. Later, it had been her idea to ask Elise, a pastry chef, to make their cake. Now Franklyn had brought her with him to their wedding. A man didn't ask a woman to a wedding unless he was serious about her.

"I'll be right back," Erica said as she slipped on a bathrobe and headed for the door.

Elise was busy studying the material where the seam had come apart. "All right," she said, then peered back down at the dress. There wasn't any damage to the material, so if she stitched it closed, Erica should have no more problems with seams ripping.

Erica was back with the needle and a spool of thread in less than three minutes.

Elise accepted them, held the thread against the dress. The color was a close match.

Erica watched her as she threaded the needle, secured a knot in the end and began sewing the seam closed.

Erica took the opportunity to observe her. She was really attractive, though not in a glamorous way. Her brown skin had red undertones, and was healthy-looking.

She had a sprinkling of freckles across her nose that gave her a youthful appearance.

The eyes in her heart-shaped, high-cheekboned face, were dark and intelligent.

She had full, bow-shaped lips that were tinted rose-red and, at the moment, were pursed as she sewed. Her thick, jet-black, shoulder-length hair was straightened and combed back from a widow's peak.

It looked very nice in the relaxed, upswept style she was wearing.

Erica didn't spend much time assessing other women's facial features, but she readily admitted that Elise had the type of face that most men would be drawn to.

And she looked fit. Erica remembered Franklyn saying that Elise biked nearly every day. No wonder she had such great legs.

Sitting across from Elise on the bed, Erica said, "May I ask you a personal question? Just tell me to mind my own business if you don't want to answer."

Elise briefly met Erica's eyes before lowering her gaze again to her sewing. "Go ahead," she said cautiously.

"You've been married before, right?"

Elise nodded. She didn't like talking about Derrick. She was content to leave him in the past, an afterthought, a vague notion, someone she didn't waste her brain cells on anymore. But she tried not to frown when Erica brought him up. She wanted to make a good impression on Franklyn's family. She liked them and hoped they would learn to like her eventually.

Erica was reluctant to go on probing unless she got some kind of signal from Elise that it was okay to proceed. And Elise was looking down at the dress in her hands.

Erica cleared her throat.

Elise looked up again. "I divorced him more than four years ago when I was twenty-five."

"You divorced *him?*"

"Yes. Actually, he left me after he passed the bar exam, but he was dragging his feet about divorcing me. So, I got things rolling instead. You would have to know Derrick Scott—I took my name back after the divorce—to understand why that was so important to me. He was controlling and abusive…"

"He hit you?" Erica cried, shocked.

"No, what he did was worse." Elise met Erica's eyes. "A punch in the face eventually heals. The wounds he inflicted on me were more than skin-deep. He was a master at derision and insults. He belittled me. Tore down my self-esteem. It was his goal to break me. But luckily, I recognized his intent and got out in time. Still, it's taken me a long time to be able to trust another man."

"Franklyn would never do anything like that!" Erica vehemently declared.

"I know," Elise said with a warm smile. "Your brother is the gentlest man I've ever known."

Erica smiled back, content. "Yes, yes he is." Franklyn was special, a genuinely good man. Looking into Elise's eyes, she knew she didn't have to tell her that.

Instead, she got to her feet, and began pacing the room. "Know what I wish we women had? A Girlfriend's Network!" Her brown eyes sparkled with excitement as she continued, still pacing. "Whenever one of our girlfriends got mistreated by some heartless guy, we'd spring into action. Maybe he'd be at a cocktail party and a gorgeous woman would walk up to him and ask, 'Is your name Derrick Scott?' He'd smile roguishly, because like most men, he'd think he was about to score. 'Yes,' he'd proudly say, flashing a sexy smile while he confidently popped a shrimp puff into his mouth. All of a sudden, the babe would pimp-slap him! The shrimp puff would fly in one direction and his smug face would turn in the other. By the time his eyes got uncrossed, the anonymous babe would be gone, lost in the crowd. A drive-by pimp-slapping! Girl, that would be so cool!"

When Erica finished, Elise was laughing so hard tears were rolling down her face.

"I'd pay good money to see that," she said.

"You and your girlfriends never got even with him?" Erica wanted to know.

"My cousin, Mariel, wanted to slash his tires," Elise said, smiling at the memory.

Mariel always had her back. "But I talked her out of it. I was satisfied just being divorced from him. I felt as if the life was slowly coming back into me."

"He was a soul-sucker, huh?"

"The worst kind of soul-sucker. He was so good at it he

could make you think you deserved every mean, vile thing he said to you. I pity the woman who's with him now."

Erica sat on the bed. "Do you ever see him?"

Elise groaned. "Unfortunately, yes. He lives in San Francisco, and we still have mutual friends. Most of the time, though, we're not invited to the same parties. Our friends have learned to keep us apart as much as possible. But, maybe once a year, I still see him. When we spot each other either I'll leave if I got there last, or he'll leave if he got there last."

"Sort of a silent agreement?"

"Yes. I don't think he really wants to be in the same room with me for too long. I might explode and embarrass him. He hates public spectacles. Thinks they're beneath him."

She finished sewing the seam, and handed the dress to Erica. "Go ahead, put it on and let me see how it looks."

Erica got up and slipped the dress over her head. Elise helped her with the buttons.

Erica turned this way and that, looking for some telltale sign that the dress had been hastily stitched-up by hand, but she found none. Elise had done a good job.

She impulsively hugged Elise. "Thank you, you saved me. I'll never forget you for this. I owe you big-time."

Elise only smiled as she patted Erica on the back. "You're welcome. And it was no bother at all, believe me."

They parted and Elise went to get her purse off the bed. "Well, I'd better go. Franklyn will be wondering where I got to. Have a wonderful wedding, Erica."

"I will, thanks to you," Erica happily said as she turned around to admire herself in the mirror just as she'd been doing when Elise had come into the room. This time, however, she was smiling at her reflection, instead of frowning at it.

* * *

Franklyn was in the solarium with his mother. Simone was going down the aisle making certain the satin bows on the chairs were straight. Franklyn thought the bows looked fine, but occasionally his mother would pause and straighten a bow that she'd determined was askew.

The guests were not supposed to be arriving for thirty minutes. The ceremony would be held here in the solarium, the largest room in the house. From the solarium the guests would walk through French doors into the even larger space of the covered back patio that had been transformed into a dining room. There were more than twenty tables. Each table comfortably accommodated six people. Simone's kitchen, her favorite space in the house because she was a professional chef, now had three caterers and a waitstaff of ten in it putting the final touches on the meal.

The wedding singer and his band had already set up their instruments on the stage and were tuning guitars and doing sound checks in preparation for their opening number.

"How is Jason doing since he moved back home?" Franklyn asked. His younger brother had given up his career as an attorney in Bakersfield to take over running the winery. A few months ago their father, Eric, had suffered a mild heart attack and decided to retire. He and Simone were supposed to hit the road in an RV shortly after Erica and Joshua's wedding.

Now, they had another passenger to take with them: Simone's mother, Monique, who was left homeless, after the devastation Hurricane Katrina caused in New Orleans—where she'd lived since birth.

"He's adjusting," Simone said, her voice low. "Jason never had the patience you and Erica did when it came to learning about the business. But he's giving it his best, which is all we can ask."

"His heart's not in it?" Franklyn asked. His younger brother had never figured he'd be the one to step into their parents' shoes and take over the winery. Like Franklyn, he'd thought Erica would be the one to do it. It seemed that she'd been prepared from birth. However, when she'd fallen in love with Joshua, a winemaker who wanted to start his own legacy, she had done what any woman would have done, she'd chosen to help him build that legacy.

Simone paused in the aisle and looked up into Franklyn's golden-brown eyes. "Don't worry about him, he'll be okay. Jason has never been bested by a challenge. And this is possibly his greatest challenge. All these years he's been thinking like a divorce attorney and now he's got to, in his words, think like a 'gentleman farmer.'" She laughed shortly. "Though, God knows, I don't know what a gentleman farmer is. We worked so hard we didn't have time to be gentlemanly about it. He'll learn that, too."

"Hard work has never been Jason's forte," Franklyn said without malice. He loved and respected his brother. Jason had simply always taken the route that did not lead to too much physical labor, that's all. He'd chosen law literally because it didn't entail anything that would get his hands dirty. He liked his expensive suits, fine cars and luxurious surroundings. His house in Bakersfield was a showplace. Franklyn knew Jason had cried when he'd had to sell it.

"That's true," Simone agreed. "He hates getting his hands dirty. He'll just have to wear gloves."

Elise entered the solarium, and Franklyn instinctively turned. His wide mouth broke into a smile. Elise's dark-brown eyes lit up in response. "Where have you been?" he asked as he closed the distance between them and pulled her into his arms.

Elise allowed herself to be enveloped in his embrace. She wasn't used to a man being so sensual. Franklyn took every opportunity to hug her, kiss her cheek, or simply pull her close to his side. The result was he made her feel safe and secure. To say nothing of all warm inside.

He dropped a casual kiss on her forehead and released her, taking a step back in order to gaze into her eyes. Franklyn never got tired of looking into Elise's eyes. In them he saw all of his dreams for the future taking shape. There'd been a time when he'd looked into her eyes, and seen only caution. Interest, yes, but she didn't trust him. She was still trying to figure him out.

Being a patient man, Franklyn became dedicated to one thing: making Elise see him for what he truly was inside. Nothing short of that would win her trust.

She was looking at him now with a bit of embarrassment in her eyes. Franklyn had forgotten his mother was present. Elise was still reticent about being demonstrative in his family's presence.

"She knows how I feel about you," Franklyn told her.

Elise began to blush.

Simone laughed. "Heck, I knew before *he* knew." She briefly hugged Elise.

"Sweetie, Franklyn takes after his father when it comes to being affectionate. And that man has never been able to keep his hands off me. Don't I look happy?"

Smiling, Elise nodded. "You look *very* happy."

Indeed, Simone's happiness shone like a beacon from within. A petite woman in her late fifties with skin the color of dark honey, she looked the picture of health. Short auburn hair with blond streaks softly framed her pretty face, and the emerald-green silk dress she wore with one shoulder on display fit her plump, yet tone, body well. Matching pumps with three-inch heels showcased her shapely legs.

Elise hoped she'd look as fabulous when she was in her fifties.

"Then take it from me," Simone told her, "soak up all that loving and give it back. You can never overdose on love."

"If there were anything I'd want to overdose on, it would be love," Franklyn said with a smile as he clasped Elise's hand in his. "Come on, let's go check out the band. I can hear them warming up." He knew by the trembling of Elise's hand that although his mother was trying to make her feel at ease, she was only making her more nervous.

In some settings, at the restaurant for example, Elise claimed her domain—owned it, even. She was the best pastry chef he'd ever worked with. But in some social situations, she was at a loss. He wondered why. She was smart, accomplished in her field, attractive, all the things that would imbue the average person with boundless confidence. He could understand shyness. He'd been afflicted with it since he was a child. But he didn't think shyness was Elise's problem. There was something deep-seated that prevented her from believing in her right to happiness. He guessed it might have something to do with her ex-husband, but he didn't know if he actually *wanted* to know what it was. If he found out Derrick Scott had done something to hurt Elise, he might be tempted to give up nearly eight years of having total control over his temper.

Eight years ago, he'd been in a very bad place. So bad that he had never confided in his mother about it, and he told his mother practically everything. He had never told his mother because he was ashamed of his behavior. His parents hadn't raised a brute, and that's what he'd been. He still had scars on his knuckles from the fistfights.

He caught a glimpse of the back of his hand now as he gently rubbed Elise's satin cheek. She would probably not want him to touch her if she were aware of the damage his hands had inflicted on some poor guy's face.

She smiled at him. "I'm sorry. I don't know why I'm so nervous. Your mother is the sweetest woman, and funny, too."

"Don't apologize," he said softly, but firmly.

He pulled out a chair for her to sit down. He sat across from her with his elbows on the table, and his eyes on her face. "Don't apologize for your true feelings, Elise. We can't get to know one another if we're not honest with each other. I'm sure when I meet your family I'm going to feel a little uncomfortable around them for a while."

Elise hadn't offered to take him home to meet her parents yet. But they'd only been dating for about four months. He was sure he'd get an invitation to Sacramento one of these days. Her parents owned a bakery there. That was where she'd caught the baking bug. Evidently, like him, she'd been cooking since she was a small child.

Elise placed her hands on her cheeks, feeling them heat up. She looked into Franklyn's eyes. His smile sat in them. Her stomach muscles constricted painfully. The thing was, whenever she was in Franklyn's presence, her body was in a continually tumultuous state. Desire coursed through her, alternating with spasms of fear and indecision. She was so drawn to him that she wanted to abandon common sense and give herself to him, fully and without reservation. On the other hand, she was afraid it was too soon, and the last thing she wanted to do was rush into a physical relationship. That could be a mistake on many levels. Her admiration for

Franklyn had lasted for nearly four years, ever since the day she'd walked into the Vineyard restaurant and interviewed for the job of pastry chef she'd been extremely attracted to him.

Attraction and acting on it were two different things. Franklyn was her boss, and she would never come on to her boss. She had to wait for him to make the first move. After three years of waiting, she was weary, *no*, plain worn out. She didn't think he'd ever make a move, even though she'd caught him looking at her with interest on many occasions. She'd figured Franklyn didn't want to risk losing a good pastry chef should his overtures be rebuffed. He was devoted to the Vineyard and, through hard work and sacrifice, had achieved a fine balance where everything ran efficiently. He didn't want to mess with success.

When he'd finally spoken up and asked her to go home with him for the weekend to attend his family's yearly grape harvest celebration she had been so happy she had immediately wanted to say yes. And then he'd tacked on the fact that she would be perfectly safe with him for the weekend because he respected their working relationship too much to jeopardize it. That declaration threw cold water on her hopes of their ever having any other kind of a relationship. He was smart enough, however, to come to her and explain that he'd lied— he was interested in more than a working relationship. In fact, he wanted her in his life outside of work.

Now they were cooking with gas!

But she felt as if their relationship had stalled somewhat. Not because of anything Franklyn had done. She couldn't ask for a more attentive lover. Not exactly lover, because they hadn't made love yet. Boyfriend, then? Nah, they were too old at twenty-nine and thirty-five, respectively, to refer to themselves in such a juvenile fashion.

The guy she was dating? No, she felt too intensely for Franklyn to put that label on him. He wasn't just someone she was dating. She adored him, and it wasn't fair of her to keep him at a distance just because her past with her ex-husband was intruding on the present.

She reached across the table to take one of his big hands in hers. Peering intently into his eyes, she said, "Franklyn, I don't know if this is the right time to tell you…. No, I take that back, I *know* this isn't the right time. But I'm going to tell you, anyway. The reason I behave the way that I do in some social situations, and the reason I have kept you at arm's length for four months is that, even though I've tried over the years, I can't get the abusive things my ex-husband used to say to me, or the feelings they caused, out of my mind. I guess you can take the abused woman out of the situation, but you can't take the abusive words out of her brain!"

The muscles worked in Franklyn's strong jaw. He took a deep breath before speaking.

Elise saw a vein appear in his otherwise smooth temple. She knew what that meant: he was trying to contain his anger. Franklyn didn't often get angry with anyone, but tempers flared in the kitchen sometimes. You couldn't help it when so many different personalities were working together under pressure.

"You're angry," she blurted out.

"Not at you," Franklyn was quick to explain. He gently squeezed her hand and maintained eye contact as he said, "A minute ago I was thinking that something must have happened to you for you to have stopped believing in the possibility of happiness."

"But I do…" Elise started to contradict him, but clamped

her mouth shut. Denying it would serve no purpose. She took a deep breath, and sighed. "I do have a problem believing in 'happily ever after.'"

Franklyn bent his head, brought her hand to his mouth and kissed her fingers. "Thank you for being honest with me. Now, tell me everything."

Elise's heartbeat sped up. Even now, when she knew she could trust Franklyn with her secrets, it was still hard to open up and say the words. "I don't want you to think I'm weak or that I somehow asked to be mistreated because I didn't do anything about it for three years."

"I won't, Elise," Franklyn assured her. His eyes narrowed. "Maybe I should tell you about my dark years. Then you'll know that I'm completely sympathetic."

Elise laughed nervously. "Dark years, Franklyn? You're the most together person I know. Always positive, you don't seem to let anything get you down."

"Then I've put on a pretty good act," he told her, smiling.

Elise leaned slightly forward. "I'm listening."

Franklyn cleared his throat. "You've noticed that I have a limp some days."

Elise nodded. "Mostly on overcast days. Sometimes on very cold days."

Franklyn smiled. She was very observant. Those were the times when the pain was most unbearable. "When I was a kid I broke my leg in several places while trying to jump onto the back of a horse who was smarter than I was. I was too dumb to know jumping from the roof of a barn wasn't a good idea, but he instinctively knew that sticking around for me to land on his back was unwise."

"Oh, *Franklyn*," Elise said, sympathy and sadness in her tone.

Franklyn only laughed, and continued, "Anyway, I've had a limp ever since."

"It doesn't stop you from doing anything you want to," Elise said with admiration.

"Not now, it doesn't," he confidently said. "But there was a time when having a limp made me feel less than a man."

Elise remained silent, urging him on with the encouraging expression in her big brown eyes. Franklyn felt revived by her support. For a minute there, he was reliving the humiliation.

"About eight years ago, I fell in love and wanted to get married and start a family."

Elise was listening intently. Eight years ago…that meant he was twenty-seven.

"But when I asked her to marry me, she laughed and said that it had been fun, but she couldn't marry a man who would be old before his time. She didn't look forward to being my nursemaid when I became a cripple."

Elise stretched her eyes in horror. Imagine someone you loved saying something that cruel to you.

"What an evil witch!" she cried.

Franklyn chuckled. "She definitely wasn't a nice woman. But the fact is, Elise, I let her get away with those kinds of comments because I thought I deserved them. I thought myself unworthy of someone better. I let my injury define me. Lessen me. Here I am, six-three, two-hundred and forty pounds, and I felt puny."

"All because of a limp!" Elise exclaimed. "Franklyn, do you know how wonderful you are?" Her tone was incredulous, disbelieving, totally astounded. "You created an award-winning restaurant with just a dream. You treat your employees with respect and kindness. The women who work for you adore you, and the men who work for you would die for you. You have a magnificent family and loyal friends. Good God, what more could a man ask for?"

Franklyn grinned at her, his eyes twinkling, and white teeth shining beneath his thick moustache. "Don't forget I've also got a good woman in my life. I couldn't ask for anything more. But eight years ago, after she dumped me, I went on a bender and courted disaster. I'd go to bars almost every night, get drunk and instigate fights. Sometimes I'd kick ass, other nights I'd get *my* ass kicked. But I loved pummeling them and I loved getting pummeled even more. I know," he added patiently. "It was sick. I wanted to prove to myself that I wasn't weak. I could take it. I wasn't going to end up a cripple before my time. Damn it, I wasn't even thirty. Then, after one hell of fight I ended up facedown in an alley on a cold and rainy night with my nose busted and several cracked ribs. When I hauled my carcass to the hospital, I decided then and there that the problem wasn't with me, it was with her. I could go on punishing myself, but the fact was she didn't love me. 'Love isn't spiteful. Love doesn't look for perfection. Love doesn't seek to tear down.'"

Elise had tears in her eyes as she turned his hand over and looked at the scars on his knuckles. "That's how you got these."

"I didn't have sense enough to wear leather gloves whenever I hit somebody."

Elise brought his hand up and placed her cheek in the palm of it. She smiled at him.

"You're such a gentle man, I can't imagine you hitting anybody."

"And I hope you never see that side of me," Franklyn told her. "I've vowed never to hit another person in anger."

Elise narrowed her eyes at him. "Except in self-defense," she said. "I love you, Franklyn. If your life is ever threatened,

you have to defend yourself. Pacifism is one thing, but promising never to strike anyone in anger again, no matter what,
is not reasonable."

Franklyn's mind froze at her assertion of love. She loved
him! She'd never said those words before. He abruptly stood
up, pulled her to him and kissed her mouth. Elise was so
stunned she was powerless to resist, and she didn't want to.
His mouth was so sweet, his method, intense, masterful and
wholly pleasure-inducing.

He held her firmly. He had to, because she was weak in
the knees. Elise felt that if she were no longer able to support
herself, she could just let go and he'd sweep her up in his arms
and carry her away. Yes, his kisses were that intoxicating.

When they came up for air she looked at him like a lovesick
idiot. She was about to ask him what she'd done to deserve
that, when his brother Jason came into the room and said,
"Hey, you two, break it up. It's not fair, flaunting your happy
relationship around someone who can't even get a date!"

Franklyn pulled Elise to his side, his arm draped about her
shoulders. "And that someone would be you, right?"

Jason dropped into one of the chairs at the table where
they'd been sitting, and with a sigh said, "You've got that
right. There are no fine sisters in this town. A brother could
die of starvation if he needed love for sustenance."

"Excuse me, Franklyn, is that you?" a sweet feminine
voice asked from the entrance.

The three of them looked up at the tall, shapely sister with
long, glistening braids. She was wearing a lovely deep-purple
sleeveless dress with a pale silver shawl. Her shoes and accessories were also in tones of silver.

Jason was speechless, so Franklyn stepped forward and
clasped Sara Minton's hand.

"Sara, don't you look beautiful!"

"Thank you, Franklyn. You look wonderful yourself." She smiled at Elise. "What a beautiful dress."

Elise smiled modestly. The jewel-toned multicolored silk dress had practically called her name when she'd seen it in Macy's. She was glad another woman found it pretty.

"Right back at you," she said. "That color is gorgeous on you."

When he could get a word in, Franklyn made the introductions. "Elise, this is Sara Minton. We all went to the same high school. I was a few years ahead of her and Jason, though. Sara, this is Elise Gilbert, the woman I adore."

Elise blushed outrageously. She also glowed with an inner pride.

She and Sara looked at each other as only sisters do when they're in the presence of a brother who can lay it down, and lay it down righteously.

"Girl," said Sara, "you can't beat that with a stick!"

And then they gave each other a high five.

Franklyn threw his head back and laughed.

Jason groaned as he got to his feet. "Lord, Franklyn, have you no pride? You don't say that kind of thing in front of two black women and survive! She's going to eat you alive now."

Elise boldly sidled up to Franklyn, tiptoed and kissed his chin. "It's true," she whispered. "I *could* eat you alive!"

Franklyn grinned as if the prospect was something he looked forward to.

Chapter 2

The wedding ceremony was held by candlelight.

Erica and Joshua could not keep their eyes off each other. After the minister pronounced them husband and wife they wept tears of joy. Their kiss was long and tender. Parting, they gazed into each other's eyes, and burst out laughing.

They had been so nervous prior to the ceremony. Now, they couldn't imagine why. This was a piece of cake. The hard part was over with. Life was going to be grand!

Enthusiastic applause erupted when Joshua swept Erica into his arms and carried her down the aisle. "Do we have to stay for the reception?" he whispered in her ear.

"Just a little while, sweetie," Erica replied, her arms around his neck.

They would stay in a local inn tonight, and tomorrow would drive to San Francisco where they would get a flight to Fiji. Two weeks in a tropical paradise, then back up north to Healdsburg. If they were lucky, they would open their winery in about three years.

Erica's brothers acted as footmen and held the French doors open for her and Joshua to walk through. She smiled at them from her perch in Joshua's arms.

"Jason, don't let Sara leave here without asking her out," she admonished as she moved past. "She came, even when she knew *you* would be here. That says a lot."

"Why don't you just keep walking with her?" Jason said to his new brother-in-law. "Straight out of the house. Nobody will miss her."

Erica, Joshua and Franklyn laughed.

Jason didn't crack a smile. He meant it. If not for his meddlesome sister, Sara Minton would have still been in his past. But, no, Erica had to chat her up to their mother who fell in love with the notion of him and Sara getting together. Now, he had both his mother and his nosy sister pushing him to date Sara. Easier said than done. Sara Minton hated the sight of him.

After he and Franklyn had secured both doorstops, Jason blended in with the flow of guests leaving the solarium and going outside to the covered patio. He happened to join the flow right when his grandmother, Monique, was strolling past. If it were humanly possible, she was even bossier than her granddaughter.

She grasped his arm with surprisingly strong fingers. "Darlin', be a dear and get your grandmother a bourbon. I don't want one of those frilly feminine drinks that sound like a fruit cocktail, either. But have it put into one of those glasses. You get me? Your mother doesn't want me drinking hard liquor. I'll be at your parents' table with the Lafons and that good-looking Lucien Davis."

She let go of him then, and veered off in the direction of

her table. Jason didn't know what to do, supply his eighty-
year-old grandmother with booze, or simply ignore the
command. Ignoring Monique was not a wise decision.
Perhaps he could get away with a watered-down bourbon.
Probably not, she'd guess the ruse with one taste. Of course,
by then, he would have gone somewhere she wouldn't be able
to find him for the rest of the evening. It might work.

He continued to his table, and was not surprised to find
only one seat unoccupied.

It was right next to the one in which Sara Minton was
sitting.

"Good evening," he said politely as he pulled his chair out
and sat down.

The other two couples greeted him warmly. Sara gave him
an intriguing smile.

He wondered if she thought he'd planned things this way.
If she had known his mother and sister better she would know
he'd had nothing to do with it. He was just a pawn in their
little games. God, help him!

"You're the brother who's a divorce lawyer, right?" asked
Neal Harrison, husband to Zola. Jason knew Zola from high
school. She was one of Erica's friends. Miss Zola had a thing
for football players. She'd dated quite a few of his teammates,
and they'd all blabbed about it. There had been a running joke
among the players about how easy Zola Robertson was. He
chided himself. Why had he thought of such of thing with Sara
sitting right next to him? Hadn't he learned that experiences
you have in high school can haunt you for years? Maybe Zola
regretted having a reputation in high school.

"That's right," Jason said with a smile. "Although, I gave
it up a few months ago to come home and run the winery."

"You gave up practicing law?" Zola asked, her fine brows

arched in curiosity. "Or gave up practicing in Bakersfield to open an office here?"

"I'm not practicing any longer," Jason informed her.

She looked disappointed. "Oh."

Jason laughed shortly. "Believe me, this place keeps me very busy."

Zola forced a smile. "I'm sure it does."

Jason hoped he hadn't read disappointment in her reaction to his news that he was no longer practicing law because she was in need of his services.

Neal was giving his wife an odd look, too. He bent and said something in her ear to which Zola shrugged, laughed shortly, and said, "Don't be silly." She took a big swallow from her water glass, set it back on the table and directed her attention to Sara.

"Sara, I went by your store a few days ago, hoping to see you, and you weren't there, but the kids had a ball in the children's section. The woman who works there was so nice."

"You mean Frannie," Sara supplied her manager's name. "She loves children."

Zola smiled broadly. It was obvious she had genuinely enjoyed her visit to the store, and meeting Frannie. "I could tell. Neal, junior, and Giselle really took to her. She's never worked as a nanny has she, because I'd steal her away from you with no guilt whatsoever."

Sara laughed delightedly. "There'd be a fight, because Frannie is indispensable."

"If you need a nanny, you can have mine," the other woman at the table, Karen Saroyan, said. "I would pay you to take her."

"Now, Karen," Sebastian, her husband, cautioned, "Tatiana isn't that bad."

"You would say that," Karen said accusingly. "She's always flirting with you."

Sebastian, a short, balding man in his midforties only smiled sheepishly. He and Karen were opposites. She was tall and exotically beautiful. He looked as though he'd probably had a note to excuse him from gym throughout his school years due to frailty.

Sara liked him immediately.

"Oh, no," said Zola to Karen's plea to take her nanny off her hands. "If I ever caught her eyeing Neal, I'd probably get ethnic on her behind. I need someone who's good with the kids, but won't come on to Neal."

"Don't I get a vote in this?" Neal joked.

"No!" said Zola, and gave him a saucy look.

Smiling, Jason saw now that he'd been wrong about Zola needing his services as a divorce lawyer. She was very much in love with her husband.

Sara had been observing Jason out of the corner of her eye throughout the conversation. She hadn't seen him since the harvest celebration. He looked even better now than he had then, and he'd looked pretty spectacular *then*. Trimmer, a couple of inches shorter and less muscular than his older brother, Franklyn, he was nevertheless just as handsome.

Jason suddenly turned his gaze on her, and their eyes met. He looked away first.

"Excuse me," he said as he rose. "There's an open bar, and I promised my grandmother I'd bring her a drink."

Sara astonished him by saying, "I'll go with you."

Jason's heart was in his throat. He tried to remain calm as he held her chair.

Sara was five-nine, plus she was wearing heels. Jason liked the fact that she was nearly eye to eye with him, and he was six-foot-one. He rarely met women who were taller than he, but he didn't like it when their heads barely came to his chest. Sara had brains and a tall, voluptuous body. She looked like an angelic Amazon to him.

When they were out of earshot, Zola commented, "I knew they liked each other."

"Honey, keep your matchmaking nose out of it," Neal warned.

Zola smirked. "You did notice that they're the only single people at this table? Someone else has got them in their sights. The matchmaking has already begun."

Across the room, at Elise and Franklyn's table, Elise was discovering that Erica and her mother had seated them with foodies. Professional foodies, at that! It was one thing to have to share a meal with people who thought they were experts on food, and quite another when they had a diploma, or a career, to *prove* they were experts on food.

Franklyn didn't toot his own horn, and you would never know he was a chef, or owned a restaurant, if you didn't know him. He was too modest to brag. You couldn't say that about the Morrises or the Hitchcocks.

Bill and Natalie Morris were food critics at rival newspapers in San Francisco. They seemed to revel in their differences of opinion. They reminded Elise of that couple who were political consultants on opposite sides, one Republican, the other a Democrat. She supposed some people could thrive in that sort of relationship.

Garrison and Bailey Hitchcock were both chefs. More low-key than the Morrises, they were nonetheless enamored with dropping names of the celebrities they'd cooked for. And the unusual preferences those celebrities had when it came to the food they consumed.

After they were served the appetizers, Garrison carefully took a bite of the salmon pâté and looked as if he were having an orgasm. "Divine, absolutely divine."

Bill and Natalie Morris both agreed that the salmon pâté was "passable."

Bailey sided with her husband and pronounced it, "Wonderful, the perfect thing to begin a meal with." She washed it down with some of the Bryant family's best chardonnay.

"Who is the caterer?" Natalie wanted to know.

Franklyn shrugged as if he didn't know. He knew, but he wasn't about to tell a critic. Elise followed his example and claimed ignorance as well. She knew the caterer well. She'd worked with her on several occasions.

"Did you see that cake?" Natalie exclaimed, aghast. "Why, it looks like something King Tut would have had at his reception had he lived long enough to get married, poor dear."

Her husband was the only one to laugh at her joke.

Elise had decorated the white cake with Egyptian hieroglyphics, as directed by Erica who wanted an Egyptian theme. Elise thought she'd done a fine job. Erica and Joshua said they loved it, and that's what counted.

Franklyn grasped her hand underneath the table and squeezed it reassuringly. Elise smiled at him. He didn't think she was going to go off on the acid-tongued little critic, did he?

"Actually," said Bailey, "I think the cake is gorgeous. I love the stark whiteness of the icing, and the gold markings. I wonder what flavor it is."

"I have it on good authority that the icing is vanilla cream, and the cake itself is made with several delicate flavorings and spices. Something new that the chef created. I can't tell you which flavorings or spices, though," Elise said.

"I can't wait to taste it," Bailey said. "I love trying new desserts. A couple of friends and I are going to compete in the Championship Pastry Team competition early next year. We're looking for another chef to compete with us. His/her specialty must be cakes. We've already got competitors in the other three categories."

"I've seen that competition on TV," Elise said. "The chefs almost have to be artists to come up with those detailed designs."

"The pastries also have to be delicious," Bailey told her. "I know chefs who *are* artists when it comes to presentation, but their creations taste like cardboard. No, in order to win you must have presentation and skill, plus the ability to wow the judges' taste buds. So, if I had a choice between some artistic prima donna and a chef who makes extraordinarily yummy cakes, I would choose the latter. If that cake over there is as delicious as it looks, I'm going to track down the chef who made it and invite him or her to join us in the competition."

Good luck, Elise thought. She was happy being the pastry chef at the Vineyard.

At the bar, Jason was being handed his grandmother's watered-down bourbon. Sara stood three feet away sipping from a glass of sauvignon blanc. He smiled at her as he turned away from the bar. "Are you still with me?"

"Sure," Sara said. She fell into step beside him. "After all, it's apparent that you're my date for the evening."

"You got that impression, too, huh?"

"That sister of yours is a piece of work."

"You won't get an argument from me!"

"How have you lived with her all these years without trying to strangle her?"

"The thought *has* crossed my mind. Unfortunately, I love her."

Sara laughed. "Yes, that'll stop you every time."

The band was playing "The First Time Ever I Saw Your Face." The singer, a sister with a deep, sensual voice was doing a great rendition. Jason paused to look into Sara's eyes. She smiled at him. From now on he would remember that that song was playing the first time she had given him a genuine smile, one without any other motive except joy behind it.

They continued up front to his grandmother's table.

The funny thing was, now that he felt a barrier had come down between him and Sara, he didn't know if he was happy about it, or just plain scared. Sara Minton was unfathomable. He knew that she had been married before and that her husband had been killed in an accident more than five years ago. She'd come back to Glen Ellen when her mother had fallen ill about a year ago. Apparently, she'd done well in advertising in New York City. Well enough to afford to buy a business and a house, and settle down in her hometown.

She seemed extremely self-contained to him, as though she were so competent that she didn't need anyone except herself, and, in fact, preferred her own company to anyone else's.

"There you are, baby," Monique said gratefully when Jason handed her the bourbon disguised as a frou-frou drink complete with a pink umbrella. She crooked a finger at him denoting that she wanted him to lean down for a peck on the cheek.

This done, Jason introduced the folks at his parents' table to Sara: longtime family friends, Sobran and Fabienne Lafon from Beaune, France, his parents, Eric and Simone, whom she already knew, his grandmother Monique, and Lucien

Davis, an elderly neighbor and dear friend with whom Monique was flirting on the sly.

Sara smiled warmly, and said, "It's a pleasure to meet you all."

Everyone agreed that the feeling was mutual, after which Jason grasped Sara's hand and beat a hasty retreat. Simone couldn't help laughing as she watched her son dragging the poor girl off. "I do believe he wants to be alone with her."

"We didn't raise a dummy," Eric said.

"Where are you taking me?" Sara asked, laughing softly. She nearly had to run to keep up with Jason as he led her toward the back double doors, down the steps and into the expansive backyard.

The sound of the party was muffled now, and Sara breathed in the crisp winter air. She was glad she had her shawl, but it wouldn't hold up to the cold if they stayed out for very long. "I'm not dressed for a trek," she said.

"We're going to the cellars, the temperature's regulated down there. It'll be chilly, but not as cold as it is out here."

He let go of her hand long enough to shrug out of his coat, and place it around her shoulders. Then, he reclaimed her hand and they were off again.

"I just need five uninterrupted minutes with you," he promised.

"Five minutes to do what?"

"To state my case."

"This isn't a courtroom, and I'm not a judge."

"No, but you've been judging me unfairly ever since we met again, and I want to air my grievances."

"You already have," Sara reminded him. "You apologized, and I accepted. End of story."

By this time, they were at the entrance to the cellars. Jason disengaged the alarm, pushed open the heavy oak door, switched on the light, and allowed Sara to precede him down the stairs.

"Ooh," said Sara, "this is beginning to feel like one of those slasher movies. Dark cellar, a woman and a man alone. Are you sure your namesake isn't going to jump from behind one of those wine casks brandishing a chain saw and wearing that godforsaken mask he always wears?"

"It isn't Halloween, Sara. It's closer to Christmas."

"A demented Santa would fit the bill."

"I'm having a hard time deciding whether I want to kill you or kiss you," Jason told her. "Keep this up. I'm beginning to lean toward killing you."

Sara laughed. She'd reached the bottom of the stairs and turned to look up at him with her back against the brick wall of the cellar. "You could stuff my body in one those casks, and nobody would be able to find me."

Jason went to her and leaned close, his face mere inches from hers. She was still holding the wineglass, but she'd drunk all of the sauvignon blanc. Jason took the glass and set it atop one of the barrels. The room was vast, big enough to house hundreds of wine barrels. With the door closed, the silence surrounding them was that of a tomb.

"Why did you come?" Jason asked her, his eyes commanding her complete attention.

"Your sister invited me, and I like your sister, so I came." Sara's formerly confident voice had lost some of its swagger. He could tell he had her sweating underneath that cool facade.

"Is that the only reason you decided to come?"

Sara's eyes narrowed. "I also wanted to taunt you. We had such fun doing that the last time we met, I thought an encore was in order."

Jason smiled at that. Indeed, the last time they'd seen one another, she had told him that hell would freeze over before she would go out with him, and he'd told her to get her ice skates ready because he wasn't through with her yet, or, something to that effect. At any rate, she'd walked off in a huff, and he'd enjoyed the sexy sway of her hips as she left.

"In other words, it's getting a little chilly in hell?" he asked hopefully.

Sara laughed, remembering what she'd told him. "The devil might actually have to turn on the heat this winter."

She defiantly raised her chin, her dark eyes daring him to kiss her.

Jason accepted the challenge, his mouth coming down on hers in a gentle kiss that made both of them sigh with pent-up longing.

"Sara," Jason breathed. "You're even sweeter than I imagined."

The kiss deepened as they wrapped their arms around each other, their bodies pressing closer. His right hand came up to hold the back of her head, her soft braids splayed between his fingers.

Sara felt herself slipping into the sensual abyss she knew awaited her if she did not gain control. And while Jason's kisses were everything she'd known they would be, she couldn't force herself to let down her guard. Even if some part of her wanted to get even for the pain and humiliation Jason had caused her when they were teenagers, she would not lower herself to that level. It was petty and mean and imma-ture. She was a woman now, a multifaceted woman, and an affair with Jason Bryant, which she had no doubt would be worth the effort, wouldn't be fair to him.

She broke off the kiss and smiled at him. She saw in his

eyes that he was confused by her actions. A flirt one minute
and a pragmatist the next. She was confused herself. Jason
had made her forget that getting involved with any man at this
time in her life was not advisable. It was downright foolhardy.

He bent to kiss her again, but she stopped him by grasping
his chin, then gently stroking his clean-shaven jaw. "Jason,
it's true, I've had time to think about what you said about my
holding a grudge after all these years. That's not what my
problem was."

She looked down. "The fact is, I'm still in love with my
husband."

Jason tipped her chin up with a finger so that she would
have to look him in the eyes.

"Your husband? But, I thought your husband had…"

"Died, yes. He died more than five years ago, but I'm
having a hard time letting go. I know it's difficult for you to
understand. It's difficult for me to understand, too. But there
you have it. I've tried everything—I got rid of all his clothing.
I boxed up his other possessions, even his photographs, and
nothing has worked. I've tried dating, but I wind up comparing them to Billy, and nobody measures up. When you've had
someone to love you completely, without reservation, without
limitations, with his whole heart, and you've returned that
love with everything that you have inside, it's impossible to
let it die." When she finished, tears were streaming down her
cheeks.

Jason pulled her into his arms and held her tightly. No, he
didn't know how a love like that felt. He'd never known a love
as deep as the one she described. He felt wholly inadequate
in the face of this revelation, this dead husband whose
memory still tormented his wife more than five years after
he had left this earth. He didn't think he could compete with

a force like that. A no-good, cheating ex-husband, yes. But the paragon of virtue that Billy must have been? No way.

He closed his eyes as he held her, breathing in the fresh, flowery scent of her skin, her hair, remembering the taste of her mouth, how she had felt in his arms when they'd kissed. He hadn't experienced that much joy in a very long time. It felt somehow wrong to want a woman like Sara. Her heart had known so much pain. Her heart had soared with the love she had for Billy. It, apparently, still soared with love for Billy.

He felt her body quiver. Her vulnerability made his heart ache.

He knew he was dog meat, then. His goose was pretty well cooked.

If it were possible, he decided then and there, he would make her heart soar for him.

Inside, at the reception, dinner had been served.

At Erica and Joshua's table, conversation was lively. Dominique Lafon was telling them how her husband, Hubert, had reacted when she'd told him she was pregnant. Hubert, Joshua's best man, was looking at her with loving eyes. "I've never seen a grown man faint dead away like that," Dominique said, laughing.

"I had a lump the size of an egg on the back of my head for days," Hubert added, smiling at his wife. "We were in a restaurant. Two waiters had to carry me out like a side of beef. I didn't wake up until a medic waved smelling salts under my nose."

"'Does he have a heart condition?' the medic wanted to know." Dominique picked up the tale. "'No,' I said, 'I just told him we're going to have a baby.' The man laughed, and said, 'That'll do it!' Now, whenever I have anything important to tell him, I preface it with, 'Baby, you might want to brace yourself for this.'"

"I'll never live it down," Hubert said.

Erica reached across the table and clasped his hand. "You're not the first man to faint at that news, and you won't be the last."

"Faint?" Joslyn, Joshua's sister, said with laugh. "Jack threw up!"

Her husband, Jack, a handsome police officer from Oakland, playfully thumbed his wife on the forehead. "Must you bring up the most embarrassing moment of my life, woman? Besides, I still maintain that I'd had bad oysters for dinner."

"Nobody else got sick that night," Joslyn countered.

"Well," Dee Davis-Wells, Joslyn and Joshua's aunt, put in, "I can top all of those stories. You see, in my neighborhood, when I was a young woman, any woman worth her salt knew how to get rid of a trifling man with just two words. My first husband, Walter, was such a man. So, when he came home from a long day of doing nothing, I looked him straight in the eye and said, 'I'm pregnant.' That man was out of that apartment so fast he left rug burns on the carpet! It's been nigh on fifty years now and I haven't seen him once since then. Mind you, I wasn't pregnant, and knew it. I was just tired of *his* freeloading behind." She was laughing so hard tears sat in her eyes.

No one else had a dry eye, either.

"Aunt Dee, I never knew you had a husband named Walter," Joslyn said between guffaws.

"Honey, that was husband number one. I was all of nineteen when I married and divorced him. You weren't even a twinkle in your daddy's eyes back then."

"How many husbands have you had?" Dominique, who had instantly liked Aunt Dee upon meeting her, innocently asked.

"Darling!" Hubert protested, seeing her curiosity as a breech of etiquette.

Aunt Dee waved aside his concern. "Hubert, don't hush up that sweet child. I don't mind talking about it. Young people should learn from older folks' mistakes. And I've made my share in my sixty-eight years, which I'm not ashamed to admit."

She directed her next comments to Dominique. "Sweetie, last count, I've been married six times. The way I was brought up, you didn't sleep with a man until you were married to him. Hence, all the marriages. It's like Liz Taylor. People are always shocked at how many times she's been married. She obviously believes in marriage. If she didn't associate sex with marriage she would never have even married once let alone eight times. At any rate, that might not be Liz's reason for marrying all those times, but it was certainly the reason I did. Plus, my daddy was a minister, and he would have committed the sin of murder if I'd lived with a man without the benefit of marriage."

She took a breath, and smiled at all the young people surrounding her. "You young ladies today have so many options. It's a wonderful time to be a woman."

Erica got up and hugged Aunt Dee. "I love you, Aunt Dee!"

"I love you, and I've just met you," Dominique told her.

Joslyn got up and hugged her aunt, too. "We all love you, Aunt Dee!"

Jason and Sara got back to their table by the time the meal was being served. Guests had the choice of filet mignon, Cornish hen, or grouper with entree options for vegans and those guests who preferred kosher meals.

"You missed the salmon pâté appetizer," Zola told them. "It was good." She wondered what they'd been up to for so long, probably kissing. She sighed softly. Weddings were so romantic. She and Neal had met at a wedding.

A couple of tables over, Franklyn was laughing at something Lettie Burrows, who'd stopped by their table for a few moments, had said. Her husband, Kendrick, wanted to slip the band leader twenty bucks to get the band to perform "The Electric Slide."

"I told him to save his money. If the band didn't do 'The Electric Slide' before the evening was over I'd eat the centerpiece at our table, and I'm not fond of the taste of flowers. But what can I say, he loves to slide."

She reached over and fondly squeezed Elise's shoulder before leaving. "I'll see you all on the dance floor."

Elise smiled at Franklyn after Lettie had gone. "They're so cute together. I don't believe I've ever seen a man dote on a woman like Kendrick dotes on Lettie."

"Yeah, they have something special," Franklyn agreed. "Lettie's been my sous chef for more than seven years, and I've never heard her say a negative word about him, or vice versa."

"Sous chef, did you say?" Natalie Morris asked. She had been eavesdropping the whole time Lettie had been talking to Elise and Franklyn. "Then you're a chef like the Hitchcocks. You're a sly one." She eyed Elise. "Are you a cook, too?"

Chef, Elise thought, but felt duty bound to defend cooks everywhere. "Yes, I'm a cook, too. Being a cook is an honorable profession. Without cooks you would not be enjoying this meal, and I see that you're enjoying it because you've just about cleaned your plate. What's more, you *liked* the salmon pâté. I could tell how you were resisting smacking your lips and licking your fingers each time you took a bite. Yes, I'm a cook. What's it to you?"

Everyone at their table, except Franklyn and Natalie's husband, Bill, seemed surprised by Elise's comments. They held their collective breaths. Then Bill Morris started laughing. Soon, the others joined in, including Natalie.

"I told you that one day the lowly cooks would get their revenge, darling," Bill joked. "Your acerbic observations have come back to bite you in the can."

Natalie smiled at Elise. "Well said, Ms. Gilbert. I'm afraid I have a hard time leaving my job at home when I attend purely social functions. You put me in my place, and I thank you. After all, I'm not here to take notes in order to write a column for the paper, I'm here to enjoy myself."

Elise was, nonetheless, mortified that she'd gotten so irritated by Natalie's attitude that she'd lashed out at her. "I sincerely apologize, Ms. Morris. I don't know what came over me."

"Hell, I loved everything you said," Garrison Hitchcock said. "Natalie once wrote a scathing review of a restaurant where I was head chef, and I've been waiting for her comeuppance."

Natalie had the grace to look embarrassed. "Did I? I've written so many scathing reviews, I can't keep up with them. I knew your name sounded familiar, though. I'm sorry. Not for the review, it's my job to tell it like I see it, but for the bad feelings. I never truly want to hurt anyone's feelings. I don't think chefs understand that I have an obligation to the customer to give my honest opinion. I admit that my opinion may be flawed on occasion. However I try to give as unbiased a view of the food's quality as I can."

"But, admit it," Bailey said, curious. "Doesn't it make you feel powerful when you write a review that's so cutting it stops people from going to a certain restaurant?"

"Honey, if I had that kind of power, I wouldn't be writing reviews, I'd be ruling the world!" Natalie returned, her eyes sparkling with mischief.

"Darling, your goddess complex is showing," Bill said, to which everyone laughed.

The ice broken now, they enjoyed themselves for the rest of the meal, keeping the conversation light, and away from the food industry. After the meal, the three couples got up to work off some of the calories by dancing.

When Franklyn took Elise into his arms, he felt her relax against him. "Don't feel guilty for what you said to Natalie," he said. "She had it coming. Most of the people we love are cooks. Your parents, my mother and lots of our friends and colleagues. I wanted to tell her to shut up already, too."

"I don't," Elise said, smiling up at him. "That's what has me wondering about myself. I'm turning into this assertive woman who speaks her mind. I don't know *what* I'll do next."

"Anything you damn well want to," Franklyn said with a grin.

Elise tiptoed and placed a kiss on his mouth. His moustache tickled her nose and top lip. Franklyn kept it groomed. It wasn't bristly, but soft and neatly trimmed, though thick and luxuriant. She giggled. "I love your moustache."

"Oh good," Franklyn teased, "because if you didn't, all you'd have to do is say the word and I'd cut it off."

"Don't get crazy on me," Elise told him. "That moustache is a part of you. I've never seen you without it. You'd look naked to me."

"Baby," Franklyn said in her ear. "Once you've seen me naked, you'll never make that statement again."

Elise grew warm at the mention of him naked. She'd seen him in his work clothes, in casual clothes, evening wear, but never so much as a naked leg, let alone his entire body. She was so turned on, she was sure he could feel her distended nipples on his chest. Franklyn nuzzled her neck, and she let out a little moan.

She had been quiet a bit too long for Franklyn. "Hey, beautiful, cat got your tongue?"

She peered up at him with innocent big brown eyes and smiled. "I was rendered speechless by the image of you naked. Think I could see that later on tonight?"

They were holding each other so close that she could feel Franklyn's member growing hard against her thigh. "I take that as a yes."

Franklyn's voice was slightly hoarse when he answered. "That's definitely a yes."

Chapter 3

"It was *you!*" Bailey cried, pointing at Elise with a triumphant expression on her face.

Elise was standing near the French doors with Franklyn, saying good-night to Eric and Simone. The bride and groom had left a few minutes earlier under a hail of birdseed and well wishes. She knew Bailey had probably found out she'd baked the cake.

Most of the guests had departed. Simone had been trying to persuade Franklyn and Elise to spend the night and have breakfast with them in the morning as she usually did when Franklyn visited home. But he'd told them that he and Elise already had reservations at the inn the family always used. After that Simone didn't protest anymore. She simply had not wanted them on the road to San Francisco at night.

Elise turned to Franklyn and his parents. "Excuse me a moment, please."

Smiling at Bailey, she took her by the arm and led her into the adjoining solarium.

"Okay, I made the cake. But I'm not much of a competitor so don't try to talk me into joining your team, all right?" She hoped her voice sounded convincingly stern.

Bailey's green eyes were fairly sparkling with excitement. "You combined vanilla and lemon flavorings, didn't you? And putting finely crushed pineapple, cooked down with sugar until it was like jam, between the layers was *genius*. I don't think I've ever tasted a cake that was so decadent, so sexy. It was an aphrodisiac. Did you notice all of the couples who were sneaking kisses after eating your cake?"

Elise laughed. "That's ridiculous, Bailey. Come on, couples kiss at weddings. It's a romantic environment. Love is in the air. As for my cake being an aphrodisiac, human beings respond positively to sweet tastes. Sweet things make us happy, remind us of our childhood when life was simpler, sweeter if you will. *Of course* we're going to associate a sweet, delicious taste with one of the most pleasurable experiences we can have—sex."

Bailey was shaking her head in the negative. "No, I'm not making this up, Elise."

She stood with her hands on her hips, her head cocked to the side, looking intently into Elise's eyes. "You've got magic in those hands, and you don't want to face it. That's your problem. Afraid of success." She narrowed her eyes. "I bet you've always had magic hands. I bet you've been baking wonderful things since you were knee-high to a grasshopper, right?" She didn't wait for Elise to answer. "Excuse my homegrown expressions, but I'm from San Francisco via Texas. It took me years to lose my West Texas accent, but I did. You know why? Not because I'm ashamed of where I'm

from, but because the people I had to impress on the way up
were turned off by it. They thought just because my speech
wasn't proper, I was a hick. That I was not intelligent enough,
so they underestimated my abilities. Relegated me to menial
labor. I had two strikes against me, Elise. I was a woman, and
I had an accent that made people think of *The Dukes of
Hazard.* You have two strikes against you, too. You're black
and you're a woman. You know how hard it is for a pastry
chef to make it in this industry. Why wouldn't you want to
take advantage of the opportunity I'm offering you? I want
to *win!* And I think we can with you on our team."

Elise was impressed by Bailey's speech. She couldn't
imagine actually changing her mind about joining Bailey's
team, but that speech deserved some kind of a reward.

"Oh, hell," she said. "Give me your card, and I'll think
about it."

Bailey grinned and reached into her purse for a business
card. She handed it to Elise. "All right, now," she warned. "If
you don't phone me within the week, I'm going to start
phoning you. I know where you work, and I'm not averse to
coming down there to pester you face-to-face."

Elise laughed. "I believe you."

Her mission accomplished, Bailey turned to leave.

"Wait a minute," Elise called.

Bailey turned around expectantly.

"Who told you I made the cake?"

"The bride," Bailey said with a smug smile. "I went
straight to the horse's mouth."

Elise laughed. Erica strikes again.

"She's right," Franklyn said on the way to the inn. Elise
had told him that Bailey wanted her to join their team for the

pastry competition. "That cake was so good, I had a second piece and I'm generally not a big sweet eater."

Uh-oh, Elise thought, remembering what Bailey had said about the cake being an aphrodisiac. She smiled. "Thank you, Franklyn." A compliment from Franklyn meant more to her than the satisfaction she might derive from competing in a pastry cook-off.

"I hope you're going to seriously think about it," he added.

"Actually, it has never occurred to me to do something like that," Elise said truthfully. "I'm happy doing what I'm doing."

"Well, that's good," Franklyn said. "Because I love having you as part of our team. You've been a real asset to the Vineyard. But don't let loyalty to me stop you from reaching for more."

He switched on the turn signal. The inn was only a block ahead on the right. Glen Ellen was a charming small town in northern California in the middle of Sonoma Valley. Franklyn had grown up there, so he knew the town well. This inn had been owned by the same family for nearly fifty years. His family routinely recommended it to their out-of-town friends and family and business associates.

The inn itself was a very large Victorian house. There were six guest rooms, all with private baths. Franklyn had reserved two adjoining rooms. When he and Elise had driven up from San Francisco that morning, they'd checked in, so their bags were already in their respective rooms.

"What if my participation requires time away from work?" Elise asked as Franklyn parked and turned off the engine.

Franklyn removed his seat belt and turned to face her. "We'd work something out. I just want you happy, fulfilled and satisfied."

Elise unfastened her seat belt as well and moved closer to him on the seat. "I'm happy coming to work at the Vineyard."

"But are you fulfilled?" Franklyn asked as he bent his head to kiss the side of her neck. Elise's body, which had been on alert the entire evening due to Franklyn's nearness, now shivered with anticipation.

She gave him her neck to nuzzle. Franklyn's moustache tickled, but she found the sensation exciting rather than annoying. She wanted to feel his moustache all over her body. "Yes," she said breathlessly. "I feel very fulfilled working with you."

"But, are you *satisfied?*" Franklyn asked. He raised his head from her neck and pulled her fully into his arms. Elise's nipples were erect and tender by this time and they felt abraded when her chest pressed against his.

They looked deeply into each other's eyes. Their mouths were so close that they were breathing in one another's exhalations. Elise ached for him to kiss her. She wanted to be joined with him in every conceivable way. "There are all kinds of satisfaction," she said softly. "Kiss me."

"I'm afraid to kiss you, Elise. I'm afraid that when we finally make love I'll never want to stop because, like a starving man, I've been craving you for so long. I may never get enough of you."

Elise sighed as a jolt of pleasure coursed through her body. "You and me both, Franklyn. Do you realize how long I've been lusting after you? Three, practically three and a half *years*. Now, take me inside and make love to me, damn it, or I'll be forced to do something desperate."

Franklyn gave her a crooked smile, and bent to take her lower lip teasingly between his, then gently and sweetly kiss her until she was breathless and malleable in his hands. When he lifted his head, it took Elise a moment to open her eyes. She smiled slowly. She had had an orgasm, and they'd done nothing except kiss and caress each other. "Maybe we'll be naked the next time I come," she told him.

Franklyn kissed her again then reached across her to open her door. Elise grabbed her purse, slid off the seat and stepped onto the pavement of the parking lot. Franklyn followed, locked the doors by pressing a button on his key ring, then took her hand.

"Your room or mine?" he asked.

"Both," Elise said. "You paid for both rooms, so both of those beds are going to be used tonight."

Franklyn threw his head back and laughed.

No one was in the lobby when they entered the inn except for the clerk behind the desk, and she looked sleepy. She waved at them and yawned as they made for the stairs. "Good night!" they called in low voices.

When they were standing in front of their side-by-side room doors, they leisurely turned to regard one another. "Are you as nervous as I am?" Elise asked.

"Probably," Franklyn admitted.

"Please tell me this isn't going to ruin our working relationship, Franklyn, because, believe it or not, coming to work for you has been a haven to me."

"It won't," Franklyn assured her. "It won't."

"All right," said Elise, her key in the lock. "See you shortly."

They disappeared into their respective rooms.

Elise immediately went to switch on the lamp next to the bed after which she walked into the closet and began peeling off the multicolored silk dress and kicking off the three-inch-heeled strappy sandals. She debated whether or not to leave the garter belt and stockings on, thinking Franklyn might enjoy watching her remove them.

However that idea was tossed out when she decided she wanted to take a quick shower. They had been at his parents' house for nearly eight hours, and after dancing for two of those hours, she was certain she must be a little funky underneath her clothes. Besides, what if Franklyn was a foot man? She wouldn't want her tootsies smelling should he actually kiss them. She was getting hot just thinking about that.

No, the thing to do was to shower, apply body lotion and put on something sexy.

Coming out of the closet completely naked, she nearly panicked. The something sexy might be a problem. She had not come to Glen Ellen with the intention of seducing Franklyn. The only sleepwear she'd brought with her was a white cotton nightgown with tiny pink roses stitched around its neckline. The hem fell about three inches above her knees. Darn her lack of siren skills. Any experienced siren would have come prepared for seduction, even if she hadn't been given any hope of succeeding at it.

Of course, she didn't have to wear the nightgown. She could open the adjoining door and stand there framed in the doorway like Botticelli's *The Birth of Venus*. Except she wouldn't cover her breasts or her other goodies.

She laughed, realizing she didn't have the nerve to do that.

Not that she was ashamed of her body. The one thing she'd gained after leaving Derrick was the sense of power that owning her own body had given her. He used to try to convince her that she was too fat at five-seven and one hundred and forty-five pounds. She exercised practically every day, biking or walking or hiking. She was in good shape. Curvy, with a nicely rounded behind, long lovely legs, a flat belly, small waist and full, natural breasts that hadn't been altered by a plastic surgeon. She realized later that Derrick was trying to mold her into a black Barbie. Big breasts, tiny waist, flat behind and long stick legs. Elise simply wasn't genetically capable of looking like that, nor did she want to.

In the shower, she closed her eyes and allowed the water to sluice away the bad memories. She knew, instinctively, that Franklyn would know how to appreciate a well-endowed black woman's body. The way his body always responded to hers told her that he would not be measuring her inadequacies with his hands as they moved over her body.

In his room, Franklyn was also in the shower. His muscular six-foot-three golden-brown body was tense with anticipation. He paused to touch the long scar that ran down the length of his left leg. It was not something he could hide. That along with the rest of the scars on his body, on his knuckles, on his stomach from a knife wound he'd sustained in one of his many brawls. God knows he was lucky to be alive. Alive, and about to make love to the woman he loved.

The only drawback was that he didn't know what sort of treatment Elise had suffered in her marriage. They had been interrupted earlier when she'd been about to tell him why being married to Derrick Scott had made her wary of other men. Had made her doubt her judgment and guard her heart so fervently.

Could Derrick Scott have been one of those insecure men who through sinister devices sought to make a woman believe she was worthless and undesirable when the opposite was true? He knew men like that. They did not feel powerful unless they were grinding someone under their heels. He prayed that Elise had not been subjected to a sociopath like that.

When Elise unlocked the adjoining door, she was wearing the nightgown and nothing else. She had smoothed cherry-almond-scented lotion over her entire body, and combed her black, shoulder-length hair away from her face, letting it fall down her back.

Franklyn stood in front of the bureau, brushing his hair, wearing only pajama bottoms, and silhouetted in the light provided by the single lamp he'd turned on. She saw him before he saw her, and the breath caught in her throat. He was beautiful to her. Not because muscles rippled under every exposed inch of his skin. He was not built like a body builder. Franklyn's body was that of a hardworking man. Nicely delineated pectorals and biceps, a flat stomach, but not a six-pack. At two hundred and forty pounds he was a big man with big feet and hands, long muscular legs and thighs and quite a nice butt.

"Knock, knock," Elise said playfully as she walked into his room.

Franklyn smiled at her reflection in the mirror as he put down the brush, turned and began walking toward her. "Hello, beautiful."

Elise did a little spin in her nightgown. "I know it's not Victoria's Secret, but it's all I have with me."

Franklyn had crossed the room and pulled her into his arms. "On you it's the sexiest thing I've ever seen."

Elise was having a great time inhaling his essence, and enjoying the feel of his bare skin on hers. She had imagined that Franklyn was gorgeous underneath his clothes, but the reality far exceeded her fevered imagination.

She resolved to go for it and stop putting obstacles in her way by recalling every horrible thing that had happened in her marriage. It was far past the time to let it go and learn to embrace the here and the now!

She went up on the balls of her feet and kissed him. Franklyn couldn't help smiling as he opened his mouth to her. He let her have her way with him, not trying to control the kiss in any way. He could feel her emotions. Knew that she wanted him as much as he wanted her, and he exulted in the knowledge.

He moaned softly and fell deeper into the kiss, fairly devouring her now, as she was devouring him. This was what happened when two people loved from a distance and denied themselves the bliss that comes with confessing their feelings and acting on them. It was sweet, so sweet, and neither of them wanted to stop.

His hands slowly moved down along her sides, feeling the curvy shape of her, fully appreciating the soft places and, when he got to her bottom, the firm roundness. He picked her up by cupping her bottom with both hands and lifting her. Elise wrapped her legs around him and he carried her to the bed.

Still, they kissed as if they couldn't get enough of each other. Elise couldn't wait to have him inside her, and, yet, she wanted to extend this anxious, delightful feeling of expectation. But she knew she couldn't have it both ways. She wanted so much. And right now! If she was impatient it was because she had waited for him for so long with nothing to appease her except longing-filled looks and the occasional sexually explicit dream about him. Dating was out of the question. To be completely honest, she didn't want anyone else, just Franklyn. Only he would do.

As for Franklyn, she didn't want to know if he'd been with anyone else since she had set foot in his restaurant. Not now, anyway. For now, she wanted to pretend she was the love of his life and other women's allure simply paled in comparison to hers.

At the bed, Franklyn let her body slowly slide down his until she was standing. Their mouths parted, and he bent to gently take her face between his hands. Then he was kissing her again, and backing her up against the king-size sleigh bed. Elise massaged his back, his buttocks, and up again to the waistband of the pajama bottoms where she slipped a hand inside and found that he was naked under them. Franklyn gasped when her hand moved around to the front and grasped his penis. He throbbed as she wrapped her hand around his long, thick, hard member. She gently rubbed the tip, and then ran her hand along its length. She ached between her legs, wanting so much to simply lie on her back, open her legs and welcome him inside her.

"Hold on a minute," Franklyn said in a soft, husky voice. He turned to retrieve one of the condoms he'd placed atop the night-stand next to the bed. He quickly tore open the plastic-wrapped condom with his teeth, and spat the wrapper onto the floor.

Watching him, Elise smiled. It was good to know she wasn't the only eager one here. "Let me," she said, and took the condom from him.

She positioned it at the tip of his penis and took her time rolling it on. The pajama bottoms, hanging precariously on his hips, dropped to the floor, and Franklyn stepped out of them. Elise giggled as he picked her up, put her on the bed, and began pulling her nightgown over her head. This done, he put the nightgown at the foot of the bed and straddled her, his heavy member on her stomach.

Franklyn bent and buried his nose between her breasts, kissing the tender skin there and enjoying the warm, wonderful scent of her body. Elise moaned and slightly arched her back. Franklyn could not resist tasting each of her nipples. He ran his warm tongue around them, up and down, and gently bit them between strong teeth. Elise softly moaned with pleasure.

Franklyn resisted licking every succulent inch of her dark-golden-brown body. Unlike his body, hers did not have any scars. She was smooth all over. The color of her skin was a little lighter where her skin was usually covered by underwear. He could tell the difference. And she had a beauty mark underneath her ribcage on the right side. Her belly, though flat, was not concave. He liked that. It meant she did not starve herself to stay in shape. He liked the fact that she did not have bones sticking out at unsightly angles. Though even if she did, it would give him great pleasure to cook for her and fatten her up.

He went lower, making a growling noise as if he were going to eat her bellybutton. Elise giggled when his mouth "bit" the flesh of her stomach. She realized he'd done that to get her to relax and also to catch her off guard when he directed his attentions a bit lower than her midsection. His big hands went to both sides of her inner thighs, gently holding them apart. First he kissed her silky inner thighs until Elise mellowed, her body letting go of the momentary tenseness she'd felt when she had guessed his intentions. Franklyn was so gentle as his tongue parted the folds of her womanhood that she could do nothing but fall further under his spell and let him catch her.

Franklyn knew the moment she peaked. He felt her release. Letting her down easy, he withdrew, and rained gentle kisses on her inner thighs. He got up, lay beside her on the bed and pulled her into his embrace. Her body still shook slightly, and he marveled at the intensity of the orgasm; it was as if she'd never before been pleasured in that way.

So, he wasn't taken aback when she said, "I didn't know it could be like that."

"You mean you've never been French kissed?" he joked. He smoothed her hair behind her ear, and smiled reassuringly.

"I've only had one lover, Franklyn."

Franklyn attempted to school his expression, but knew he failed to hide his surprise.

"Elise, you're twenty-nine."

"Yes, and I was twenty-one and a virgin when I got married. Twenty-five when I got divorced and I haven't gotten close enough to anyone except you since then. Once you have a virgin's mentality I guess it sticks, even after a relationship fails and you suddenly find yourself free to do whatever you please."

Franklyn hugged her closer. "Are you ready for a fresh perspective on sex?"

"More than ready, I'm ripe," Elise told him, grinning.

Franklyn's erection had lessened while he'd been performing cunnilingus on her, but now she felt him growing harder by the second. He grasped her around the waist and rolled over in bed, winding up with her on top of him. "Come on, I want to watch your beautiful face as you have your way with me," he said, a humorous light in his eyes. He lay on his back with his hands behind his head. "Ride me." He raised his hips, thrusting his hard member into her crotch. Elise gave him a sensual smile and got up on her knees. She took his penis in her hand and placed the tip at the opening of her sex. Slowly, she lowered herself onto him. She didn't think that this would also be a carnal delight for her. After two orgasms, already, she had thought that she would now be a little desensitized, but no. As she took the length of him inside of her, her vaginal muscles contracted around him causing rivulets of luscious pleasure to course through her. Perhaps it was because she loved him so much. Perhaps it was simply because she'd never been made love to by a man who cherished *her*. Whatever the reason, she could have cried with the joy it gave her.

Franklyn could not stop watching her. Her eyes were closed, and her breathing a bit labored. Her head was slightly tipped back, and her breasts thrust forward. Her skin seemed to glow, and her lips were pouting so prettily it made him harder just looking at her mouth.

When she had him fully inside, Franklyn reached up and grasped her buttocks. Elise cried out, it felt so good. Then she started moving her hips back and forward, slowly in the beginning. Franklyn was tense, trying to hang on so that they could come together this time, but it was difficult to do so because she was exquisite, a feast for the eyes, and the senses. He was an experienced man, in spite of his tendency to pick his lovers with discrimination after one disastrous relationship. He knew the difference between having sex and making love. As far as he was concerned, being with Elise was his first time. She'd taken his virginity. He had *thought* he had made love to the woman who'd broken his heart. He knew now that he'd been mistaken.

Elise suddenly opened her eyes and peered down into his. "Franklyn, I can't believe this..." The orgasm bloomed within her, spreading warmth throughout her from the top of her head to the tips of her toes. Or so it seemed. She felt compelled to thrust harder, and she did, practically wearing out Franklyn, who was thrusting upward right along with her. He came with a roar. Her entire body covered with perspiration, she collapsed onto his chest. He laughed softly and held her firmly in his strong arms. Turning her head to the side so that they were looking into each other's eyes, she said, "Now, I'm totally satisfied."

"Yes," Franklyn said. "But are you fulfilled?"

Elise laughed. She could still feel his penis throbbing. "I'm fulfilled right now, yes."

They lay there smiling at one another for several minutes after which Franklyn asked her if she was ready to tell him what she was about to when Jason had interrupted them earlier that day.

"All right," she said. "But first, let's shower together and get into my bed."

Franklyn smiled. "You were serious about using both beds."

"You bet I was." She sounded cheerful, but when he'd mentioned discussing Derrick, she'd felt a dark cloud descend upon her. She knew it was in Franklyn's nature to get at the truth, though, and she understood that. He had, after all, been bamboozled by a woman whom he'd felt confident enough in to propose to, only to discover that she didn't really love him or respect him. He deserved to know what he had gotten himself into when he had made the decision to woo her. That was only fair.

"All right," said Franklyn, rising. When he'd gotten to his feet, he reached for her.

Elise gave him her hand and he pulled her up out of bed and into his arms.

In his shower, which was in a big claw-foot tub, they soaped each other, not with the intention of inciting passion, but simply to take the opportunity to get to know one another's bodies better.

Elise didn't mind getting her hair wet. She would towel it dry afterward and put it in a single braid down her back. She liked the thicker texture after it air-dried overnight. She did not relish pulling out the hair dryer and styling it. That would reduce the amount of time that she could be spending with Franklyn.

"You have red highlights in your hair!" she said, admiring his dark-brown, curly hair.

"I guess we had a red-headed ancestor somewhere down the line," Franklyn said with a smile. "Dad also has them."

"But not Erica or Jason?"

"No, they got Mom's black hair. Whom do you resemble most? Your mom or your dad?"

"I think I look more like my dad. He's about six feet, and my mom's very tiny, barely five feet. He's dark-skinned and she's fair, so I'm in between. All three of us girls have skin that's somewhere between his shade and hers."

"Eye color?"

"I got my dad's—dark brown, almost black. I did get my mother's long hair, but her eyes are green."

"Green?"

"My mother's dad was African-American, but her mother was Irish. They met during the Korean War. She was a nurse in the British army, and he was a GI assigned to bringing in the wounded or the dead from the battlefield. He was bringing some wounded to the M.A.S.H. unit one day, and she saw him and was instantly smitten. She pursued him. A black man back then didn't chase after a white woman. It was still hard for them to carry on an affair. They had to meet in secret. After the war, he went back home, and she followed several months later. I suppose living in California things weren't as bad for them as if they'd been living in Mississippi, but they still had it tough. They got married, had four kids. She died about five years ago, a car accident. Grandpa lasted two years after she was taken. He died in his sleep in the same house they'd shared for about fifty years."

"What did he do after coming out of the army?"

"He was a baker. That's who started the family business.

My dad and mom run it now, but they're training my sisters to take over for them when they retire."

"Baking's in your blood," Franklyn said with real respect shining in his eyes.

"I guess you could say that," Elise returned happily.

The water was getting cold. They rinsed off, and stepped from the tub onto a thick bath mat. Franklyn patted her body down with a warm, soft towel, and she returned the gesture. He caught her eyes on the scar on his leg and smiled, wondering if she was going to ask him about it or not. She surprised him by gently rubbing her hand over it. It was a little lighter than the rest of his skin and slightly raised. "Your parents must have been terrified for you that day," she said softly.

Franklyn felt tears prick the backs of his eyes. He blinked them away. It was true, he didn't think he'd ever seen his parents in a more emotional state than they had been when they had come running and found him in a twisted heap on the ground. He hadn't told Elise, but not only had he fallen from the barn's roof and broken his leg, but the horse had stomped his leg. His parents had been afraid the leg would have to be amputated.

"Yes, they were," he said, his voice cracking. He cleared his throat. Taking the towel from Elise, he carefully placed it on the towel rack as he had done with the one he had used to dry her body with. He hated damp towels in the morning.

Turning back around to face Elise, he said, "Some of us have wounds on the outside, and some of us have wounds on the inside. Then there are the unfortunate few who have them on the inside *and* the outside." His smile was so enigmatic that Elise could not tell which one he considered himself to be.

A few moments later, they were in her bed. She was

wearing the white nightgown and he'd put the pajama bottoms back on. "In the past," she said, beginning her story, "I'd watch one of those talk shows that feature scorned wives, and they'd be sitting there telling the audience that they never suspected their husbands of cheating on them. Hadn't noticed any signs. They were perfect princes before they were married. Well, I used to scoff at those women, calling them clueless, until I became one of them. That's how Derrick's abuse was—I never saw any clues that he would turn into an abuser before we were married. He was so charming that everyone, my family, my friends, adored him and told me how lucky I was to have a man like that love me. I couldn't have agreed more. When we met I was fresh out of culinary arts school. He was in his last couple of years of law school. I was helping my cousin, Mariel, a caterer, by serving at a party one night, and I served him a drink. He immediately started flirting with me. I ignored him. He followed me back to the kitchen, and I gave him my number just to get rid of him. He was that persistent. I forgot all about him, and then about a week later, he phoned and asked me out. I told him I was busy, but he kept calling back. In hindsight, that should have been a clue as to his single-mindedness. But, really, most women believe when a man is that persistent he's simply overwhelmingly attracted to her, and that's a turn-on."

"So he wore you down, and you went out with him."

"Yes, and I found myself drawn to him. He was smart, and a good conversationalist. And his ambition seemed like a good thing. I'd recently met a few guys who didn't have any ambition, so that was a plus. Also, he didn't seem to mind that I didn't want to have premarital sex. He said he thought that was commendable. I sincerely didn't think things were moving too fast when he asked me to marry him after only three months. When I said I would, I *did* think it was rushing things when he suggested we get married within the month. My parents thought I was pregnant."

Franklyn laughed softly. "They obviously didn't know about your vow of chastity."

"No, they didn't. My dad was furious. 'Ellie,' he said, 'you have to know someone for longer than three months before the lust even wears off. Wait a year before you marry him. Sure, we all like him, but marriage is a very serious commitment.' I should have listened. Inside of a week, I learned that I would have to support us until Derrick graduated. He'd had a falling out with his parents who are very well off, and he didn't see fit to tell me until after we were married. My parents had paid for the wedding. The one thing that redeems me is the fact that it was a very simple affair and they didn't spend a lot of money on it. I got a second job to help make ends meet while Derrick concentrated on school. Most evenings he would already be asleep when I got home, had a quick shower and climbed into bed. Then, he'd be gone when I got up. When we did see each other, on weekends, I would have to clean and do the laundry because he never found time to do it between classes. Whenever I complained he would say, 'Babe, think of the future. When I get my degree, you're never going to have to clean again. You'll have a housekeeper. I'll set you up in your own business so you won't ever have to work for anyone else. Please, just be patient.' And I would look at all my hard work as an investment in the future. But as soon as he got his degree and started working at a law firm, I became a hindrance to him. He would take me to social gatherings and on the way home say, 'Hon, why don't you dress like Harry's wife? She's so sophisticated. You would look good in clothes like that if you would lose ten pounds.' It got so that I couldn't do anything to please him. I was not overweight. I weighed less than I weigh now because he was making me such a nervous wreck that I'd forget to eat. You know me, Franklyn, I don't forget to eat!"

Franklyn held her closer against him. "I love everything about your body."

Elise took a moment simply to appreciate the sincerity of his statement. Then she took a deep breath and continued. "Toward the end, it was apparent he was trying to make me leave him. There are some men who don't have the guts to call it quits, so they do everything within their power to harass, irritate and drive a woman nuts until she either has to save herself by getting out of the situation or kill the sonofabitch."

"Elise!" Franklyn said, as if he were scandalized.

Elise laughed. "I was mad as hell at the end. I'd realized that he had married me expressly to use me up. In the beginning he used a subtle form of brainwashing to make me believe I was doing it to insure our future. When he was done with me, he became more vicious. He didn't pretend to be nice anymore. It was a constant barrage of 'My parents were right, I married beneath me,' or 'I don't take you anywhere because you're an embarrassment,' or 'Your ass is so big it leaves the room ten minutes after you do.'"

"Where does he live?" Franklyn asked, his tone menacing. "I want to go kick *his* ass right now."

"It doesn't matter where he lives," Elise said. "Because by the time I left him, I was so done with him that if I'd seen a bus bearing down on him from behind, I would not have shouted a word of warning. That's how badly I wanted to be rid of him. However, like any dog who has been repeatedly kicked, I came away with residual scars on the inside. I started thinking I was not worthy of love. So, I kept to myself, concentrated on work, and as you know now, even when I found myself falling in love with you, I wouldn't do anything about it. You had to make the first move. And, honestly, Franklyn, I thought I was going to have to wait forever for you to make your move."

Franklyn smiled and nuzzled her shoulder. "We both had to let go of past hurts in order to move forward. But now that we've done that, nothing and no one is going to get in the way of our happiness. I promise."

Elise turned to face him. She kissed him on the forehead. "So do I."

Chapter 4

The Vineyard was open for lunch and dinner from Tuesday through Saturday. Located on Stockton Street in the Telegraph Hill area, it had been a mainstay in the neighborhood since 1996. Its cuisine was Californian/French and Franklyn's menu featured fresh produce that had been grown locally, as well as seafood from the Pacific Ocean.

He personally went down to a market in the Chinatown section of Stockton Street every morning to choose the seafood that would be served that day; but had made a deal with a local greengrocer to have fresh vegetables delivered to the restaurant by 7:00 a.m.

Franklyn arrived at six-thirty and adjusted the thermostat in preparation for the arrival of the first shift that clocked in promptly at seven. Those who were on the first shift worked from seven until three. The second shift worked from three until eleven.

Franklyn remained at the restaurant the entire two shifts, taking a two-hour break from three until five when his assistant chef took over the cooking while he took a nap in his office. No one disturbed him during that time. Over the years, Lettie Burrows, who worked the second shift, made certain that everyone knew that those two hours were sacred, and he wasn't to be bothered unless the restaurant was on fire. Elise, who worked the first shift, but sometimes would work the second shift if Franklyn needed a waitress to fill in for someone under the weather, was well aware of this rule. So she was surprised when the phone rang in her apartment after 3:00 p.m. on the first Tuesday after their trip to Glen Ellen, and it was Franklyn calling.

"You're supposed to be sleeping," Elise said, after recognizing his cell's number.

"I was lying here thinking about you," he told her, his tone husky. "What do you have planned for the evening?"

"Mariel has been trying to get me to check out her yoga class, and I promised I'd go with her tonight at seven. We should be done by nine and after that I'm coming home and soaking in the tub."

"Think you'll be asleep by eleven-thirty?"

"Not hardly. Would you like to come by?"

"Definitely. I miss you so much." This was said with passionate intensity.

Elise smiled. They had seen each other less than an hour ago, but she knew exactly what he meant. "I miss you, too."

At work, they were not affectionate. Both of them thought it was unprofessional to act like lovers. As in most workplaces, gossip was rampant at the Vineyard, and they didn't want to add fuel to the fire. Upon getting ready to leave the restaurant when her shift was done, Elise did not even seek Franklyn out for a goodbye kiss.

"See you then," Franklyn said softly.

"Get some rest, you're gonna need it," Elise teased.

Franklyn laughed shortly. "I'm looking forward to it. Bye, darling."

"Bye, sweetie."

Immediately upon hanging up, Franklyn lay back down on the comfortable leather couch in his office. A lazy smile crinkled the corners of his eyes, and curled his full lips. If he had his way, Elise would be his wife by next Christmas. He'd never been happier, but he suspected she needed more time to settle into their relationship.

Unfortunately, they both carried baggage from previous relationships. He was a patient man and he was more than willing to bide his time. He'd waited nearly four years to tell her how he really felt about her. He could wait six more months before proposing. By then, there could be no comparison to her past relationship.

He closed his eyes, relaxed now after speaking with Elise and making a date to see her later. Soon, he was asleep with a smile on his face.

"You actually think this is *calming?*" Elise asked.

She and Mariel were bent from the waist with their derrieres in the air and their palms flat on an exercise mat. Thank goodness they were wearing leotards and tights.

"It is," Mariel insisted, barely able to draw a breath. "You'll see, after a while you'll be addicted to it. I've been coming nearly a month, and I love it."

"I'm already addicted to chocolate, and I find that much more enjoyable."

"Franklyn will love the more flexible you," Mariel whispered. "Have you tapped that yet?" Her thick, dark eyebrows arched inquisitively.

"Uh-uh," Elise returned. Meaning it was none of Mariel's business.

The music, a purely instrumental composition that sounded like whale song or stampeding elephants, depending on whenever the bass drums chimed in, was sufficient cover for their intimate conversation. Twenty others stretched and pulled their muscles into submission alongside them in the class. Low groans were heard intermittently.

Mariel twisted her neck in an odd angle until she could glare at Elise. "Don't give me that. Who pushed you to say something to that walking advertisement for virility?"

"You did," Elise admitted.

"And who told you to accept his invitation to Glen Ellen four months ago? I did!" Mariel got back into position, the neck thing being too painful to maintain. "You owe me."

"I owe you intimate details about my love life?" Elise screeched, although softly.

"What do you think I am, some kind of a freak? I don't want the blow-by-blow details. I just want to know if you've tapped it yet."

"Yes," Elise said in a very low voice.

"What?"

"I said yes!" Elise hissed, slightly louder.

Mariel laughed softly. She stood up straight. "Hell, I was getting dizzy. Let's go get some coffee."

Elise straightened, too. Everyone else in the room was still in position. "What about your devotion to yoga?"

"Do I look Hindu to you?" Mariel asked, totally serious. She stepped around a tall sister who had her eyes closed and a contented smile on her face. Elise followed her cousin. "*She* seems to be enjoying herself."

Mariel was moving faster now. In the back of the room, they collected their purses and jackets. She crooked a finger at Elise. When Elise got closer, she whispered, "That girl's on mood enhancers. You'd look happy too if you were as drugged as she is."

Elise pulled her baggy jeans from the cubbyhole where she'd earlier stashed her belongings and slipped into them, then she put on her brown suede clogs. Beside her, Mariel pulled on a long multicolored cotton skirt whose hem fell to her ankles. She bent and pulled on a pair of three-inch-heeled black leather ankle boots. They shrugged into their jackets.

Following Mariel to the front door of the dance studio on Post Street, Elise said, "Are you quitting?"

"Nah, I'll be back. My mind just wasn't on it tonight. I'd rather be talking to you in a warm coffee shop."

Cold air greeted them as they stepped outside. Elise pulled her jacket closed, and hugged her shoulder bag tighter against her side. People joked about California having wonderful weather, but if you wanted to freeze your butt off, December in San Francisco was a good time to do it.

"Besides, I've got some news," Mariel said as they hurried across the street to a small coffee shop that did not have a famous name. "My company's doing the catering for his law firm, for their Christmas party on Saturday, December twenty-fourth. I didn't want to do it, but I let Laura talk me into it. Okay, I admit it, I was swayed by the money."

Elise didn't have to ask who "his" was. Derrick.

This time, though, when he was mentioned, her stomach muscles didn't tighten painfully, she didn't cringe, and she didn't have vivid flashbacks about some regrettable episode between the two of them.

"In spite of its size, San Francisco is still a small town. You can't avoid running into him forever."

Mariel stopped in her tracks in front of the coffee shop and turned to stare at Elise. Her short red feathery curls were blowing in the wind. "Girl, his stuff must be mighty good for you to say something like that."

Elise laughed and reached for the door. "It is."

Mariel jumped up and down in glee. "All right, now!" Once again under control she followed Elise inside. They quietly sat down at a booth next to the window so that they could people-watch while they chatted.

The shop was busy, nearly every booth and table occupied. They knew it would be a while before the waiter, a tall blond Adonis with wavy shoulder-length hair, got around to them.

Mariel whistled at him and blew him a kiss.

"I take it you've been in here before," Elise said with a smile.

The guy sent Mariel a kiss through the air, and Mariel smiled seductively at him.

"Not only have I been in here, I've been out with him. Our first date was at his apartment and he cooked for me. He's sweet."

Elise was busy removing her jacket and getting comfortable. She sneaked a peek at her watch. It was eight-fifteen. "Sweet, as in he's a nice guy?"

"His name's Paulo, and he's a blond Italian. Owns this place and two others, but every Tuesday night, he's here. He likes to get to know his customers."

"How well?"

Mariel smiled coyly. "Now, cousin, I've only been out

with him once. You know my rules. Never on the first date, seldom on the second, and he has to be damned lucky to get that far on the third date. You know what a careful girl I am."

"He doesn't look Italian," Elise said.

"What does an Italian look like?"

"Shorter and darker?"

"His people are originally from Scandinavia. You know the world is changing. You don't look part Irish, either, but you are."

"Is it something you think can go somewhere?" Elise asked. Her cousin, at twenty-seven, had never been married. She'd been engaged once and had called it off two months before the wedding because she suspected she couldn't be faithful to one man for the rest of her life. She liked variety in her men.

"No," Mariel answered without having to think too long about it. "I haven't met the man yet who makes me want to settle down. When I meet him, I'll know. Paulo is fun to be with. He's a good cook and a good kisser. He's also a gentleman. Three for three, that's good enough for me."

Elise knew not to press the point. Mariel had a very good reason to be wary of marriage. Her parents had divorced when she was ten. Neither of them had been able to find anyone they could live with since then. Her mother was on husband number three; her father was on wife number four. Sometimes it appeared to her as if they were competing against each other to see how many times they could get married. What was really sick about the situation was that every time they were between relationships they would get back together simply to have sex. Mariel had caught them together once when she'd gone over to her mother's apartment without phoning in advance.

"What I really want to hear is how your weekend in Glen

Ellen went," Mariel said, leaning forward, her dark-brown eyes eager. "How was the wedding? Were his relatives as friendly as they were the first time, or were they more reserved this time?"

Elise told her everything, starting at the beginning with the road trip, how she had repaired Erica's dress, meeting all of the foodies at their table, and how she'd been rude to food critic, Natalie Morris.

"I know her," Mariel said, laughing. "Kudos! Wish I could have seen her face. She said a chef friend of mine was a pretender who would do better being a short-order cook in Roswell, New Mexico. At least, there, people were used to aliens and wouldn't be shocked to find his gelatinous gook on their plates. He's not a bad chef, he was just having a bad day when she showed up in his restaurant. The boy developed an ulcer behind her acidic remarks. Hung up his chef's hat and is now selling cars. Making a lot more money, but *still...*"

Elise was laughing, too. Wiping the tears from the corners of her eyes with a paper napkin, she said, "Well, I let her have it and then apologized, of course."

"Of course. You're too nice," was her cousin's opinion. "I wouldn't have apologized to that mean hussy. So, what happened after you left the reception?"

"We went to the inn where Franklyn had reserved two rooms."

"*Two* rooms? Girl, you made the man reserve two rooms? Why couldn't you just come out and tell him you had plans to jump his bones before you came back to San Francisco?"

"Because neither of us had plans to make love. It wasn't until after I told him about Derrick, and he told me about his past relationship with the woman who turned down his marriage proposal that a dam broke, and we realized that we didn't want to wait any longer."

Mariel was looking at her with her mouth open. "Some woman turned down a marriage proposal from Franklyn?"

"Yes, thank God," Elise replied.

"Yes, that's good for you," Mariel agreed. "But she must have been a pure idiot to do that."

"Let's not dwell on it," Elise said. "Her loss is my gain." She looked sober. "Promise me that when you see Derrick, you're not going to make a scene like you did last time."

"All I did was throw a drink in his face," Mariel said. She smiled slyly. "But that idea Franklyn's sister had about pimp-slapping guys who have mistreated women sounds pretty good."

"Mariel, you wouldn't!"

"Me?" Mariel cried, innocence personified. "I meant, *I?* No, my dear cousin, I wouldn't slap him. He knows me. I'd get one of my girlfriends, someone he's never met to do it for me. Then she'd get out of there, quick, and no one would have witnessed the assault save one big-headed attorney who deserves much worse but only got a little slap from a hot chick he thought he was going to take home that night. I like Erica. You ought to bring her around to meet the girls sometime."

"Seriously, Mariel," Elise entreated. "Just ignore him. After all, you're going to be in the kitchen, right? You don't even have to see him if you don't want to."

Mariel pouted. "But it's so much fun when I see him."

"Okay," Elise warned. "He almost pressed charges last time. You may see the inside of a cell this time."

"Oh, he wouldn't dare!"

"You don't think so? The only reason he didn't press charges the last time is because I pleaded with him not to."

Mariel hadn't known about that. Her cousin had gone

begging on her behalf? To that slime? Frowning fiercely, Mariel said, "I'd better stay in the kitchen because if I do see him, I'd probably be the one doing the slapping." She met Elise's eyes, her own narrowed. "Don't you ever do that again. Never beg him for anything. Not even if I'm on death row and he's the only one who can save me." Her gaze turned contemplative. "There must be some way for me to exact revenge. It isn't every day I'm given the opportunity to be in the same place at the same time as your ex-husband. I'll think of something." She hummed, thinking. "I can't put anything in his food. Bad for business."

"I wish you would simply get over it," Elise told her. "Call in sick that day if you don't trust yourself to behave."

Paulo finally came over to their table. He looked scrumptious in tailored black slacks, a bronze-colored long-sleeved silk shirt open at the collar and black oxfords.

He smiled down at them. "Mariel, who is this enchanting creature?"

Mariel looked at Elise as if to say, didn't I tell you? Peering up at Paulo, she gave him an appreciative smile. "This is my cousin, Elise Gilbert. Elise, this is Paulo Santini, owner of this quaint coffee shop."

Paulo accepted Elise's proffered hand and kissed it. "A pleasure."

"Good to meet you, Paulo," said Elise.

Smiling, Paulo released her hand, and stood erect. "What can I get you ladies?"

After they'd told him what they wanted, he bent close to Mariel. "I'm leaving here in half an hour. Would you like to have dinner with me?"

Mariel looked down at her casual attire, thinking she would have liked some warning so that she could have had time to go home and change. Seemingly reading her thoughts, Paulo said, "Don't worry, I plan to cook for you."

Mariel never turned down a home-cooked meal, nor a man who could produce said meal. "I'd love to."

Paulo smiled his pleasure, and took his leave.

"Wow," Elise said in his absence. "Talk about Old World charm. Are you sure he's for real?" She glanced down at her watch again.

"Girl, if he isn't, don't wake me up from this dream," Mariel returned. She pursed her lips. "And would you get on out of here? It's obvious you have to get home to primp for Franklyn."

Elise grinned. "What gave me away?"

"You kept looking at your watch, and I can feel the pent-up sexual energy coming off you. I do know a little about sexual energy. You have lots of it stored up that needs to be expended. Go home."

Elise began pulling on her jacket. "We'll do this again real soon. Enjoy your date with Paulo. He could be the one."

"Honey, it will take a very special man to break through this hard shell around my heart," Mariel told her jokingly. Her smile didn't quite reach her eyes though.

Elise stood and kissed her cousin on the cheek. "Love you, girl."

"Love you back," Mariel said.

Elise turned to go.

"Oh, Elise?"

She turned back around. "Yes?"

"This is your time to shine. Grab every good thing life has to offer."

Elise stood smiling at her cousin, wondering where those platitudes had come from. She waited for Mariel to crack a tasteless joke, but she did not even crack a smile. She was totally serious. "I'll try my best." Elise's voice broke with emotion.

Tears shone in Mariel's eyes. "I'm just so happy for you," she said by way of an explanation.

Elise went back to the table and hugged her tightly. "You nut!" She gave her a squeeze for good measure, then released her. "Dry your eyes. Gotta look gorgeous for Paulo. I'm gone."

She hurried out of the coffee shop.

Mariel picked up a napkin and blew her nose, after which she went in her purse, retrieved her makeup mirror and made sure her face didn't require overhauling. Paulo came back to the table a couple minutes later with cups of coffee. He sat down and clasped her hands in his.

"I think that the day I met you was a very lucky day for me." His Italian accent lent a lovely lilt to his soft tones.

Their eyes met and held, and Mariel's heart thudded in her chest. What was this? She actually felt giddy with happiness. Her cheeks felt warm, and, if she wasn't mistaken, that sick feeling in the pit of her stomach didn't portend nausea but something else much scarier, like attraction. Her first instinct was to call off their intimate dinner date at his place. She went against her better judgment, though, and said, "I think you may be right."

Paulo brought her hand up to his cheek and turned his face so that he was now kissing her palm. His skin was lightly tanned. Hers was a deep, rich chocolate with golden undertones. He thought her skin was beautiful, and longed to touch her all over. But he sensed that Mariel was the type of woman who needed to learn a man slowly.

Fortunately, he was a man who liked discovering all the layers of a woman.

* * *

Having lived in San Francisco for nearly ten years, Elise was very familiar with the bus system. When she wasn't riding her bike, which she used to go back and forth to work, she took the bus. The cable cars, while terrific tourist attractions, were not a practical way of getting around the city because they only ran three routes and oftentimes did not go where she needed to go. She lived in a nice neighborhood, on Filbert Street, in a three-story Victorian house that was owned by a writer who traveled a great deal. Elise's apartment took up the entire third floor with outside stairs leading to her door. She'd been there nearly four years, ever since her divorce.

The writer, Hilary Chesterfield, wrote mysteries about a retired schoolteacher with wanderlust. Like most fictional sleuths, murder followed her wherever she went. Because Hilary was wildly successful and a retired schoolteacher herself, she enjoyed traveling to the places her heroine traveled to in each book. She was now in Tahiti. In exchange for looking after the house in Hilary's absence, Elise's rent was low.

Hilary e-mailed to check in whenever she found a free moment, which wasn't often.

On the bus en route to home, Elise read for the second time the information about the pastry competition for which Bailey Hitchcock was gathering a team. The organization that sponsored the competition had an online presence, and Elise had printed all of the information pertaining to the next competition, which would be held in Phoenix, Arizona, in mid-March.

Elise didn't know why she'd looked up the competition online, except that with Franklyn and now Mariel telling her to seize the day, she felt buoyant in spirit. Maybe it wasn't such a stretch of the imagination to believe that she could do more with her life. Not that she wasn't happy working at the Vineyard. Two years ago Franklyn had even given her a separate dessert menu that promoted her name. It wasn't unknown for diners to come to the Vineyard expressly for coffee and one of Elise's rich desserts. Franklyn was very generous in that respect, wanting her to gain as much recognition as possible. When she thought about it, he had always been in her corner, cheering her on, building up her confidence. She wanted to prove to him that his faith in her wasn't unwarranted.

A two-year-old baby girl with big brown eyes stood on the seat in front of Elise's and opened her tiny palm, offering Elise a handful of plain M&M's.

"Oh, thank you very much, but I've already got some." Elise reached into her bag and produced an unopened bag of peanut M&M's. "See?"

The little girl snatched the bag of M&M's before Elise could jerk her arm back.

"Emily!" cried the child's mother, a slender brunette with equally big brown eyes. "Give those back, you little thief." She turned to give Elise an apologetic smile and both women burst out laughing. "I'm so sorry," she said to Elise.

"Please, I'm a chocoholic myself, I understand," Elise said. "Let her keep them."

"I would," said the mother. "But she's allergic to peanuts." She bent to peer into Emily's chubby little face. "These have peanuts, sweetie. Remember how you itch like crazy when you eat them? Give them back to the nice lady and say sorry."

Emily's bottom lip protruded with obstinacy, however she did not disobey her mother. She stood on the seat, handed the M&M's back to Elise and said, ever so softly, "Sorry."

Elise smiled at her and accepted the package, putting it back in her purse. "Apology accepted, sweetie. Next time, I'll have some plain ones in my purse."

Her stop was coming up on the right, and once the bus came to a halt, she rose. "Bye," she said to the little girl.

"Buh-bye," intoned the charming miniature chocoholic, with an angelic smile.

"Take care," said the mother, a humorous glint in her eyes.

"You, too," Elise said and exited at the back, hopping onto the sidewalk and walking up the street to the Victorian three blocks away.

It was a quarter past nine by the time Elise got home. She stepped into the small foyer after unlocking the side door, nearly bumping into her ten-speed bike on its kickstand next to the wall. The hardwood floors were polished to a high gleam. Hilary had not spared any expense when it came to renovating the home she'd inherited from her parents. As an only child, she'd inherited not only the house but a sizeable bank account. Even if she weren't a successful author, she would still be set for life. Never married, no children, few relatives, she had only herself to be responsible for. Elise worried that Hilary was deeply lonely. Hilary insisted that she was too busy to be lonely.

After locking the door behind her, Elise put her jacket and shoes in the foyer closet, then walked barefoot through the small living room and down the hall to the master bedroom. She had one other bedroom that she used as an office/sewing room. She'd made all of her curtains and slip covers for the secondhand but well-made furniture in her apartment.

Weekends, she haunted estate sales and yard sales in the wealthier neighborhoods, surprised by what rich people considered throwaways. She had a talent for refinishing furniture, and could see the beauty underneath the worn, battered exterior of a piece of discarded furniture. Her bookshelves, made of maple, were salvaged and redone. They ran the length of the south wall in her living room. She had hundreds of books, all of which she'd read. The ones signed by her favorite authors were lovingly wrapped in plastic to preserve their pristine condition.

Other pieces she'd bought brand-new, like her couch, upholstered in rich, caramel-colored silk. It was big, bold and roomy, and so comfortable guests had been known to fall asleep in its generous folds.

In the bedroom, she went straight through to the walk-in closet and removed her jeans, leotard and tights. She hung the jeans up and tossed the leotard and tights into the dirty clothes hamper. As she walked back out into the bedroom wearing only panties and bra, the phone rang and she plopped down on the bed next to the nightstand to answer it.

"Elise," came Mariel's voice, "I'm still at the coffee shop waiting on Paulo to finish up. Talk me out of going home with him so that he can cook for me again."

"Your first date was at his place, and he cooked for you, right?"

"Yeah."

"Then what are you so afraid of?"

"The last time I wasn't feeling this way."

"What way?"

"Like I want to rip his clothes off and screw his brains out."

"You seldom make love on the second date. That's a hard and fast rule."

"I've never broken that rule," Mariel affirmed, although not too confidently.

"And you won't break it tonight," Elise told her. "If things get too hot, go into his bathroom and splash water on your face. Don't go back out until you feel you're in control."

"See, I phoned you because you were supposed to tell me to cancel the date altogether."

"Do you want to cancel?"

"No," Mariel stated emphatically.

"Then it wouldn't do any good for me to tell you to cancel. You're not a child."

"I don't know, Elise, I'm not feeling like myself."

"The Mariel who always controls every situation with men?"

"That's my girl!" Mariel said, cheering on her alter ego.

"Maybe you don't sound like that Mariel because you're no longer 'that' Mariel."

"You're making about as much sense as I'm making," Mariel complained.

"Remember when you told me that when you met the man who could break through the barrier you've built around your heart, you'd recognize him?"

"Uh-huh," Mariel said cautiously.

"Obviously, your radar is off and it's coming through as confusion. You don't know if you can trust yourself with Paulo because you're afraid he *is* the one!"

"But he's white, Elise," Mariel whispered.

"Surprise, surprise," Elise said, trying not to laugh. "All those fine brothers you've gone through and it's a white boy from Italy who breaks through your reserve."

"You're not funny at all," Mariel said.

"I'm not trying to be funny. A while ago you were talking as if Paulo was someone you could have a little fun with. Now that you're developing a serious jones for the boy, you have to bring up the fact that he's white, well, Italian, anyway."

"My parents would freak!"

"So what? They're living their lives. You have a right to live yours. When have they ever asked your opinion about one of their lovers?"

"Girl, if they had, they would have gotten an earful, I tell you."

"There you go," Elise said. "Mariel, you are one of the most level-headed people I know. You love to kid around, but I've never known you to make a decision that you haven't thought out. I don't think you have it in you to jump in feet-first without making sure the water's fine. There is something about Paulo that you like on an instinctual level."

Mariel was silent for a while. She sighed. "Or maybe I just like the way he looks in those black slacks he has on."

Elise laughed. "That's a given."

Mariel laughed, too. "I'm going for it. Meaning the meal, not hot monkey sex. If I have to stay in his bathroom all night, I'll do it."

"Let me know how it goes."

"I'll call you tomorrow. G'night."

"Good night."

After hanging up, Elise got up and went to soak in the tub.

Chapter 5

The Vineyard closed at ten. Tonight there was a couple at table two lingering over Elise's triple chocolate cake drizzled with strawberry sauce, otherwise the dining room was empty of patrons.

Franklyn closed the kitchen door after spying on the couple, and when he turned around Lettie was smiling at him. "I think you have someplace you want to be tonight."

"Now, Lettie," Franklyn said, smiling, allowing the swinging doors to swish closed behind him. "Whatever gave you that idea?"

"Let me see," said Lettie as she approached him. She was five-two, if that, and on the plump side. She wore her black hair in braids that were now in a ponytail. "There's the rose in the office refrigerator. I saw Annette put it in there this morning." Annette Duchamps was the florist who provided the flowers, mostly hardy varieties like carnations, for the tables.

Franklyn had forgotten he'd asked Annette to leave one perfect long-stemmed red rose in the office refrigerator this morning. He was glad Lettie had reminded him.

"Anything else?" Franklyn asked, feigning ignorance of the rose's significance.

Lettie laughed as she turned back around and returned to what she'd been doing before she had decided to have some fun with Franklyn. "All right, be like that," she said as she cleaned one of the stainless-steel sinks. She went into her mumbling mode, which she only did when she was frustrated. "As if I haven't been waiting years for you to find someone. Now, you're gonna make me beg for the details."

"What did you say?" Franklyn asked, a humorous light in his eyes.

"You heard me," Lettie said, still mumbling. "You've got ears like a bat."

"You say you've waited years to get a cat?"

The chef's apprentice, the four waiters and waitresses, and the two dishwashers all laughed at Franklyn and Lettie's antics. They were used to their boss and his sous chef's witty repartee. For years Franklyn had been the straight guy in his and Lettie's routines.

"Yes, I'm getting a cat," Lettie said. "You know I have a house full of dogs. They'd eat a cat alive. They're not too fond of *you* when you visit, come to think of it!"

"It's too bad they're so little, their mouths don't open wide enough to take a big plug out of me," Franklyn joked. Lettie owned four Pomeranians. Franklyn referred to them as hairy rodents. "Oh, I forgot, you can't own a cat, you've got a house full of rats."

Lettie held up a huge aluminum colander. "Keep that up, and you'll be wearing this as a hat."

"Don't get mad at me because your dogs have pointed ears, pointed muzzles and long, curling tails. If those aren't hairy rats posing as dogs, what are they?"

"They're purebreds, that's what they are. They're very intelligent."

"They would have to be to fool everybody into thinking they're dogs when they're really rats. As purebreds they're living the good life. If it were known that they're actually rats, they'd be exterminated."

"I'm going to exterminate you!" Lettie cried, and threw the colander at him.

Laughing, Franklyn adeptly caught it. Walking by one of the dishwashers, a middle-aged man with graying brown hair and pale gray eyes, he handed it to him. "I'm just glad she wasn't holding a knife."

Lettie was laughing so hard her belly shook. "Sorry, Franklyn, you know not to insult my babies."

"Yes, ma'am," said Franklyn, going to her and kissing her cheek. "I lost my head. I'd better go finish the receipts."

"Tell Elise hi for me," Lettie said for his ears only. She usually left before he did. He would inspect the kitchen after the staff cleaned it, do the receipts, adjust the thermostat and finally lock up. He was always the last person to leave.

"Will do," he promised.

Lettie watched him go, her love and admiration for him shining in her eyes. She was so happy for him and Elise, she found it hard not to pry. She'd known Franklyn for fifteen years, long before he owned the Vineyard. At twenty-one he'd come to work at a restaurant where she was a sous chef. Some might think Lettie lacked ambition or she simply wasn't good enough to become a head chef, and that's why she had been a sous chef for so long. The fact was, being the right-hand woman to an excellent chef made Lettie feel needed and successful. Plus, she didn't want the responsibility of being head chef. Her life with her husband, Kendrick, who was a police officer, was just the way she wanted it. They worked the same hours, generally, and that gave them a lot of time together which they thoroughly enjoyed. After raising three children, they liked being in their house in Oakland alone. Except for the Pomeranians, and they were little or no trouble.

Franklyn had been a very ambitious chef, though, and good at what he did, as well. He moved on from the restaurant after only a few months, but he'd jokingly promised Lettie, "When I open my restaurant, I want you to be my sous chef." They stayed in touch, and Lettie took him up on his offer four years later when he opened The Vineyard. Over the years, she had met his family and had grown close to them, as well.

Nearly an hour later, Franklyn locked the doors of the restaurant and walked around the corner to where he'd parked his black, late-model Ford pickup. The name of the restaurant was emblazoned across the driver's-side door along with the number to call in order to make a reservation.

Usually, he would take the receipts home with him, and in the morning drop them off at the bank, but since he wasn't going straight home tonight, he'd left the receipts in the office safe. They'd done well tonight. He was lucky to have a loyal clientele, a solid reputation as a good, innovative chef and excellent word-of-mouth advertising.

Operating a restaurant in the black wasn't the easiest thing to do, but if you worked hard, had a good head for business, and were lucky enough to have loyal employees who cared about the business, it was possible to be a success. He looked at chefs like Wolfgang Puck and Emeril Lagasse and realized that it could be done. He loved what he did for a living, and it hadn't taken his becoming a household name for him to own a lucrative business. He owned his apartment. Last year, the building he'd been renting a place in for years decided to offer their longtime renters the opportunity to buy their apartments. Consequently, he owned a two-thousand-square-foot apartment with a view of the bay. Not huge by some people's standards, but roomy in comparison to plenty of other city dwellings. It would be big enough for him, Elise and two children.

It was chilly tonight. As he hurried down the walk to the truck, Franklyn wished he'd thought to wear a hat. After a shower in the bathroom in his office, his hair was still wet. He didn't relish catching a cold. As the owner and head chef, it was inconvenient for him to take sick days.

He gently laid the single red rose on the seat next to him as he slid behind the wheel of the truck. After starting the ignition, he saw by the illuminated dial of the clock that it was ten minutes past eleven. Elise's place was only a five-minute drive if traffic wasn't heavy, which it wasn't at the moment.

Franklyn loved driving at night. The city was lit up spectacularly, especially at this time of year. San Franciscans never did anything in a small way. Businesses, private homes, well-kept and dilapidated, were festively festooned with the season's brightest decorations. Ever since he was a kid, Christmas had been Franklyn's favorite time of the year. He didn't care if the rest of the year was lousy, as Christmas approached he cheered up and opened his heart to the wonderful possibilities the magic in the air seemed to promise. This year, he was in love. And was loved in that special way only a good woman could provide.

He switched on the radio as he drove. Otis Redding's "White Christmas" was on the R & B station he liked listening to. He sang along with Otis.

Elise knew she shouldn't be watching *Penny Serenade,* one of her favorite Cary Grant movies. She knew it was filled with tragedy, and that she always cried, even though she'd seen it countless times. However, when she'd been channel-surfing an hour ago, she could not resist stopping. Then she'd gotten comfortable on the couch and, well, that was it, she was hooked.

After her bath, she'd put on a short silk nightgown in a deep rose shade, and slipped into the matching robe. Both fell only halfway down her thighs. Her hair was in a single braid, and she had on one-carat ruby stud earrings. Her skin was smooth and fragrant due to a generous application of shea-butter skin lotion.

She was curled up on the couch when the doorbell rang.

She had left the light on because she was expecting Franklyn. However, she peered through the peephole before opening the door, nonetheless. She tried to remain calm as she threw the deadbolt, removed the chain and unlocked the door. Her hands shook a bit; she wasn't used to having late-night gentleman callers.

Swinging the door open, she moved back so that he could enter. Franklyn stepped across the threshold, grabbed her about the waist with one arm, and closed the door with the hand in which he held the rose, careful not to crush it.

They were both smiling as their mouths met in a deep, satisfying kiss. The kiss was lingering because of the length of time they'd been apart, intense because they had hungered for each other's touch in that absence, passionate because that was the only way their hearts knew how to express the love they had for each other.

"I wanted to kiss you so many times today," Franklyn breathed between kisses. "I'm surprised I didn't burn everything I cooked." He suckled on her lower lip a moment then hungrily kissed her full on the mouth again.

Elise was content to enjoy the feel of Franklin's hands on her, his mouth on hers, his body pressed urgently against hers. There was a time when she could only imagine how Franklyn would taste, and now the intense male scent of him wafting into her nostrils causing pheromones to race through her body like wildfire. She hadn't realized until now how the smell of a man wreaked havoc with your nervous system.

She was discovering erogenous zones on her body that she never knew existed. It was as if she really was a virgin, and was experiencing physical love for the first time.

Franklyn finally raised his head and held her to his chest. He buried his nose in her hair which smelled like fresh flowers. He suddenly remembered the rose, and laughed abruptly. He presented it to her. "For you."

Smiling up at him, Elise accepted the still-fresh and fragrant rose. She kissed his chin. "Thank you, it's beautiful." She inhaled the heady scent, and turned out of his embrace. "Let me put it in a vase." She met his eyes. "How was the dinner shift?"

"Busy," Franklyn said, wanting to follow her into the kitchen. Instead, he made sure he'd locked the door as he thought he'd done when he'd come in, then he went and sat on the couch. Damn it if he wasn't so enamored with this woman, he didn't even want to be two feet away from her when they were together. She looked so delectable in that gown and robe, which were, coincidentally, nearly the same shade as the rose he'd given her. She was like a flower herself, blossoming right before his eyes.

He remembered exactly what she'd been wearing when she had come to be interviewed for the position of pastry chef more than four years ago. He had asked her to come in the morning because he knew he could spare a half hour at that time of day.

The restaurant was closed, and he'd asked one of the waitresses to let her in and show her to his office. She'd knocked on his door promptly at eight o'clock.

"Come in!" he'd called, not bothering to rise because he was doing the books using the computer and he had been entering figures when she'd knocked.

He heard the door open and close. Still looking at the computer screen, he said, "Have a seat. I'll be with you in a sec."

He finished what he'd been doing and shut down the program. The computer screen returned to its desktop image and he swiveled around in his chair to smile at her.

She had not taken him up on his invitation to sit down. She was standing a few feet in front of his desk wearing a navy blue pantsuit with a white blouse open at the neck, and a pair of black high-heeled sandals. His gaze had gone to her pink-lacquered toenails for some reason, and he'd swallowed hard. She was sexy as hell, but trying to look prim and proper. Her long, thick black hair was restrained in a severe bun at the back of her head. And in her hands was a pile of pink bakery boxes. He had not recalled asking her to bring samples of her work, just herself and her credentials, which he already knew were excellent. The food industry in their area, while big business, was in many ways a close-knit community. He had already heard from very reliable sources that she was a first-rate pastry chef. But if her creations were as appealing as she was, he was looking forward to tasting them.

He got up and made room on his desk for her boxes. She smiled at him and set the boxes down. Offering him her hand, she said, "Elise Gilbert."

He frowned. "I'm sorry, your application says Elise Scott."

She looked slightly uncomfortable. "I was recently divorced."

Thank God, he thought, but managed a sympathetic expression. "I'm sorry."

"I'm not. It was for the best." She forced a smile. "At any rate, I was glad you phoned. I left the application with your sous chef nearly a year ago. I've been working as an assistant pastry chef at the Regency Hotel, but I'd really like to work in more intimate surroundings."

"You want to do your own thing," he correctly surmised.

She nodded slowly. Their eyes met, and she shyly lowered hers but then raised them again and smiled at him. "I'm not going to lie to you. I've never been a head pastry chef. It's not because I lack the credentials. It was simply because when I was married I was trying to make ends meet, working two jobs, and did not take the time to focus on career advancement."

"You were just working for the paycheck."

"Exactly." Her gaze shifted to the boxes on his desk. "Now that I'm only working for myself, I want to see where my talent can take me, and when I came in here a year ago I saw an area that could use improvement, your dessert menu. I like your restaurant. Your menu, the ambience, your reputation for demanding excellence from yourself and those who work for you. But I think that if you would add a more diverse dessert menu, it would garner even more praise from critics and patrons alike."

Then she proceeded to seduce him with ten different desserts ranging from crème brûlée to exquisite layer cakes with dense fillings presented with sauces that were so delicious they brought tears to his eyes. Being a chef, his palate was trained to detect anything off in a recipe, too much salt, too much sugar, too much of any one flavoring. Her creations maintained a nearly perfect balance of dulcet experiences for the tongue.

Being a perfectionist, he never bestowed upon anyone the title of perfection, but she came very close that day.

"You're hired," he said around a mouthful of strawberry shortcake that was like no other strawberry shortcake he'd ever consumed before.

He saw in her eyes that she wanted to jump up and down with glee. However, to her credit, she managed to control her happiness, and shake his hand instead. Of course, touching her for the first time sent a chill through him. Thanks to his always wanting the very best for his restaurant, he'd hired a woman he was certain he'd love to have in his bed. Being who he was, though, he could not woo her because she was now his employee and unwanted attention from an employer to an employee was called sexual harassment. He would have to wait until the feeling was mutual, and then they would still need to tread carefully.

Elise reentered the room carrying the rose in a single-bloom vase. She set it on the coffee table and joined him on the couch, falling into his open arms. "You smell good," she said as she started unbuttoning his long-sleeved denim shirt.

"I just showered." His mouth was on the sensitive area behind her ear. "I couldn't come to my baby without washing the day's stink off me."

She took his earlobe between her lips and sucked it.

Franklyn's member, already semi-erect, grew harder. Her right hand went inside the shirt she'd unbuttoned to caress his chest through his T-shirt. His nipples were also erect.

Franklyn turned his head and their mouths met. Tongues moved sensuously around each other causing spirals of pleasure to ignite all over their bodies. Elise pushed him back onto the couch as they continued to kiss. Franklyn's hands raised the hems of the nightgown and the robe simultaneously. He discovered she wore nothing underneath. He eagerly ran his hands up and down her nude form, ending by cupping her full breasts and gently rubbing the nipples. Elise moaned softly, feeling her female center grow wet and ready to receive him.

Her hands went to the zipper of his jeans.

Franklyn placed his hands over hers. "Let me."

Elise rose and took a step back, allowing him to get up. She watched as he removed his jeans and shorts. He watched her watching him, and had to smile. She had lost some of her shyness. Franklyn removed the rest of his clothing and stood before her, fully erect. Elise went to him and grasped his penis firmly in her hand. Once again, she encouraged him to lie on his back on the couch. "I want to taste you."

Franklyn's penis pulsed in her hand at that statement.

She knelt on the couch and bent down. Franklyn closed his eyes and willed himself to maintain control as her mouth descended. Her tongue teased and tantalized him. She took him and made him hers, and she took great pleasure in doing so. Franklyn didn't know if she was ready for the reaction of a male who was being pleasured by the woman he loved. It wouldn't be something gentle to behold. It would be utterly explosive. He would roar with release because it felt so good he wanted to holler.

He could not look at her while her mouth was on him

because he would be lost. The sight of those luscious lips, wet and plump, would send him over the edge.

He allowed it to go on only a couple of minutes. That's all he could take, then he reached down and pulled her up to his chest. "That was amazing, but too much of that, and I wouldn't be any good to you for a while, and we're just getting started."

Elise smiled and kissed him. He pulled her fully into his arms, rose on his powerful legs and carried her back to the bedroom, all without breaking the kiss.

The bed, queen size, sat four feet off the floor. Elise had put steps at the side of the bed to facilitate getting in and out of it. Franklyn climbed the steps, put her on the bed and climbed in after her. "I feel like Tarzan," he joked about the bed being so high. It was a canopy bed, and Elise had hung mosquito netting around the edges.

She was not bothered by the pests, but just had always wanted a bed so equipped.

"I *have* dreamed of you in a loincloth," she teased him.

Franklyn removed her nightgown and robe and flung them onto the dark-green leather armchair beside her bed. "Whenever I dream about you, you don't have anything on you, except me."

Elise reached under her pillow and produced a condom. "I like your dream better."

Franklyn didn't have the patience to wait for her to put the condom on him, he did it himself. Done, he straddled her and buried his face between her breasts. His penis was at the entrance of her womanhood. Elise slowly rose up and he entered her. She squeezed her vaginal muscles around his shaft, experiencing the excruciating pain and pleasure that came with sexual stimulation. Franklyn trembled slightly.

He was so hard that he too was experiencing sweet pain at first, then his enjoyment was of such a voluptuous nature that he sighed and threw his head back in ecstasy. "Man, I love you."

Elise wrapped her legs around him. He pulled her tightly against him, his arms all the way around her as he practically lifted her off the bed. His thrusts were deep. She answered them with abandon and extreme confidence. It was no longer a matter of who was pleasuring whom, because they were equally under a sensual spell whose aim was fulfillment.

Just before he came, Franklyn had the presence of mind to pull his penis out of her and place its engorged length directly over her clitoris. He then held her tightly against him, rubbing against her until she quivered with powerful release. He felt her intake of breath, heard her sigh as she peaked. It was only after this that he had an orgasm that momentarily left him weak in her arms.

Their bodies were covered with a thin sheen of perspiration as they held each other.

He kissed her fragrant neck. "I could hold you like this forever."

Elise was so relaxed in his embrace that she didn't want to move. "Same here."

"But I can't. You need your sleep. I know your boss, and he doesn't like it when his employees are late."

Elise grinned lazily. "Yeah, he's quite the tyrant. Tell you what, I'll set the clock to wake us at five. That'll give us both time to make it into work before he shows up."

"Sounds good to me," Franklyn said softly. He kissed her forehead and climbed out of bed. "How about a quick shower, and then we'll get some sleep?"

"Go ahead," Elise told him. "The towels are in the closet next to the bathroom. I'll be there in a minute."

She watched him go, then she sat up in bed, reached for the clock on the nightstand, set it for 5:00 a.m., and then gingerly climbed down from the bed and went into the bathroom.

"Where did you get that?" Franklyn asked her when she walked into the room.

He was indicating to an old-fashioned washstand that Elise had found at an estate sale three years ago. She'd refinished the oak and resurfaced the porcelain bowl. Now it was used as a shelf for her bath oil, candles and lotions.

"An estate sale in Nob Hill," she told him. "I love restoring old things."

"You have very good taste," he said appreciatively.

Elise stepped into the shower with him. "Yes, I do," she said, looking at him with open admiration. Franklyn just smiled and kissed her cheek.

Chapter 6

"Where is Amy?" Mariel asked her partner, Laura Watson. Both women were in the employee lounge of the law firm of Crenshaw, Davis and Benson. The lounge was equipped with a stove, a refrigerator and generous counter space, all of which the catering duo put to good use while they worked. It was Christmas Eve, and the two were working instead of at home with loved ones, but someone had to provide the food.

The annual employee Christmas party was in progress in the conference room on the other side of the door. Tables and chairs had been removed from the large space, and a full bar had been set up in one corner of the room. Soft music drifted on the air.

Someone from the law firm had decorated for the party in red and green: huge red-velvet bows, poinsettias and holly, not forgetting the requisite mistletoe. Mariel thought it all looked grotesque and commercial, but she figured after a few drinks no one would notice.

"I don't know," Laura said of Amy's absence. "She was supposed to be here at seven like the rest of the servers."

Mariel removed aluminum foil from a tray of miniature shrimp egg rolls and put them in the oven to stay warm. "Well, the party has started, and she isn't here yet. I hope nothing's wrong, she's usually pretty reliable."

"Me, too," Laura said, frowning with worry. Laura, forty-two, mothered everyone she got close to. "I'll try to phone her if she isn't here in the next ten minutes."

"All right," Mariel said. She picked up a tray of fried wings with a bowl of peppery hot sauce in the center. "I'll circulate until she gets here." She headed for the door, looking very professional in a black tuxedo skirt, crisp white blouse, and black suede high-heeled sandals. Her red hair was in a smooth bob tonight instead of in its customary feathery curls.

"You're a doll," Laura said thankfully. She loathed having to serve. By the end of the night, her corns would be speaking loudly.

"Hey, no problem," Mariel said. Actually, she liked to walk among those she cooked for because she got the chance to see their reactions to the food. She and Laura had been in business for five years now. Like Elise, Mariel had gone to culinary arts school, however she didn't want to work as a chef for someone else. "Don't work for someone else when you can work for yourself," her mother, a successful beauty salon owner, had always told her when she was growing up. She saw her mother, a single mother of three, work hours that would have broken a man. Her mother's example instilled in Mariel a work ethic that she'd never shirked.

An upbeat song by the Black Eyed Peas was playing in the

background. The law firm's employees and their guests were standing around in groups chatting, laughing and generally enjoying each other's company. Pretty sedate for an office Christmas party, but it was still early. Mariel had been at Christmas parties where scantily clad women danced on desktops, and drunken men swilled champagne from their pumps. It was embarrassing what people would do at a year-end shindig.

She paused at a group of eight—four women and four men. Chicken wings were casually taken from the tray, and dipped in sauce, some double-dipped, but what were you going to do, slap their hands?

Mariel smiled at them and was as unobtrusive as possible. That's how they liked their servers—there when they wanted something to eat or drink, but not really *there*. You didn't engage a server in conversation unless you had a question about the food or drinks. She liked it that way, not wanting to have to entertain them *and* serve them.

The tray empty now, Mariel turned and headed back to the employee lounge to get another round of hors d'oeuvres.

As she was walking through the crowd, she heard an all too-familiar voice braying with laughter. She looked in the direction of the sound, and narrowed her eyes in anger. Derrick Scott, looking every bit the successful attorney in an expensive dark-blue suit, was the center of attention in a group of ten or more. They seemed to be congratulating him on something, or just brown-nosing, she couldn't tell. Against her better judgment, she turned around and began walking in their direction. She planned to slowly walk past to see if she could hear what they were talking about.

She kept her face averted just in case Derrick looked her way.

"Scott, here, was brilliant," one man loudly said. He was middle-aged, thin, with a florid face attributable either to ill

health or good booze. From his voice's volume, she assumed
it was the booze. "Caught the prosecution with its pants down
and swooped in and freed our client on a technicality. Any
first-year law student should have known to guard against
malfeasance."

Mariel would have to look up that word, *malfeasance,*
later, but she thought it referred to bad conduct. She stopped
near them, the tray held away from her as she bent and pretended to wipe something from her hose.

"You shouldn't accuse someone of molestation when your
own conduct is less than honorable," Derrick said smugly.

Everyone laughed.

Mariel cringed. That's like the pot calling the kettle black,
she thought. A creep defending a creep. She was sure he'd
been well-compensated.

"Now that Scott's becoming a partner, we're gonna assign
him to more high-profile political cases," the red-faced man
said, patting Derrick on the back.

Partner! Mariel screamed in her head. She straightened up,
rolled her eyes and turned to go back to the employee lounge.
She'd heard enough. When people like Derrick Scott pros-
pered there was something wrong with the universe.

She angrily glanced over her shoulder at him. He happened
to look her way at that moment and visibly blanched. She
smiled evilly at him. He swallowed hard.

She hoped he'd choke on his own saliva.

A few minutes later, she was offering up the minishrimp
egg rolls when someone tapped her on the shoulder. She
didn't even need to look up at him to know it was Derrick.
That's how supremely confident he was. He probably thought
he'd head trouble off at the pass by confronting her.

She allowed the party guests she'd been serving time to

partake of the hors d'oeuvres then she casually walked away, sure that he would follow her. He did.

She stopped walking and turned around to face him once she'd found a private alcove adjacent to the employee lounge. "What is it? I'm working."

"What are you doing here?" Derrick ground out. Six-foot-two, trim and muscular, his square jaw looked stiff with irritation.

"Already answered that question," Mariel said.

"No, you're spying on me!"

"For what purpose?"

"I don't know. You're her cousin, maybe she wants something on me."

"Don't be paranoid. I own the company your firm hired to cater this party. I guess you're not in on that kind of menial decision-making." Mariel popped the gum she'd been chewing all night, and put a hand on her hip. "Don't worry, I'm not in a drink-flinging mood tonight."

"You'd better not be," he warned, still furious with her.

"And don't you refer to Elise as *her*," Mariel warned him. "You know her name, although I'm sure she'd like to forget yours."

"I saw you eavesdropping on our conversation," Derrick accused her, not convinced she wasn't spying on him for some nefarious purpose. He had good reason not to trust her. Mariel was Elise's cousin and her best friend. She'd been Elise's moral support throughout his and Elise's marriage. And she made it known that she hated his guts for the way he'd treated Elise. She'd thrown a drink in his face the last time they'd been in the same room together, and he couldn't prove it, but he *knew* she was the person responsible for letting the air out of all four of his tires. He'd had to have the car towed to a garage to get the tires reinflated. He wasn't going to forget that anytime soon.

"For your information," Mariel told him. "No one cares about you, Derrick. You never cross Elise's mind. She's too busy living her own life, falling in love and getting married to a real man this time!"

Derrick was shocked by the news of Elise's impending nuptials. It had taken him completely by surprise that he should even have any leftover emotions for the stupid woman. She had, after all, simply been a means to an end. He needed support to finish law school, and she'd been gullible enough to allow him to use her. It was cold-blooded, but you had to be cold-blooded if you were to be successful in life. His own parents had cut him off without a cent when he was twenty-one. It was his mother's doing, really. His father would have continued footing the bills for him. But his mother, who had conveniently divorced his father when he was twenty-one and bled the poor man dry, held the purse strings. She told him that until he realized that there was more to life than money and the luxuries that money could buy, he could consider himself on his own financially. She'd thought she was doing it for his own good. Well, he still spoke to her because he figured she had to die someday, and leave him everything. He *was* her only child. But he hadn't genuinely felt any emotional attachment to her since she'd treated him so cruelly. Now, the thought of Elise actually being happy rankled. Why should she have a wonderful personal life when all he had was partnership in a law firm? He had a disturbing thought—what if his mother's blathering about true happiness lying in human relationships, rather than monetary gain, was right?

Mariel had to restrain herself from laughing aloud when she saw the confused and, yes, irritated expression on

Derrick's face. She realized she was laying it on thick. Elise and Franklyn were not engaged, but Derrick didn't know that. Let him ruminate. Let him stew. Let him roast in hell!

Derrick cleared his throat as though something was suddenly clogging it.

"Who is she marrying, some cook she met?" he asked derisively.

"Yes, he's some cook she met. He just happens to own the restaurant."

Derrick would be an utter flop at poker because Mariel could read his face like a book. Her last statement had caused him further irritation. He tried to cover his true feelings with a forced smile and a nonchalant air. "Congratulate her for me," he said as he turned to leave.

"I'll do no such thing," Mariel said to his retreating back. "Because I know you don't mean it!" She did laugh then, and went back to serving the mini egg rolls.

Elise was going to kill her when she told her what she'd done. She'd wait until after Christmas to call her. At this moment, Elise was en route to Sacramento with Franklyn. Mariel glanced at her watch. It was seven forty-five. They were more than likely already there.

Payton and Nedra Gilbert lived on a tree-lined street in one of Sacramento's oldest neighborhoods. All of the houses were unique, not cookie-cutter like the houses in the newer subdivisions. Their house was a Sears Honor Bilt that Payton's parents had built in 1940. People didn't believe it when they were told that Payton's parents had ordered their house from Sears and boxes had arrived in two railroad cars with a leather-bound instruction book. They'd built it with the help of friends and family. Payton and Nedra owned one of the few mail-order homes left standing. They had, of course, made improvements on the original design over the years. The house had formerly been a mere fifteen hundred square feet. Today, due to added rooms, it was closer to three thousand square feet.

The wood siding had silvered over the years, and the color blended in nicely with the many trees and shrubs on the large corner lot. Payton's prowess as a gardener was evident in the lush lawn and the various flowering plants in the front and back yards.

When Elise and Franklyn pulled into the driveway and parked behind two other cars, Elise experienced a moment of panic. She hadn't brought a man home since she'd brought Derrick here to meet her folks. And that hadn't turned out well.

She wasn't afraid that Franklyn wouldn't be welcomed by her family because they were good people and never rude to guests. What she feared were the questions. There would be plenty of them. From her mother and father and her two sisters, who were both happily married even though they were younger than Elise. Her sister, Dasia, already had two children. Elise felt like she'd been left in the dust.

She paused with her hand on the door's handle so long that Franklyn asked, "Elise, what's the matter?"

She smiled at him. "I just don't want them comparing you to Derrick. There *is* no comparison."

Franklyn laughed shortly. "I'll have to win them over with my charm."

"Family. The Inquisition will seem tame compared to the questioning they're going subject you to."

"I'm ready for them. Don't worry." His hand momentarily went to his coat pocket.

"Okay," Elise said as she went to open the door.

"Wait, let me get that," Franklyn said as he hurriedly got out of the truck and jogged around to her side. "Someone might be watching. I don't want to have points taken off for not being a gentleman."

He helped her out of the cab of the truck. Elise kissed his chin and put her arms around him. Franklyn hugged her back. Behind them someone cleared his throat.

Elise looked up at her father who was walking across the lawn in the twilight. He had a lit cigar in his hand. Her mother had forbidden him to smoke them in the house.

"Daddy!"

She clasped Franklyn's hand and went to hug her father. Payton, six feet tall, stocky, with dark-brown skin and a shiny bald head grinned at her. "Hey, sugar."

She had to let go of Franklyn's hand when her father pulled her into his arms in a big bear hug. He squeezed her tightly and then set her away from him so he could get a good look at her. "I guess life has been treating you right because you're beautiful, daughter."

Elise was beaming. "You're looking fine too, Daddy." She reclaimed Franklyn's hand. "I know I've mentioned Franklyn a lot over the years, but here he is in the flesh. Franklyn, meet my dad, Payton."

Payton shook Franklyn's hand and smiled at him. "Good to meet you, Franklyn. Welcome to our home."

"Good to meet you too, sir. Thanks for inviting me."

"Elise is our eldest, and she never brings anyone home to meet us. Curiosity was eating us up," Payton joked. "Come on inside. Her mother and sisters are dying to meet you."

Elise and Franklyn followed Payton onto the porch and inside. Icicle lights framed the entire house, a beautiful wreath was on the front door, and as soon as they stepped into the front hall, they could smell the scent of the pine Christmas tree, a huge seven-footer in the corner of the living room.

Hearing the door open and close, Nedra Gilbert came to see who had arrived. All day long they'd been getting visits from friends and relatives. Tomorrow would be even busier. But she hadn't seen Elise in months. Her daughter hadn't even come home for Thanksgiving, spending the day in San Francisco with Franklyn, instead, so she was delighted to see her.

Nedra was tiny, unlike her daughter. Her head barely came to Elise's chin. She had very light-brown skin with a sprinkling of freckles across her nose, auburn hair and light-green eyes. Hugging Elise with all her might, she cried, "It's about time you came to see us!"

Elise laughed and kissed her mother's forehead. "I know, I know. I'm a terrible daughter."

Nedra smiled up at her. "You're a wonderful daughter."

They parted and Elise introduced her to Franklyn. "This is Franklyn, Mom. Franklyn, my mother, Nedra."

"So, we finally get to meet Franklyn," Nedra said, sizing him up, and liking what she saw. "Lordy, he's good-looking, isn't he? And big, too. He could put you in his pocket, Elise."

Everyone laughed good-naturedly, the sound of which brought Elise's sisters—twenty-four-year-old Chassie and twenty-seven-year-old Dasia—into the room. The women hugged and kissed their big sister, leaving two different shades of lipstick on her cheeks.

Chassie, tall like Elise, with dark-brown hair and golden eyes, looked Franklyn up and down admiringly. "Dang, Elise, he makes Derrick look like a boy."

"Chassie!" Nedra reprimanded her.

"Well, it's not as if we weren't all thinking it," Chassie said, unrepentant.

Franklyn liked her honesty. It was best to get everything out in the open right away. He planned to be in Elise's life and, therefore, their lives for a lot of years to come.

"It's all right," he said with a smile. "Comparisons are inevitable. You all don't know me yet. I want you to know, though, that I have been in love with Elise for nearly four years, and all I want to do is make her happy."

Dasia, around five-five and full-figured, grinned impishly. "Amen, amen!" She turned around as if she was looking for someone. "Where's my husband, I want him out here so he can see what a romantic guy looks like. Aaron!"

A thin, brown-skinned man with a scraggly goatee appeared in the doorway. He had been in the family room watching ESPN with his brother-in-law, George, when he'd heard his wife's distinctive screeching. He was a couple of inches taller than Dasia, and looked like he was one meal away from starvation; in reality he was a bottomless pit when it came to putting food away.

"Yes, baby?" he said before he saw the new arrivals. When he spied Elise, he grinned broadly, transforming his thin face into something close to handsome.

"Hey, girl, how you doin'?" He hugged her.

Elise found herself giggling, it never failed to amuse her how Dasia rode roughshod over Aaron, and Aaron, totally besotted with her sister, humbly ignored her sometimes-rude behavior. Aaron was a sweet guy. He worked hard as a plumber, had bought Dasia a beautiful house and was a doting father to their one- and two-year-old children.

Elise glanced briefly at Dasia's stomach, wondering if maybe number three was on the way. Dasia got especially hard to live with when she was pregnant. She had poor Aaron jumping up to do her bidding all day long.

"Aaron, it's good to see you, too. This is Franklyn Bryant."

"Your boyfriend?" He looked delighted by the prospect.

"Yeah," Elise said.

Aaron pumped Franklyn's hand. "Hey, man, welcome, welcome."

"Thanks," Franklyn said, liking Aaron already.

George stuck his head in the room, his eyes falling first on his wife, Chassie. "What's all the noise? Oh, Elise, you made it. What's up, girlie?"

Elise went to hug her other brother-in-law. George was six-three and the size of a tree, at least that's how Elise thought of him because he was solid. Gentle as a man could be, but strong, dependable and Chassie was his world. They hadn't been blessed with children yet. They'd been married less than a year.

"You must be Franklyn," he said as he came forward to grasp Franklyn's hand in a firm grip. "The women have been talking about little else all afternoon. Aaron and I were beginning to feel inferior."

Franklyn liked him, too. He laughed shortly. "Now you see you had nothing to worry about."

"I don't know," said George, a smile on his face. "I hear you can cook. Aaron and I are lousy cooks."

Payton laughed louder than anyone else and ushered everyone into the living room where they sat on the over-stuffed couch and chairs. The fireplace was lit because the temperature was in the forties tonight, and the room had a red-golden glow to it.

As soon as they were all seated, of course, Nedra asked if she could get Franklyn and Elise anything from the kitchen. Were they hungry or thirsty? How about a cup of Payton's eggnog? He'd put too much rum in like he always did, but a cup would definitely help them sleep tonight.

"Mom," said Chassie, "I don't think Elise or Franklyn have any trouble getting to sleep at night."

Sitting beside Aaron on the couch, Dasia seconded that with an, "I know that's right!" To which her husband pinched her on the sly and whispered, "Don't embarrass Elise, she'll never bring anyone else home to meet us."

Chassie's meaning went right over her mother's head. Nedra asked Elise, "How is Mariel? I invited her here for Christmas, but she told me she had to work tonight and probably wouldn't be up to the drive in the morning."

"Yeah, she had a party to cater," Elise told her, not going into detail. "But she's doing well, I saw her just last week."

Payton's brother, Wilfred, was Mariel's father. He lived in San Diego. Her mother lived in Oakland, so she saw her more often. Payton and Nedra loved their niece and had been including her in their holiday celebrations since she was a child.

Nedra sighed. "I'll have to call her tomorrow and wish her a merry Christmas."

The conversation turned to how long Elise and Franklyn had been dating.

"Around five months now," Elise said, looking at Dasia who had asked the question.

Dasia's thick eyebrows rose in surprise. "You worked with Franklyn for four years, and you mean to tell me you never flirted with him the whole time?"

Elise laughed. She looked at Franklyn with her love for him reflected in her eyes.

"Oh, we flirted subtly for years, but neither of us could say anything because Franklyn is my boss, and if I didn't feel the same way about him, I could have cried sexual harassment. And as for me, after going through a messy divorce, I had to be darn sure of him before I told him how I really felt about him. So, it took us a while to come to that point."

"But four years!" Dasia cried.

"Honey, I've been in love with you all my life," Aaron reminded her. Aaron's family had lived on the same street when he and Dasia were growing up. They grew up together, went to the same schools, but it wasn't until Aaron got his plumbing license and started building a house for Dasia that he finally got up the nerve to tell her how her truly felt about her. It had taken Dasia another year before she had fallen in love with the boy who'd rarely even spoken to her, let alone shown a romantic interest in her. She reached over and tenderly grasped his hand. "How could I forget that?" she asked softly.

Elise smiled. Aaron was good for her sister.

"I think it's very romantic that you two loved each other from afar," Chassie said. "And I'm happy for you."

Forgetting her romantic moment with her husband, Dasia turned on her sister, "I'm happy for them, too. I never said I wasn't happy for them."

Elise whispered to Franklyn, "Don't mind them, they always spar like this."

"Well, you keep asking nosy questions," Chassie pointed out. "Elise brought Franklyn home to meet her family, not to be interrogated. Chill out!"

"I *am* calm," Dasia insisted. "You're the one with her butt on her shoulder."

"If you weren't pregnant I'd wipe up the floor with you," Chassie told her.

"Pregnant!" Aaron said, stunned. He stared at Dasia. "Dasia?"

"I was going to make it a Christmas gift, honey," Dasia said of her announcement.

She glared at Chassie. "You've got a big mouth."

"Well, you made me mad," Chassie defended herself.

"You promised to keep it quiet. Okay, well, I'm going to tell on you." She turned to George. "George…"

"Honey, I'm going to have a baby!" Chassie hurriedly said before her sister could get the words out. Chassie threw her arms around her husband's neck. George held her tightly against his chest. He felt a little disoriented. Giddy, even. Soon, a huge grin spread across his face. Tears shone in his dark eyes. "Oh, baby, I'm so happy. I know we've been trying a while now, but after months of nothing happening, I thought there might be something seriously wrong with me."

"With you?" Chassie asked, incredulous. She repeatedly kissed his lips. "Baby, there is absolutely nothing wrong with you. You're going to be a wonderful father."

Nedra sat fanning her face with her hands. "Oh, my Lord, two more grandbabies on the way. All this love, and on Christmas Eve, too. I don't think I can take any more good news."

Franklyn wanted to tell her that there was more good news. He had been carrying a flawless two-carat diamond solitaire ring around in his coat pocket for two weeks now, waiting for the right time to ask Elise to be his wife.

He had never imagined the right time would be during his first visit home to meet her relatives. But he felt compelled to get on one knee in front of Elise, and propose.

When he rose, and knelt before her, all the women in the room collectively drew in a breath and held it. All except Elise who was bug-eyed with shock.

A man getting on one knee meant only one thing. He was a traditionalist and was about to ask you to marry him. "Elise," he said, taking her left hand in his. "After meeting your family, I can't think of a more perfect time to ask you to marry me. You and I have had similar experiences that made us wary about falling in love. Yet, we fell for each other. Hard. From the look on your face, I know this comes as a surprise to you. But the fact is, *I'd* hoped that we would be married *before* Christmas, so credit a guy with some restraint. Will you marry me?"

Franklyn was so intent on gazing into Elise's eyes, trying to gauge her feelings, that he almost forgot about the ring in his pocket. He reached in and removed the ring in its brown velvet case.

Elise's mind was racing, but one insistent directive was screaming inside her head: Yes, say yes! Say yes right now before the man thinks you don't want to marry him!

"Yes!" she croaked.

Franklyn heard her, but no one else was close enough.

"What'd she say?" asked Payton.

"I think she said yes," Chassie said.

Franklyn was kissing Elise. Elise was crying. Nedra was crying. Dasia was peeking around Aaron trying to get a glimpse of the ring.

Franklyn and Elise eventually came up for air, and that's when he put the ring on her finger. Elise looked down at the ring and back up at Franklyn. Everything was happening too fast. Did she deserve to be this happy? What had she ever done to merit having a man like Franklyn love her? But he did, and she loved him. Why couldn't she let go of the doubts about her character, live in the present and plan a future with this wonderful man? That nagging voice was persistent though. From this point on she had to be exemplary in every aspect of her life. Franklyn must never regret having proposed to her. "I love you so much," she whispered.

Franklyn kissed her again. "Good, because I'm yours from now on."

Elise smiled happily. "And I'm yours." They pressed their cheeks together. Elise turned her head to the side and that's when she remembered that her family was in the room witnessing everything. Franklyn got up and sat beside Elise on the couch. Her family crowded forward then, hugging Elise, congratulating him and shaking his hand.

"This has been some night," Payton said, still amazed by everything that had transpired in the last few minutes. He sat down in one of the chairs and sighed heavily. Nedra went to sit on his lap, and comfortingly put her arm about his shoulders. "Yes, my head is still spinning." She kissed his cheek and softly added, "But I certainly do like her choice, don't you?"

Payton smiled up at her and whispered, "It's a marked improvement."

Later on, after Dasia and Chassie, who lived in town, had gone home with their husbands and the children, Franklyn and Elise sat on the deep front porch talking. It was nearly midnight. Payton and Nedra had retired for the night. Nedra had told them she'd made the beds in Elise's old room and in the guest room. Elise had earlier explained to Franklyn that her parents were uncomfortable with their daughters bringing boyfriends home and sleeping with them under their roof. He had naturally understood.

They cuddled on the porch swing, both of them in jackets because the temperature had dropped farther while they'd been inside. "I've decided I'm going to try out for the pastry competition," Elise told him quietly.

"That's good," Franklyn said without hesitation. "I'm glad

you decided to do it. What changed your mind? You didn't seem too enthusiastic when Bailey asked you."

"It's part of my makeover," Elise told him.

"Makeover?"

"Yeah," Elise began. "Some brides want to shed a few pounds before they marry their guy. Some may want to get their teeth fixed. Some may have to get their finances straight before they can come to the marriage feeling as if everything's out in the open and the marriage is starting on the right foot. But with me it's the residual negative feelings I have about myself that came from being involved with Derrick Scott. I didn't accept Bailey's challenge right away because I doubted myself. Well, I'm not going to refuse to do something because I'm afraid anymore. I'm going to feel the fear and do it anyway. This way, when we get married, I can look you in the eyes and honestly say I'm the best I can be. You deserve no less than that."

Franklyn squeezed her a bit tighter. "Do you think I'm coming to the marriage a perfect specimen?"

Elise smiled up at him. "No, I know you're not perfect, Franklyn. I'm not aiming for perfection, either. This is just something I need to do to prove to myself that he didn't win. He does not continue to influence my choices in life in any way!"

"The best revenge is living well," Franklyn said.

"Who said anything about revenge?"

"Of course you want revenge, Elise. He used you. And you never did anything to get even."

"You sound like Mariel."

Franklyn laughed. "Sometimes that cousin of yours makes a lot of sense."

Elise was silent, thinking. Revenge? Yes, she did want to

see Derrick suffer, but she would get just as much satisfaction simply knowing, for herself, that what he did to her didn't leave her incapacitated in any way. Franklyn was right, the best revenge was living well.

"Okay, you've got something there," she told him. "Revenge might be my goal, but it'll be a kind of quiet revenge. He'll never know about it, but I'll get the satisfaction of knowing that I've risen above the effects of the verbal abuse and emerged a happy, sane person."

"I see what you mean," Franklyn assured her.

Elise peered up at him. "Did you ever get revenge on her?"

"Oh, yeah," said Franklyn. "I quit abusing myself with booze and fistfights. I killed her memory by making the Vineyard a success and falling in love with you. I'm nailing her coffin shut by marrying you."

Elise kissed him for that.

Chapter 7

Because he was sleeping in a strange house whose sounds he wasn't accustomed to, Franklyn woke at four in the morning and went downstairs to get a glass of water. He wore a pair of light-blue pajamas and was barefoot, but the floors were mostly carpeted. As he passed Elise's bedroom door, he resisted knocking softly upon it.

While he was pouring the water, he heard footfalls and looked up to find Payton standing in the doorway. "Couldn't sleep?" Payton asked.

Franklyn put the water pitcher back in the refrigerator and closed the door. "I think it's because your street's so quiet. I'm used to more noise when I sleep. Plus, I get up early anyway. It's a hard habit to break."

"I hear you," Payton said. He went and got himself a glass of water, drank it and set the glass in the sink. "I'm on my way to the shop." They referred to the bakery as *the shop,* as Nedra's parents, who had started the business, had done.

"You're going to be open today?" Franklyn asked, surprised. Many businesses closed their doors on Christmas Day even if they were open every other holiday on the calendar.

"Only for a few hours," Payton said, smiling. "It's tradition."

Nedra came into the room, also dressed for work. "Hello, Franklyn, what're you doing up this early? Couldn't sleep?"

Payton saved Franklyn a reply by answering for him. "He habitually gets up early," he said to his wife before crossing the room to kiss her on the cheek.

"Why don't we take him with us then?" suggested Nedra. She tied a red scarf beneath her chin and strolled over to the coat tree where her husband helped her into a tan wool coat. She looked up at Franklyn. "Every year we open the shop at 8:00 a.m. and serve free coffee or hot chocolate for the kids, and hot donuts to our friends and neighbors. We'll be back here by eleven-thirty. I'll leave a note for Elise telling her where you are."

Making donuts at four in the morning. To the average man that might not sound enticing, but Franklyn wasn't a normal man, he was a chef. "Thanks, I'd love to help out."

Nedra smiled her pleasure. "Then run upstairs and get dressed. I'll write the note while you're gone."

Twenty minutes later, they were pulling to the curb in front of the Gilberts' bakery in Old Town, a section of Sacramento that had been historically preserved. Payton turned off the ignition in the van and proudly said, "Here we are!"

Franklyn, dressed in jeans, a long-sleeve shirt, black athletic shoes and his leather jacket, opened his door in the back, stepped down and opened the door for Nedra who had been sitting up front with her husband.

The bakery was large, the storefront beautifully restored, reminding Franklyn of another era. Gazing up at it in awe, he said sincerely, "It's a beautiful store."

Nedra took his arm as they followed Payton to the front door. Franklyn noticed the absence of steel mesh covering the picture windows and glass doors. "You don't have a problem with break-ins?"

Payton laughed. "The city has cameras on the streets in this neighborhood, and we have a security system. We're careful. Nedra just found bars on the windows aesthetically repulsive, her words not mine."

"We're insured," said his wife. "What are they going to steal from a bakery? It would take lots of muscle and a huge truck to steal the equipment, and they can have all the stale donuts they want. Like any smart business, we take the receipts with us when we lock up at six."

Payton had the door open by then and they walked into the cool building. The air was chilly, and smelled like baked bread. Franklyn supposed that scent had permeated the walls of the bakery over the years. He liked it.

Payton locked the door behind them and switched on the lights. The black-and-white checkerboard floor gleamed with polish. The display cases were spotless. There were about six tables with four chairs each, and as many booths along the walls upholstered in red leather. It reminded Franklyn of a fifties diner. He could imagine coming here every morning and opening up as Payton and Nedra must have done for the past thirty years.

"Come on back," Payton said, turning on lights as he walked into the kitchen where all the real work was done.

Stainless-steel countertops, huge mixing vats with equally huge mixers, all stainless steel. The kitchen fairly gleamed. The floor was white tile in here, and scrupulously clean.

Nedra went to the big refrigerator and began pulling out bowls of dough that they'd mixed last night before closing up. Payton was on the other side of the kitchen readying the fryer for the copious amounts of oil he'd soon be pouring into it. Franklyn knew that most donuts were fried, but he'd rarely seen it done since pastry-making was neither his forte nor something he'd shown much interest in over the years. He did, however, know the basics.

Nedra explained that they allowed the dough to warm up once they took it from the refrigerator. It would be more pliable then, and they could make quick work of shaping the donuts before dropping them into the hot oil. After the donuts came out of the oil they were allowed to sit a minute or two, then they were dipped in the icing.

They were making only glazed donuts this morning. They were a customer favorite, and they were best enjoyed piping hot. The three of them chatted amiably while they waited for the dough to warm up and the oil to get hot. Nedra had poured the dough out of the steel bowls onto floured kneading boards so that it would warm up quicker.

"This was always Elise's favorite thing to do," Nedra told Franklyn. "That girl could shape a donut in a second. She has this thing she does with her wrist, a quick flick and there you have it, a donut. I never did get the hang of it."

"Your pop was quick like that," Payton said. "Elise must have gotten it from him."

Nedra smiled at her husband, remembering her papa. "He did have agile fingers. Momma was a terror in the kitchen, though. Papa put her out front. She was very good with the customers, and they loved her Irish accent. Thought it was quaint. I really don't know how they managed running a business being an interracial couple back in the day, but they made it look easy. I had a happy childhood."

"How about you, sir?" Franklyn asked. "Where did you grow up?"

"I'm still living in the house my parents built in 1940," Payton told him. "I used to see Nedra at my high school, but I would never say anything to her. I thought she was white with a deep tan."

Nedra laughed. "I had to approach *him*. Back then, here in California, the schools were integrated, but the races still kept pretty much to themselves. There wasn't any interracial dating that I noticed. Payton would look at me, but never say a word. One day I cornered him at his locker and asked him to go with me to get a soda after school. 'Are you crazy, girl?' he asked. 'Negro boys don't take white girls for sodas.' 'Well,' I said to him, 'Do *Negro* boys take Negro girls for sodas, because that's what I am, you dope!' As we know, if you've got one drop of black blood, you're black. He had to meet my parents before he really believed me though."

They had Franklyn laughing out loud the entire time. When the dough had gotten sufficiently warm, Nedra instructed him in the fine art of dough manipulation. After a few bad starts, he finally got the hang of it and was shaping the donuts nearly as swiftly as Nedra. Once they got a long baking tray full, they carried them across the kitchen to Payton who placed them in the hot oil and in what seemed a very short time took them back out again. Golden-brown donuts were soon being produced at a speed that amazed Franklyn. Soon he was assigned to glaze-duty. Nedra shaped the dough. Payton fried the donuts and Franklyn dipped them in the sugary glaze. By eight they had made five hundred of the sweet treats, and Nedra went to open the front door.

At least fifty people were waiting on the sidewalk to get in and get first crack at the warm confections.

Nedra passed out coffee and hot chocolate in paper cups. Franklyn handed out the donuts, and Payton stayed in the kitchen doing triple duty. They didn't think five hundred donuts were going to last them until eleven o'clock. Folks were steadily making the bell ring over the bakery door as they entered.

There were a lot of "Merry Christmases" shouted out with good wishes thrown in. Franklyn observed it all with a warm feeling growing in his heart for Payton and Nedra. They were indeed beloved in their neighborhood. As a couple they complemented each other. Nedra often finished Payton's sentences, and Payton seemed to anticipate Nedra's needs as if by some psychic connection. Franklyn supposed that's what happened when you had been married to someone for more than thirty years.

At eleven, Nedra locked the door, the last customer having left ten minutes earlier with a cheery, "Merry Christmas and a happy New Year!" in his wake. When Franklyn and Nedra went to the kitchen to check on Payton, they found him washing the stainless-steel bowls that the dough had been in. "How'd it go?" he asked.

"Beautifully," Nedra told him.

"Nearly two hundred people showed up by my count," Franklyn said.

Payton grinned. Franklyn wondered at his level of pleasure, seeing as how he had not been present to see any of the customers come in and reap the benefits of their efforts. It was a prime example of being good for goodness' sake.

Now he knew what that verse in the popular Christmas song truly meant. He had never given it much thought until this moment.

Elise had brunch ready for them when they returned to the house: smoked sausages, scrambled eggs cooked with onions, peppers and cheddar cheese, fresh Southern-style biscuits, and fresh fruit. They sat around the kitchen table talking and eating heartily.

Nedra told Elise all about the morning's activities at the bakery, applauding Franklyn's efforts. "Next year he'll probably be able to do it without Payton and me."

"Oh, now, Nedra, don't go enlisting the boy a full year ahead of time. Let's sneak up on him when it gets close to this time next year," Payton said, laughing.

"That is if Elise will be fit to travel this time next year," Nedra said.

Franklyn paused with a forkful of scrambled eggs halfway to his mouth.

"Tell him, Elise," Payton said, looking as if he were privy to some top-secret information. "Or warn him."

Elise laughed. "Don't pay them any attention, Franklyn. The fact is, Dasia, Chassie and I were all born either on December 25 or within days of the date."

"Your birthday's January third," Franklyn remembered.

Elise nodded. "Dasia was born on Christmas Day, and Chassie was born on December twenty-seventh. Dasia's boys, Aaron, junior, and Kahlel were born on December twenty-eighth and January first, respectively."

"That's really coincidental," Franklyn admitted.

"It's not coincidental," Nedra said. "It's just how this family does things. I was born on December twenty-sixth and Payton was born on January first."

"It's getting weirder," Franklyn said.

Payton laughed. "Don't be surprised if your child is born somewhere between Christmas Day and January third, Elise's birthday."

Nedra looked embarrassed. "Listen to us. The children haven't been engaged twenty-four hours yet, and we're already talking about grandchildren. We are so greedy!" Then, she smiled at Franklyn and Elise and asked, "You *do* want children, don't you?"

Elise wished they'd change the subject. She and Franklyn hadn't seriously discussed having children. She assumed they would, but she didn't really know how soon Franklyn wanted children.

"Of course we both love children," Elise began reluctantly. Her eyes drifted to Franklyn's face, imploring him to save her.

"We haven't decided on the number or anything but I think it's safe to say that Elise and I definitely want to have children."

"Leave them alone, Nedra. It's obvious that's something they haven't gotten around to talking about. They just got engaged. They don't even know how long the engagement will last."

Franklyn reached over and clasped Elise's hand. "That's true. Short or long? I prefer a short engagement."

"How short?" Elise asked, feeling more trepidation at the thought of making wedding plans than she thought she should be feeling. Butterflies clamored for space in her stomach. She had no qualms about marrying Franklyn, but what bride-to-be didn't get nervous when thinking of buying her dress, sending out the invitations, booking the place where the wedding would be held and the reception would be held. Plus, she didn't want her parents footing the bill this time. They'd paid for that fiasco with Derrick. This time she would pay for the wedding, so it definitely had to be a simple affair.

"Three months?" Franklyn bargained.

Actually ninety days didn't send Elise into a panic. "I can work with three months," Elise told him, smiling into his golden-brown eyes, and thinking, God, this man is incredible!

"Three months is good," Payton said. "Your mother and I will, of course, pay for the wedding. You will be getting married here in Sacramento, won't you?"

Elise had given that no thought whatsoever. The last time she'd been married in the family church and the reception had been held right here in the backyard.

"First of all," she told her parents. "We haven't talked about where we want to get married. Franklyn's family is in Glen Ellen. Most of our friends are in San Francisco. Secondly, I don't want to put a financial burden on you. I'll pay for the wedding myself."

Franklyn squeezed her hand. "*We'll* pay for the wedding."

"Honestly, Elise," Payton interrupted. "Your mother and I always regretted your first wedding."

"Well, so did I!" Elise said, laughing.

"That's not what I meant," her father said, frustrated. "What I meant was, you and Derrick got married so quickly that Nedra and I always regretted we didn't have time to plan the ceremony better. Your sisters got beautiful weddings. You were married in the church and we served hot dogs and burgers in the backyard afterward. We would like the opportunity to send you off in style."

Elise sat dumbfounded. From the expressions on her parents' faces, they were sincere. She knew they could be silly about their superstitions. Could they actually believe her marriage to Derrick had fallen apart because they hadn't given her a more lavish wedding?

They had also probably expected her and Derrick to have

children. She'd nipped that in the bud by going on birth control pills *and* making him use a condom every time.

She wasn't going to work two jobs to support them plus get pregnant. As soon as the divorce was in the works she'd stopped taking birth control pills, figuring it would be a very long time before she'd let another man near her. And it had been.

She had to set her parents straight right now. "Mom, Dad, I don't want you thinking that my marriage with Derrick didn't work out because of anything you two did, or didn't do. Even if you had spent twenty thousand dollars on it, it would have still failed. I never told you this, but he mistreated me. He was verbally abusive, and toward the end he admitted that he'd married me only so that I could support him while he went to law school. I didn't tell you any of this because I didn't want to worry you, but that's the real reason I divorced him."

"He didn't cheat on you?" Nedra asked. That was what Elise had told her parents. She'd told no one in her family the truth.

"It was less embarrassing to admit infidelity than to admit I was a fool," Elise said.

"But, honey, you weren't the fool, he was," said her father. "He was a fool for not recognizing how wonderful you are. You can't fault yourself for being gullible. Gullibility is a characteristic of someone in love. You *want* to believe in them. That's why you're so lucky to have found someone who will be truthful with you and will insist on your being truthful with him, no matter how much the truth hurts. I can tell that's what you and Franklyn have. Now stop being stubborn and let your mother and me give you two a nice wedding. We ain't committing to twenty thousand but we can go up to at least ten."

"Ten thousand *dollars?*" Elise said, her voice squeaky.

"Honey, how much money do we have in Elise's wedding fund?" Payton asked.

Her parents were notorious for starting funds. The Christmas fund, the girls-gotta-go-to-college fund, the-spoil-the-grandkids fund, the retirement fund.

"Twelve thousand dollars," said Nedra. She kept the family's books.

"Why would you even *start* a wedding fund for me?" Elise asked, incredulous.

"Well, honey," Nedra said. "We thought it was wise to start one when you got divorced at twenty-five. Twenty-five is an awfully young age to decide to stay single for the rest of your life. We know you swore you would, but we didn't believe that for a minute."

Elise was shaking her head in disbelief. "Okay, you win."

Her mother got up, trotted around the table and hugged her tightly. "Great! You and Franklyn decide where you want to get married. We're not going to force our opinions on you. We want your day to be everything you two can imagine it should be. And if you should give us a grandbaby a year or two afterward, well, we'll take it!"

Elise met Franklyn's eyes across her mother's shoulder. He was smiling at her with tender affection. Elise glanced down at the ring on her finger, then back up at Franklyn. Her mind was still in the stratosphere. She was marrying Franklyn Bryant, the man she'd loved longer than any other man in her life; the man she hadn't expected would ever declare himself to her. It all seemed impossible. But she was beginning to believe in the impossible.

When they got back to Elise's place, Elise dropped her overnight bag and shoulder bag onto the foyer table, and asked Franklyn to make himself at home while she ran to the bathroom. Chuckling, Franklyn said, "Why didn't you tell me you needed to stop? I would have been happy to."

"I hate using public restrooms," Elise said as she hurried down the hall.

Franklyn went and sat on the couch, picked up the remote from the coffee table, and switched on the TV. *A Christmas Story* was on TBS. The hapless kid who would do anything to get a BB gun for Christmas had his tongue stuck to a flagpole. Franklyn turned. There was only so much humiliation he could watch the poor kid go through.

He was watching Whoopi Goldberg portraying Santa on Lifetime Television when Elise came into the room and sat beside him. "Whew," she said. "So, what's the verdict? Think you can stand my relatives for the next fifty years?"

Franklyn got closer and put his arm about her shoulders. "I had a good time," he told her. "Your parents are as nutty as mine. They're great! As for your sisters, they will get along just fine with Erica. Jason, on the other hand, is not going to be happy to have two more outspoken women in the family. Mom and Erica have been giving him hell for years."

"If he doesn't like outspoken women, why is he falling so hard for Sara? She's definitely a woman who knows her own mind."

"Jason's ruled by his gonads. He finds Sara very attractive. What I want to see is him hanging in there long enough to get to know the real Sara and discovering that he not only likes the package, but what's inside."

"I have a feeling he will," Elise said, trying to stifle a yawn. She had been up very late last night talking to her sisters. They had plenty of advice for the bride-to-be, and were even more delighted to point out the horrors of pregnancy so that she would be prepared when her time came. She'd tried to change the subject numerous times but there was no turning Dasia and Chassie off once they got going.

"You look like you could use a nap," Franklyn observed. "Want me to get out of here so you can rest?"

"No!" Elise said hurriedly. "Except for the drive, this is the first time we've really had the chance to be alone."

Franklyn placed a kiss on her forehead. "I know, and I've missed holding you. But there's work tomorrow." He got to his feet, preparing to leave.

The Vineyard would be open from Tuesday until Saturday: New Year's Eve. When the doors closed, there would be a New Year's Eve party in the dining room at the restaurant. Spouses and boyfriends or girlfriends were invited. It would last until the wee hours of the morning.

Elise rose too and looked at him, puzzled. However she didn't do or say anything to stop his going. Maybe he had something important to do today. It was nearly 5:00 p.m. They'd gotten a relatively early start from Sacramento. Her parents had only tried to delay them a few dozen times. Those delays were easily thwarted, then they were on the road.

She tried not to frown with frustration as she walked him to the door. "Okay, if you have to go." She would have preferred spending the evening in bed with him. If this was what happened after you got engaged, you could keep it!

She waited for a chaste kiss at the door.

Franklyn, however, swiftly turned around, pulled her into his arms and laid one on her that left her reeling. "To hell with sleep. We're young. We can sleep when we're too old to make love."

"God forbid that ever happening," Elise said, laughing.

Franklyn picked her up in his arms. "Bedroom or bath?"

"Let's shower first. I feel grungy."

* * *

Tuesday afternoon, Elise was in the kitchen at the Vineyard putting a tray of custards in the oven when the double doors of the kitchen swung open and Bailey Hitchcock strode in, a determined expression on her face. Dressed for battle in black jeans, a long-sleeve black shirt and black leather boots, Bailey looked like a furious female Johnny Cash. She was the woman in black.

"Elise Gilbert!" she shouted.

Franklyn looked around, taking his attention away from a capon that he was basting. He smiled. Elise had obviously forgotten to phone Bailey as she'd promised to. He placed the capon back in the oven and went on to his next task.

Across the room, Elise sighed and began pouring more custard into baking dishes. Getting harassed by Bailey or not, she had a schedule to keep. The other workers in the kitchen were so used to boisterous voices and other disturbances in their workplace that they, too, went on with their various duties. Not that they were not paying strict attention to everything that was transpiring around them.

"Didn't I tell you that if you didn't contact me within the week, that I would come down here looking for you? It's been nearly three weeks! We have deadlines, you know. We have to submit the team's line-up and then we have to be approved. Someone from the judging board will come to interview you. They'll want to know what sort of training you've had, and how many years you've been working as a pastry chef."

Elise finished another tray of custards and put them in the oven as well. This done, she turned to face Bailey. "Has the deadline passed? Is that why you've burst in here yelling at the top of your lungs?" she asked with a smile.

"You haven't heard how loudly I can yell," Bailey said, a

smile curving her bright red lips. "I was hog-calling champion at my high school three years running. Wanna hear one?"

"No, thank you," Elise said. "Maybe you can do one after we win the competition."

Bailey did a wonderful imitation of a cheerleading split right in the middle of the kitchen, heels and all. Elise was so impressed she went and gave her a hug.

After they parted, Bailey grinned at her. "You're all right, Gilbert. This could be the beginning of a beautiful friendship."

"Or it could be the beginning of a disaster waiting to happen," Elise joked. "However this turns out, you can count on me to give my best effort."

Bailey frowned, then brightened. "I don't know what you just said, but okay. I'll let the guys know. They're Justin Goldsmith, who studied at Ecole Lenotre in Paris, and Daniel Martinez who went to the California Culinary Arts Institute and does amazing things with pulled sugar."

"Good for Daniel, because I'm basically a baker," Elise said truthfully. "I had to do all that in culinary school, but I haven't done it since. Just not my thing."

"It doesn't have to be your thing," Bailey assured her.

As they were talking, Elise was leading her out of the kitchen, Bailey taking the hint that it was time for her to go with graciousness; after all, she hadn't exactly been invited. "Okay, okay, I'm going. I'll call you after I hear from the interviewer who will be calling you to set up an appointment." She stopped walking to turn and regard Elise with all seriousness. "Thank you, Elise. I know this isn't the sort of thing you enjoy doing, being in the limelight, I mean. But I swear it'll be good for your career. You'll see."

"You're welcome," Elise sincerely said. "And I agree with you. Why not give it a shot?"

Bailey grinned, her green eyes glowing with triumph. "I knew you had it in you. You, my dear, can be as competitive as the rest of us." With that, she left, not giving Elise the time to rebut her last statement.

Elise smiled, spun on her heels and went back to work.

A short while later, she was walking past the pantry in the back of the restaurant when someone grabbed her arm and yanked her inside. Whomever it was had neglected to turn on the light in the many-shelved storeroom, and it was pitch-black inside. Elise knew it couldn't be anyone except Franklyn, but pretended she was about to scream anyway. His big hand came down over her mouth at the first indication of a squeal.

Then, his mouth descended on hers in a long, hungry kiss. Elise moaned against his mouth, enjoying the masterful way he brought the art of kissing up a level each time they kissed. He seemed to find such pleasure in gently sucking her lower lip, tasting the sweetness of her tongue, raining dry kisses on her throat, sucking her earlobe. She never knew what he'd do next, and the anticipation often left her weak with sensual longing for hours on end. Life was so sweet.

They parted, and Elise said, breathlessly, "Who are you and where did you learn to kiss like that?"

"I am who you vish me to be," Franklyn said, his French accent deplorable.

"You know I'm engaged to Franklyn. You can't be pulling me into dark closets like this. He's going to get suspicious."

"I apologize. You're so zexy I couldn't rezist. But, if you are sincerely true to Franklyn, I vill not do it again." His French sounded more like German.

"What he doesn't know won't hurt him," Elise said, pulling him down for another passion-filled kiss. Afterward, they stood in each other's arms catching their breaths.

"Franklyn, I'm having a problem waiting until Saturday night's party to tell everyone we're engaged. I want to do a Bailey and shout it out! Last night, after you left, Mariel phoned and told me she had something important to tell me but she didn't want to tell me over the phone. I reminded her that she's invited to the party and that she could tell me then, but I really wanted to tell her. She and I have never kept secrets from one another. She's the only one in my family I told the truth about Derrick, and she kept that secret from the rest of my family for me. I felt bad not telling her we're engaged."

"Well," Franklyn said, "I spoke with Jason last night, and wanted to tell him, too. Thankfully, he was so obsessed with trying to figure out how he's going to get close to Sara now that she's confessed she's still in love with her deceased husband, I could barely get a word in edgewise."

"Oh, no—she's still in love with her dead husband? I feel for Jason, even though you say he's just interested in her because she's gorgeous."

"I may have been wrong," Franklyn allowed. "He's not behaving like his old self. He wanted strategies. He actually asked me for advice about a woman. He always used to say that he was the professor and I was the pupil when it came to women."

"What did you tell him?"

"To be her friend, and not try to get her into bed. Just be there for her, let her see that he's someone who can be trusted. It's obvious she's attracted to him. She needs to feel secure with him, and I believe that his staying close to her will allow her to see that loving a dead man is nothing nearly as won-derful as loving a warm-blooded male."

Elise tiptoed and kissed his chin. "I think that was very wise of you."

She grasped the doorknob then, and opened the door. Her eyes had to readjust to the light. Franklyn went in one direc-tion and she went in another.

No one saw them enter or exit the pantry.

Franklyn had spared no expense on the year-end party for his employees. He'd hired valets to park their cars as they arrived, and although the party was held in the big dining room (there were two at the restaurant) of the Vineyard, his people had had nothing to do with the food preparation. For that he'd hired one of the finest caterers in San Francisco.

The previous week he'd handed out Christmas bonuses. As he watched some of them arrive tonight he knew that some of the money had been spent on their attire. They fairly sparkled tonight, especially the ladies in black or deep red or in stunning metallic dresses in gold or silver. It was a night to dress up and everyone was putting on the ritz. Elise, whose hand he was holding right now, was wearing a beaded jacquard halter dress in a golden-brown shade that was nearly the color of his eyes and a very sexy pair of gold strappy sandals. She was wearing her ring tonight, something she hadn't done at work all week. He wore a black tuxedo with a red bow tie, crisp white pleated shirt, black cummerbund and highly polished black wingtips.

Elise squeezed his hand when she saw Mariel come through the door with Paulo in tow. Mariel had hedged when Elise had suggested she bring Paulo. They both looked attrac-tive tonight, Mariel in a red Grecian-style dress that showed off her long neck and equally long legs, and Paulo in a dark-blue pinstriped suit with a pale-blue shirt underneath. His feet were encased in black Italian leather loafers. Elise thought they made a lovely couple.

She and Mariel rubbed cheeks. "You're glowing in that dress," Mariel told her.

"Likewise," Elise said, smiling. "You're gorgeous."

Mariel's smile appeared a bit nervous to Elise. She hoped there was nothing wrong. Could she be wondering how people would react to her and Paulo as a couple? In San Francisco? Everywhere Elise looked she saw interracial couples. That couldn't be it.

"Hello, Paulo, good to see you again," she said cheerily.

Paulo smiled graciously and came forward to kiss her hand. "Elise, a pleasure."

"Oh, I'm sorry, where are my manners?" Mariel said. "Paulo Santini, this is Franklyn Bryant, owner and head chef of this lovely establishment."

The two men shook hands. "Good to meet you," said Franklyn.

"The pleasure is mine," Paulo said, looking around them. "This is a beautiful restaurant. I own three coffeehouses in the city."

"Oh?" said Franklyn with interest. "Which ones?"

"The Cup of Joes," Paulo told him.

"I like your set-up," Franklyn complimented him. "Let me buy you a drink and you can tell me more."

He knew that Elise and Mariel had private business to discuss. He could always be amused by discussing the service industry with a fellow owner.

When Elise was alone with Mariel, she gushed, "I've got something mind-blowing to tell you!"

"I've got something to tell you, too," Mariel said. "But you go first. My news can wait." In fact, she was dreading having to tell Elise that she'd boasted so much to Derrick about how wonderful Elise's life was going without him that she'd gone overboard and said she and Franklyn were getting married. Elise was going to be livid. Hadn't she asked her not even to say a word to that weasel?

Mariel took a deep breath and forced another smile. Let Elise tell her news first, and maybe her news would be so good that what she had to say wouldn't matter at all.

"Don't keep me in suspense, Elise. Spill it!"

She realized that for some reason Elise had been holding her left hand up and moving it around in the manner of those television chicks who brought out the prizes on game shows. Mariel focused. Then she saw the two-carat platinum diamond solitaire on Elise's ring finger. The finger where engagement rings usually resided.

She screamed before she could cut it off. Grabbing Elise around the neck, she pulled her cousin to her and hugged her tightly. The two women rocked back and forth. Finally, Mariel let go of Elise and stood back, shaking her head in amazement.

"Franklyn asked you to marry him. When? Where? How?"

Elise was beaming. She was thankful for the gutbucket blues on the sound system. Buddy Guy was loud and raucous and sexy. She hadn't seen any heads turn when Mariel had screamed. They probably thought it had been part of the song.

"Christmas Eve, in front of my entire family in Sacramento," Elise told her.

"And you didn't call and tell me?" Mariel asked, sounding hurt. She was not one to wallow in self-pity, though, and quickly recovered, whereupon she hugged her cousin again. "I'm so happy for you both!"

Elise set Mariel away from her so that she could look her in the eyes. "Thank you, sweetie. I know you mean that from your heart. Now, what did you have to tell me? Something wonderful about you and Paulo?" Her eyes danced with excitement.

Mariel twisted her lips in a scowl. "I wish it were something about me and Paulo. But it isn't. We're taking things slowly. No bedroom antics to report yet. We're just enjoying each other's company."

She sighed as though she were reluctant to say what she had to say, then she quickly launched into her tale about running into Derrick at his firm's Christmas party and the resultant gloating she'd done about Elise just to make him squirm. When she'd finished, she smiled brightly. "Isn't it wonderful that, in actuality, I told him the truth and wasn't just saying what I did to make him regret ever treating you so badly? All's well that ends well?" she said, ending on a hopeful note.

Elise had been watching her cousin with her mouth slightly open, in utter amazement. Mariel had done some crazy things over the years because of her sense of justice, especially when someone she loved was wronged, but this one took the cake. She had topped *herself*. Elise wished she had been there watching Derrick's face when Mariel had told him she was getting married.

"Girl," she said to Mariel. "That was so good, I wish you had it on tape."

Grateful that she wasn't mad at her, Mariel hugged her yet again.

Chapter 8

Mariel and Paulo joined Elise and Franklyn at their table up front where Lettie and Kendrick were waiting. There were two seats left empty because Jason and his date, whoever she might be, hadn't arrived yet.

Mariel knew Lettie and Kendrick from past social gatherings of the Vineyard's staff. She was delighted to see them again.

Lettie looked lovely in an elegant deep-russet flowing caftan. Kendrick looked sharp in a brown suit with an off-white shirt and caramel-colored silk tie.

"Hey, girl, long time no see," said Lettie. She liked Mariel. She was down-to-earth and knew how to keep things light and festive.

"Hey, yourself," said Mariel. "Who is this handsome man you're with tonight? What happened to your wonderful husband, Kendrick?"

Kendrick was eating up her compliment. He'd recently

dropped thirty pounds. He knew he looked good. He was a policeman and he could get into his dress blues again.

"Lettie's been starving me," he said. "She says it's for my own good. She wants me to live long so she can henpeck me to death."

"Don't pay any attention to him," Lettie said. "It was the doctor who put him on the diet. I just enforced it." She turned her attention to Paulo. "Who is this Brad Pitt look-alike?"

Mariel introduced them to Paulo.

As soon as Paulo spoke, Lettie smiled broadly. "You're Italian."

"Sì," said Paulo. "Do you know the language?"

Lettie laughed shortly and turned to Kendrick for support. "Honey, how long ago has it been since we were in Italy? Twenty years?" She smiled at Paulo. "I can recall only a few words and phrases—*arrivederci,* goodbye. *Buon giorno,* hello. *Gelato,* ice cream. *Non capisco,* I don't understand. I said that one a lot. And *ristorante,* restaurant."

"She said that one a lot, too," Kendrick joked.

"The food was to die for," Lettie agreed. "I could eat my way through that country, given the opportunity."

"You almost did," Kendrick said dryly. Lettie elbowed him in the side.

"What part are you from?" Lettie asked Paulo.

"Milan," Paulo told her, his dark-blue eyes lit with amusement and genuine interest.

"When I think of Milan, I think of commerce," Lettie said. "Except for maybe Rome, it was the most industrialized city we visited."

"You are very observant," Paulo told her, pleased to be conversing with someone who had visited his home. "My father's family has always made women's clothing, and Milan has been the company's headquarters for many years now."

Lettie was nodding sagely. "I was simply stunned by some of the skyscrapers. Italy is an ancient country with over two thousand years of history. The skyscrapers almost seemed out of place."

"I know how you feel," Paulo said softly. "I, too, sometimes felt as if industry was taking over. It's one of the reasons when I visited San Francisco ten years ago, I fell in love with the city. Yes, we have skyscrapers here, too, but in some ways San Francisco has a small-town feel. That's what I wanted to achieve with my coffeehouses, a small-town flavor, if you will."

"Which coffeehouses?" Kendrick asked. "I'm always in one or another. I'm a policeman."

"Cup of Joe," Paulo said.

"I go to the one on Post Street practically every day," Kendrick told him. "Nice places, and you don't charge an arm and leg like another well-known coffee place I'm not going to mention."

Everybody laughed.

Soon afterward, a Michael Bublé cover of the Nina Simone song "Feeling Good" came over the sound system, and Kendrick reached for Lettie's hand. "Come on, sugar, it's not Nina, but that's our song."

He and Lettie smoothly took the dance floor, moving like a well-oiled machine due to having danced together for more than thirty years. Paulo rose and asked Mariel to dance. She smiled sweetly and let him sweep her onto the dance floor.

Elise and Franklyn rose simultaneously, their eyes locked in sensual acquiescence. It was indeed a sexy number, lovingly sung by someone who understood the history behind the song, and who gave tribute to the woman who had made it a classic, Nina Simone.

Elise forgot where she was momentarily. She forgot everything except Franklyn, who held her confidently and sumptuously against him, his big hand splayed on her bare back. Elise relaxed, and would have closed her eyes, being in his embrace gave her such a feeling of exultation; however, if she had closed her eyes she would have missed his eyes boring into hers with such sensual intensity. She melted. Her senses came alive with Franklyn's sheer presence, how he smelled of Calvin Klein Eternity for Men, not too much, just a hint, along with a freshly showered aroma all his own. How his golden-brown skin contrasted so nicely with that dark, thick moustache that gave him a rather swashbuckling attitude. He would have made a fabulous pirate.

The song ended, and somehow Franklyn had managed to bend her backward, his mouth on the base of her throat, his face almost in her ample cleavage. Neither of them knew they were the center of attention until the music ended, and thunderous applause brought them out of their self-induced trances.

"Go, Franklyn!" called one of the busboys, a nineteen-year-old college student who was there with his high-school sweetheart.

Franklyn laughed shortly. "Don't try that," he announced, "with anyone you're not engaged to." He nodded imperceptibly at Elise who showed everyone her ring.

"We're going to be married," she said, her voice breaking with emotion.

The room erupted in cheers and more clapping. Elise and Franklyn were engulfed in a sea of people wishing them well, hugging them, kissing their cheeks, and generally showing them some love.

"It's about damn time!" Lettie cried. She had tears in her eyes. Kendrick had to give her his handkerchief and hold her in his arms while she wept.

As the night wore on, Franklyn held out little hope that Jason would show up. It was nearly midnight, and his brother wasn't there yet. He would have invited his parents and Erica and Joshua, too, but they had other plans. His parents and grandmother, Monique, were somewhere on the road in his parents' new Winnebago.

They had left a day after Erica and Joshua's wedding and said they would not be back home for at least three months, depending on the degree they drove each other crazy in the tight confines of the Winnebago.

Erica and Joshua planned to celebrate their first New Year as husband and wife in their home in Healdsburg. Franklyn couldn't fault them for that. He couldn't think of a more romantic way to bring in the New Year. Next year, he was sure he and Elise would be celebrating their first in their new home.

Franklyn and Elise, nonetheless, placed Happy New Year calls promptly after kissing in the New Year. Franklyn took her into his office where they could have some privacy.

His mother answered the phone after the second ring. "Hello?" Her voice sounded distant, as if she were on the moon instead of somewhere in New Mexico, which was where they had been a couple of days ago when he'd last checked in.

"Happy New Year, Mom!"

"Franklyn! How are you, darling? Happy New Year to you and Elise, too!"

"Are Dad and Grandma up?"

"Yeah, they're both here watching folks celebrate in Times Square on TV."

"Good," Franklyn said, smiling at Elise. "Tell them Elise and I are engaged."

Simone screamed in his ear. "Oh, baby, I'm so happy for you both!" He heard her give the news to his dad and grandmother. More whooping ensued. Then, she came back to the phone. "Sweetie, put Elise on, please."

Franklyn handed Elise the phone.

She smiled and put the receiver to her ear. "Hello, Mrs. Bryant, Happy New Year."

"Same to you, you darling child," said Simone. "Welcome to the family. I know you and Franklyn are going to be happy together."

"Thank you, Mrs. Bryant, that's so sweet of you."

Simone laughed shortly. "Just calling it like I see it. I'm going to let you and Franklyn get back to celebrating your engagement. Put Franklyn back on a minute, please."

Elise handed the phone back to Franklyn. Grinning, he said, "I'm here, Mom."

"I know I don't have to tell you always to treat her like a queen."

"No, you don't have to. It'll be my pleasure to do that."

"I know it will be," Simone returned. "Well, good night, sweetie, and congratulations again!"

"Oh, Mom, where are you guys?"

"We're in Las Vegas."

"Don't let Grandma near the gambling tables," Franklyn joked.

"Not that Las Vegas," Simone said with a chuckle. "Las Vegas, New Mexico, population *maybe* close to twenty thousand, if that. Very quiet."

Franklyn laughed. "Then I suspect Grandma's pension is safe."

"Get off this phone and go make love to your woman," Simone told him.

"Mom!" Franklyn cried, trying to sound aghast but failing.

Simone laughed delightedly. "You're thirty-six. I hope you're not embarrassed that your mother knows you're not celibate. Good night, dear."

"Good night," Franklyn said, still laughing softly. He pressed the end button on the cell phone and smiled at Elise. "Mom said to go make love to you."

Elise laughed. "I liked your mother the moment I met her."

Franklyn gave the phone to Elise next and she phoned her parents and sisters to wish them a Happy New Year. Franklyn sat on the corner of the desk, watching Elise's animated face as she briefly chatted with her relatives in Sacramento.

After she was finished, he phoned Erica and Joshua who were apparently in the middle of something because Erica sounded breathless. Franklyn's face flushed with embarrassment just listening to her, and he quickly ended the call, not giving them the news about his and Elise's engagement.

He then told Elise about it, and she burst out laughing. "Well, they *are* newlyweds," she said reasonably.

Finally, he dialed Jason's cell phone number. Jason picked up after several rings.

"Hey, Franklyn. Sorry I didn't make it to the party but Sara's mother passed away yesterday morning."

"I'm sorry to hear that, Jason," Franklyn said, a frown drawing his brows together.

Elise immediately noticed the difference in his demeanor and raised her brows in an askance gesture. Seeing it, Franklyn said, "Please give Sara our condolences. We'll be sure to send flowers."

"Thanks, bro," Jason said, his voice weary. "She's really broken up about it."

Franklyn decided that he could tell Jason about the engagement at another time as well. "Yes, I imagine she is. Let me know if there's anything I can do. I'll let you go get some rest."

"Okay. Good night, Franklyn," Jason said. "Tell Elise hello for me."

"Will do," Franklyn said in closing.

He hung up the phone and sighed. "Sara's mother died yesterday."

"Oh, no," Elise said, sympathy apparent in her expression and tone.

"She'd been sick for a long time. Sara came home to stay so that she could look after her."

"She's a good daughter."

"Sara's good people," Franklyn agreed.

He rose and took Elise by the hand. "Come on, we've got guests to see after."

When they reentered the dining room they saw that the number of guests had dwindled significantly in their absence. The party was winding down. They returned to their table to find Lettie and Kendrick preparing to call it a night.

Lettie was gathering her purse and her coat. Kendrick helped her into it, and affectionately squeezed her shoulders when he was done.

"We had a ball," Lettie said to Franklyn as she walked over and kissed his cheek.

"But old folks can't stay up as late as you whippersnappers."

"Speak for yourself, woman," Kendrick said with a pronounced yawn.

Lettie took her husband's arm. "I'd better go put him to bed." To Paulo, she said, "Wonderful meeting you, Paulo. I hope we can get together again sometime soon."

"It was my pleasure, dear lady," Paulo said with a gentle smile. He took her hand in both of his and held it a moment. He and Kendrick firmly shook hands.

Lettie and Kendrick then said their good-nights to Elise and Mariel, kissing both women on their cheeks. When Lettie kissed Mariel's cheek, she whispered, "Italy is shaped like a boot with the toe pointing to Africa. You two make a lovely couple. Don't let anyone tell you otherwise."

Mariel smiled broadly. "Thank you, Lettie," she whispered back.

Shortly after Lettie and Kendrick departed, Mariel and Paulo also decided it was time to go home. "I've eaten too much, drunk too much, danced too much," Mariel said. "I guess it's time to go home and sleep too much."

She hugged Elise. "Love you, girl." Smiling up at Franklyn, she said, "Franklyn, welcome to the family. We're nutty, but lovable."

Franklyn hugged her briefly. "I'm not unfamiliar with nutty relatives."

To Paulo, he said, "Don't be a stranger."

They shook hands. "You are a lucky man," Paulo said. "To have such friends and such a woman to love you."

"That I am," Franklyn couldn't agree more. "Gilbert women tend to make a man feel lucky, so watch out."

Paulo took this as an indication that he wasn't alone in recognizing that there was more to his relationship with Mariel than casual dating. Although he was having a very hard time trying to discern exactly what it was Mariel wanted from *him*, he knew he wanted something more permanent with her than mere dinner and dancing.

By 2:00 a.m., all of the guests had gone, and the clean-up crew was just about finished in the kitchen and the dining room. Franklyn and Elise pitched in, thinking that everyone would get out of there sooner with their added elbow grease.

After the last of the clean-up crew had left, Elise and Franklyn helped each other on with their coats and slowly walked to the door hand in hand. The place was so quiet after the noise of the party, Elise was feeling kind of nostalgic. This had been her fourth New Year's Eve party here at the Vineyard. This time, however, she'd been Franklyn's date. The last three years, it had pained her to watch him walk through the door with a different woman on his arm. She had also come with dates, all of whom were now distant memories.

Franklyn turned to her as they stood at the glass double doors to the restaurant. Moonlight shone in and illuminated Elise's face. He reached up and gently stroked the satin skin of her cheek. Peering deeply into her eyes, he said, "This has been the best New Year's I've ever experienced, and it's all because of you. I love you so much I honestly don't know what I would do if anything should happen to break us up. I would probably lose my mind."

"Don't talk like that," Elise said. Her heart had skipped a beat when he'd said it because ever since he'd proposed, she'd been having fatalistic thoughts as well. What if she truly didn't deserve this kind of happiness? People more worthy than she had gone through their lives searching for, but never finding, their soul mates. What made her so lucky? But then she told herself that God made the sun shine on everyone and if you were fortunate enough to be out on the day the sun came out, then bask in it!

"Listen," she said fiercely. "Nothing's going to happen to break us up. I don't want to ever hear you say that again. I've waited too long for you. I will not *let* anything happen to us. Ever!"

"Okay," Franklyn said consolingly. He kissed her cheek. "I guess the old Franklyn came through for a minute there. The old insecurities." He sighed. "I'll try my best to keep him from coming to the surface again."

"You do that," Elise said with a smile. "Now, come on and make love to me like your mother told you to."

Franklyn laughed softly as he unlocked the door. "Let me get that out of my mind. The last thing I want to hear in my head while I'm making love to you is my mother's voice."

Zora Neale Hurston wrote in *Their Eyes Were Watching God* that women forget all those things they don't want to remember, and remember everything they don't want to forget. In the next few weeks, that was exactly how Elise was conducting her life.

She focused on the wedding. She focused on Franklyn and enjoyed learning more about the man she was going to marry. She focused on work, and her friends and her family. She kept all her ducks in a row, not allowing any stragglers to step out of line. She concentrated so hard on making everything perfect that it was no wonder that she got blindsided when she did. It didn't come as a surprise, but it was still unnerving.

The wedding date had been set for May sixth, and it was going to be held at the Vineyard. Elise and Franklyn wanted something low-key but elegant. They hired Mariel and Laura's company to cater the event.

Elise's parents complained that the couple had made those choices in order to save *them* money and made the situation more equitable, in their minds, by insisting that Elise splurge on her wedding dress. Elise countered that volley by buying wholesale.

How many times was she going to wear a wedding dress? It made no sense to her to buy a five-thousand-dollar dress only to have it molder in the closet.

The end result was, they were going to have a beautiful wedding for a little over half of the amount in her wedding fund.

Now that plans for the wedding were finalized, Elise could turn her attention to the pastry competition whose date was rapidly approaching. Her team had been accepted by the nit-picking judges that selected teams based on their experience and quality of work.

Elise had met her teammates, all of whom were way more intense when it came to the competition than she was. She was doing it to prove she *could*, plain and simple. They seemed to be doing it to further their careers, which wasn't bad but put a whole new spin on the words do or die. They were so keyed-up Elise expected them to keel over with strokes if they didn't win. She would be happy with second place. The second-place prize was ten thousand in cash and a brand new double oven. Elise *really* wanted to win that oven.

On March seventeenth, a Friday, Elise arrived at the Phoenix, Arizona, resort where the event was being held. The team had traveled separately even though they all lived in the Bay Area. She walked through the lobby's doors, her sandals resounding on the tile floor. Removing her sunglasses, she looked around. Spanish Colonial-style architecture characterized both the adobe facade and the interiors.

"Welcome to the Saragossa," said an attractive male clerk in his early twenties. He was smiling, revealing an enviable set of teeth. Elise recognized Saragossa as a city in Spain. Today, the city was called Zaragoza.

"Thank you," she said, returning his smile. She leaned her zippered clothing bag against her jeans-clad leg, and put her overnight bag on the floor. "I'm Elise Gilbert. I have a reservation."

Maintaining his cool smile, he quickly looked her up on the computer. "You're with the pastry competition," he said, sounding surprised by that bit of information. Surprised and delighted. "You're in room 412. Would you like assistance with your bags?"

"No, they're pretty lightweight. Thank you."

He handed her the room's card key. "Please sign here."

Elise signed the registry, which must have been just a formality because she'd been assured that all of her expenses for the three days and two nights she would spend at the Saragossa had been taken care of. She carefully read what she was signing. It just said Guest Registry at the top. Her signature was on a thirty-something line down the gold, gilt-edged page. "Am I among the first to arrive for the competition?" she asked.

"Oh, no, since I've been on duty, six others have checked in. You're all on the fourth floor."

"All right, thank you." She gave him a parting smile and picked up her bags. She didn't ask him which rooms her teammates were in. He would have told her that to protect their guests' privacy they didn't give out that information; however, there was a house phone in the lobby that she could use to phone the hotel operator and the operator would connect her to the person's room. Which was fine with her. She had no doubt that Bailey would be tracking her down soon. She had the feeling that Bailey considered her the team's dark horse, the unknown quantity. Elise would either put them over the top, or sink them.

As Elise stepped onto the elevator, she smiled at the notion. Bailey's problem was that she was a control freak. Still, she liked the Texas spitfire.

The room was spacious with a queen-size bed, a sunken bath and all the amenities. Upon entering it, Elise made certain the door had locked behind her, then she switched on the light next to the door, walked over to the bed, where she deposited her bags, went straight to the drapes and opened them. It was a breathtaking view of the expansive grounds peppered by native cacti and various imported flowering plants that must have cost a small fortune to keep watered in this arid climate.

Other guests strolled the scenic manicured paths or rode about in golf carts. Elise turned away to go rummage in her purse for the schedule of the competition she'd been sent. Today was basically check-in day, and at seven this evening there would be a welcome dinner with admonitions to get plenty of rest because the competition would start bright and early the next morning.

After satisfying her curiosity about the schedule, she began peeling off her traveling clothes, jeans, two layered T-shirts, one in turquoise the other in fuchsia, and a pair of pristine white athletic shoes, in case she had to run to catch her flight. Franklyn had seen her off at the airport, kissing her with such passion that it would last her until they were together again, and telling her to phone him when she arrived.

Naked, she slipped on the bathrobe the hotel had provided, sat on the edge of the bed, picked up the phone and dialed the Vineyard's number. A minute later, she was patched back to the kitchen and Lettie answered.

"Hey, Lettie, it's me, Elise. Is Franklyn available to talk?"

"Hi, Elise!" Lettie cried. "Hey, Franklyn, Elise is on the phone!"

Everybody yelled to be heard over the cacophony of the kitchen.

"He'll be here in a minute, sweetie. How's Arizona?"

"Hotter than I thought it would be. I was glad to get to my room and take off all the clothes I had on."

"It'll be cooler at night, just like here," Lettie told her. "Here he is now. Good luck in the competition!"

"Thanks!" Elise yelled. She knew that Franklyn had probably already taken the receiver out of Lettie's hands. She was proved right when the next voice she heard was his.

"That was quick. How was the flight?"

"Smooth all the way," Elise said.

"And how are your nerves?"

"Jagged around the edges, but I'm working on it."

"You have nothing to be nervous about. Just do what you do," Franklyn said, his voice so confident that Elise felt comforted all the way in Arizona.

"I can't imagine being away from you for two nights," Elise cooed. Since they'd been dating, and more importantly since they'd been engaged, a day hadn't gone by that they hadn't looked into each other's faces. She had brought a photo they'd had taken on the pier at Fisherman's Wharf, but it wasn't the same. And Franklyn had a favorite photo of her on his nightstand.

"I miss you too, baby, but you'll be back Sunday night. I'll pick you up at the airport and pamper you all night long."

"Mmm, sounds good," Elise said. She sighed. "Well, you'd better get back to work. I love you."

"I love you, too. Go, get 'em!"

Elise laughed. "Consider 'em gotten."

After they hung up, she went and showered. As she was toweling off, someone knocked on her door. She quickly put on the bathrobe and walked over to the door.

"Who's there?"

"Cynthia Patterson, remember me? I'm on the staff."

Cynthia had come to Elise's apartment to interview her early in the process.

Elise quickly unlocked and pulled open the door. Cynthia, tall and cranelike, stood in the doorway with her black-rimmed glasses sliding down the bridge of her nose and a clipboard held against her flat chest. "Greetings, Ms. Gilbert!" That's how she talked. It was never hi, but Greetings! or Greetings and Salutations! She sounded like a member of an official delegation sent to meet the first aliens to land on Earth.

"Hi," Elise said, moving aside to let Cynthia enter. "And, please, call me Elise."

Cynthia started to walk inside, then quickly turned to go back out again. "Oops, I almost forgot your introduction packet."

She bent to pick up a huge white plastic shopping bag from outside the door where she'd left it. Returning inside, she smiled at Elise and closed the door behind her.

"This is for you," she said, placing the bag in Elise's arms. "In it you'll find your chef's hat and uniform. We asked you to bring a pair of good work shoes in black. You did remember them?"

"Yes," Elise said. She met Cynthia's gray eyes. "I also brought my uniform."

"Oh, no, you can't wear your restaurant's emblems on TV," Cynthia said.

"TV?" Elise asked, taken aback. "No one mentioned that the competition was going to be televised."

"I know we didn't," Cynthia explained. "It was in the agreement you signed, though. We don't mention it because we don't want the contestants to have time to worry about how they're going to do on TV. It can be nerve-racking, and we want you all as calm as possible. Believe me, once the cameras start rolling you'll get used to it so quickly you won't even notice them."

Elise didn't think she could ever ignore the fact that her image was being shown across the planet. "I think I'd notice," Elise said.

Cynthia changed the subject. "Also in the bag is a pager so that anyone on the staff can contact you no matter where you are during the competition. Things will move rapidly once we get started, and plans can change in a nanosecond. So, keep the pager on you at all times, no matter where you go."

"Got it," Elise said.

Cynthia smiled appreciatively and glanced down at the watch on her bony wrist. "It's nearly five. Some of your fellow contestants are meeting in the lounge downstairs to get acquainted before dinner at seven. Drinks are free, of course, with a two-drink limit. We don't want you all to get plastered." She laughed, sounding like a twittering bird. "There will be wine with dinner."

Elise laughed along with her. She wondered how that laugh sounded when Cynthia got plastered. "I'll come down as soon as I'm dressed," she promised.

"Good," Cynthia said happily. "Your teammates will be there, as well."

Satisfied that she had sufficiently briefed Elise, she left.

Half an hour later, Elise walked into the dimly lit lounge wearing a simple off-white sleeveless shift whose hem fell a couple inches above her knees and a pair of palest yellow leather sandals. Her shoulder bag was in the same shade. The place was packed nearly to fire-safety limits.

"Elise!"

Elise had no trouble recognizing the hog-calling champion of West Texas. She grinned and walked in the direction from which the voice had come. Bailey, Justin Goldsmith and Daniel Martinez sat at a booth in a dark corner. Bailey hopped up and hugged Elise. "You made it!"

Daniel got up and allowed Elise to slide onto the bench, while he stayed on the aisle. Justin did the same with Bailey. Elise assumed it was some protective male thing, keeping the women safely on the inside. "You never doubted I'd come, did you?"

"Frankly, Gilbert," Bailey said, squinting at her, "the thought did occur to me. You've gotten fat and complacent since you got engaged. *We're* still hungry. I'm worried that you don't want this as much as we do."

"Fat!" cried Elise. She was in the mood to have fun with Bailey and intended to make her squirm a little. "I was hoping you all wouldn't notice I've picked up a few pounds. I'm pregnant. But don't you worry, the mood swings, such as they are, are pretty mild. I won't throw food at our competitors or screech at the judges, at least not much, anyway."

Bailey went pale. Justin looked uncomfortable with a woman talking about her body. Daniel's reaction puzzled Elise. He met her eyes and smiled warmly.

"You're joking, right?" Bailey said prayerfully. She took a sizable gulp from her beer mug. "Oh, Lord, that's all we need, a PMSing female under pressure. Thar she blows!"

"Oh, now you're making whale jokes," Elise said tearfully. "I may cry."

Daniel placed his arm about her shoulders. "Bailey didn't mean it. You know what a witch she can be when things don't go her way. Don't worry about your condition getting in the way, Elise. You'll be fine, you'll see. My wife, Dorie, is expecting our first child. She had terrible mood swings in the beginning, but lately she's always in a good mood. Your hormones will settle down." He spoke so soothingly, and with such compassion that Elise felt bad about teasing them.

Bailey, however, was not moved. "Oh, I think I'm gonna throw up. Our chances are spiraling down the drain, and you're spouting saccharine platitudes."

"See what I mean?" Daniel asked Elise. "Pure evil when she doesn't get her way."

"I bet she flew here on a broomstick instead of in a plane," Elise said, getting into the rhythm of Daniel's flow.

"See that beauty mark on her chin?" he asked. "Used to be a huge witch's mole until she had it surgically removed, the better to fit in with the rest of humanity."

Elise laughed, and Bailey punched her on the upper arm. She was laughing, though, and her strength had been minimal at best. "Stop that, you're hurting my feelings," she said, giggling.

"Remember the witch in Hansel and Gretel?" Daniel asked. "She was Bailey's second cousin twice removed. She's who inspired Bailey to become a pastry chef. Bailey hopes to one day build a gingerbread house and lure unsuspecting children, too."

"Now that's going overboard," Bailey protested, unable to stop laughing. "All I'm trying to do is insure that we're all on the same page. I didn't mean to beat up on Elise."

"Apology accepted," Elise said calmly. "And I'll have you know that I'm here to win just like the rest of you."

"Okay, okay, I believe you," Bailey said between tear-filled guffaws.

Justin handed her a dinner napkin to wipe her face.

Bailey blew her nose. She took a calming breath and regarded Elise. "Are you really pregnant and hormonal?"

"Nah," Elise told her. "But even if I were, I'd still be a team player."

"Wonderful," said Justin, deadpan. "Now, shall we get off the subject of hormonal females, and discuss something more pertinent like the presence of Shoji Yamaguchi in the competition?"

Bailey, Daniel and Justin all fell into reverential silence. They knew something that Elise, the only one at their booth who did not follow the various competitions around the world, did *not* know. Shoji Yamaguchi had virtually ruled every competition he'd ever been in. He was the Iron Chef of pastry. Energetic, flamboyant, fiercely competitive. He did not take prisoners.

"Who is Shoji Yamaguchi?" Elise asked.

Her teammates burst into laughter.

"You are such a greenhorn," Bailey said affectionately.

Chapter 9

That night, in San Francisco, Franklyn arrived home after work and, feeling restless without Elise's company, went to the exercise room and did thirty minutes on the treadmill and several reps of a tried-and-true weight-lifting routine. He liked the way his muscles felt after the cardiovascular and weight-bearing exercises. Nicely taut and spent but with an underlying added strength that contributed to his physical, emotional and spiritual well-being. The endorphins loosed into his system were better than any artificial mood-enhancing drug.

There had been a time when he'd gone overboard with the weight-lifting—going to the gym and closing the place, he'd be there so long. That was during the turbulent years, when he'd tried to fool himself that as long as he worked out hard, he could also play hard. He felt invincible. But the only thing he was really doing was killing himself with booze and hand-to-hand combat. The human body wasn't designed to be a punching bag. The time at the gym only insured that when he died he'd leave behind a good-looking corpse.

Today, he worked out seven days a week for about forty-five minutes. The treadmill, weight-lifting and, when he could get away, hiking and rock-climbing. He loved being outdoors, possibly because he'd been raised on a farm and the land was in his blood.

He also stayed in shape because he feared that if he didn't his muscles would atrophy and his limp would become more pronounced. In shape, he was able to support his infirmity. If he allowed himself to become weak, he might become that cripple that Vanessa had said he would be before his time.

Vanessa. God bless her!

As he finished several reps, his leg muscles burning, he could still see her beautiful face twisted into an ugly caricature of herself as she'd told him she didn't want to be tied down with a future cripple. She was young, hot and knew somebody was waiting for her out there. Someone who could make her really happy, someone who would truly deserve her. She'd obviously been wasting her time with him, even though she had to admit she had enjoyed herself. She wished him well with his little restaurant so close to the section of Chinatown on Stockton Street that you could smell the chow mein in the air.

If he had been the obsessive type, he might have tried to follow her life and keep up with what was happening in it. He wasn't a glutton for punishment, though, and didn't care. If he had been the vengeful type, he might exult in her downfall. Again, he could take no joy in knowing she had somehow suffered after dumping him. He actually hoped that she had, in the intervening years, met the man who was now making her happy.

Two NEW Kimani Romance™ Novels
Two exciting surprise gifts

YES! I have placed my
Editor's "thank you" Free Gifts
seal in the space provided at
right. Please send me 2 FREE
books, and my 2 FREE Mystery
Gifts. I understand that I am
under no obligation to purchase
anything further, as explained on
the back of this card.

PLACE
FREE GIFTS
SEAL
HERE

DETACH AND MAIL CARD TODAY!

168 XDL EF2P   368 XDL EF2Z

FIRST NAME   LAST NAME

ADDRESS

APT.#   CITY

STATE/PROV.   ZIP/POSTAL CODE

Thank You!

(K-ROM-12/06)

The Reader Service — Here's How It Works:

If offer card is missing write to: The Reader Service, 3010 Walden Ave., P.O. Box 1867, Buffalo, NY 14240-1867

BUSINESS REPLY MAIL

FIRST-CLASS MAIL   PERMIT NO. 717-003   BUFFALO, NY

POSTAGE WILL BE PAID BY ADDRESSEE

THE READER SERVICE
3010 WALDEN AVE
PO BOX 1867
BUFFALO NY 14240-9952

NO POSTAGE
NECESSARY
IF MAILED
IN THE
UNITED STATES

Whatever happiness *was* for Vanessa Charles. He had to admit, he really did not know the woman well. After all, he'd been foolish enough to believe she was in love with him. Vanessa had been truly adept at hiding her real emotions.

Elise was not. Elise was all too human. She wore her heart on her sleeve for all the world to see, and she didn't have a deceptive bone in her body. Elise. God bless her.

After doing one hundred sit-ups on a slanted board, Franklyn got up and walked through the house to the kitchen where he withdrew a bottle of water from the fridge and drank half of it in one swig.

Wiping the sweat off his face with a hand towel, he went to the living room, plopped down on the couch in front of the TV and used the remote to switch it on. He checked the local stations first just in case there was any breaking news. An infomercial was on the first station, an old black-and-white film on the second, and a news brief on the third. He left it there. A woman who'd been carjacked was telling how she'd stopped at an intersection and two men had appeared out of nowhere and demanded she unlock her door or they'd shoot her through the window. "I thought of speeding off and taking my chances," she told the reporter. "But I would have had to run over the one standing in front of the car." She was nursing a huge lump on her forehead. "Now, I wish I had. He could have just taken the car, but he took the time to beat me in the head with the butt of his gun before jumping behind the wheel and taking off. I hope they get caught, and rot in jail!"

The reporter, who was supposed to remain unbiased and report the incident, had to add her two cents by saying, "You can't blame her for those sentiments. Back to you, Phil."

Franklyn turned the channel before it could get back to Phil. He looked around for a minute or two, finding nothing of interest, and then cut the power on the TV. Rising, he decided that without Elise his Friday nights lacked flavor, and went to take a shower and go to bed.

Around 2:00 a.m. his phone rang. He quickly picked up thinking it might be Elise. It was.

"I'm sorry for phoning so late. I know you were asleep but I have to talk to somebody or I'll go crazy," Elise said.

"What's the matter, sweetheart?"

"The competition's going to be live tomorrow and Sunday," she told him in a near panic. "They waited until today to spring it on us. I've tried to reconcile myself to the fact, but the more I think about it, the more I just know I'm going to make a fool of myself on national television!"

Franklyn sat up in bed and turned on the lamp on his nightstand. "What network?"

"Some big food channel out of New York according to Bailey who had to get every last detail. I don't do well in front of an audience. I threw up during a play when I was seven. Some of the other kids were sympathetic but some of them started calling me Regan."

"Regan?" Franklyn asked, puzzled.

"That's what the girl's name was in the movie *The Exorcist.* Some kids have a gross sense of humor."

Franklyn had to shove a pillow in his face to keep Elise from hearing him laugh. He could kick himself for finding that funny, but it was. "Elise, you're a big girl now. And the fact is, you cook before an audience every day. The kitchen staff. I've often thought you look beautiful while you're cooking. I've gone home and had to take a cold shower after watching you cook all day. Stop worrying, you're a feast for the eyes. Pretend you're in the kitchen at the Vineyard. Concentrate on your recipes. Remember how wonderful it was learning how to cook from your parents. Recall all the excitement in the beginning when everything was a mystery, and you knew that cooking was chemistry, the best kind of chemistry. If you got all the ingredients in the proper proportions, you knew you were creating magic. You make magic every day, sweetheart. Don't let the presence of TV cameras rob you of that. Ignore them."

Elise remained silent on her end for what seemed like a long time.

"Elise?"

"I love you so much for what you just said." Her voice sounded teary. "Okay." A deep sigh. "I'll go out there tomorrow and simply do what I do."

"Create magic," Franklyn said confidently.

"Cook from the gut," Elise corrected him. She didn't think she created magic, she thought she cooked instinctively. Long experience had taught her how different flavors would taste when combined without having to actually combine them. Years of working with ingredients told her which consistency worked well with another. She cooked by the seat of her pants. Even measurements had become instinctive over the years. She could hold flour in her hand and tell whether it was a cup or a cup and a half. A pinch of this, a pinch of that. Like her grandfather used to cook. Maybe what her father had been telling her all these years—that she'd inherited cooking genes—was true.

Feeling much calmer now, Elise said, "I can do this. I'd much prefer being there next to you, but I can do this. Thanks for listening."

"I always will," Franklyn said. "Get some sleep, baby girl."

"Don't tell anyone it's going to be televised in case I *do* throw up!" Elise said with a laugh. "Good night."

"'Night," Franklyn said.

He hung up the phone, turned out the light, snuggled underneath the covers and made a mental note to phone everybody he knew to tell them to watch Elise on the Food Network. It had to be the Food Network. It was the biggest network devoted to cooking on television, and they were based in New York. He had every confidence that Elise would blow the competition away. She might *feel* insecure, but something in her nature made it impossible for her to go out without a fight. Look at how she'd handled her divorce from Derrick Scott. When he'd dragged his feet about going through with it, probably hoping to keep her a slave a little while longer, she had gotten it done. Plus, received alimony. That wasn't something she bragged about, the alimony part, but she'd known she had deserved some compensation after working two jobs to support them while Derrick was in law school, and she hadn't allowed him to take advantage of her in the divorce. Verbal abuse aside, she didn't let him use her in that respect.

No, Franklyn wasn't worried about Elise.

The competition began with twelve teams consisting of four pastry chefs per team culled from some of the finest hotels, bakeries and restaurants across the United States. The resort had set aside the largest room they had, the grand ballroom, and each team was assigned to a fully equipped kitchen in there. The teams were numbered from one to twelve. Elise's team was number eight.

Saturday morning, Elise found herself at the top of the day's schedule. Her specialty was cakes. So when the team was assigned the task of baking a cake, icing it and decorating it, and doing it all within two hours, Elise was designated to carry out the assignment.

Therefore, twelve pastry chefs, one from each team, were in their individual kitchens baking cakes. Elise was required to wear her uniform and her chef's hat at all times during the competition.

Her wavy black hair was neatly pinned in a chignon. She wore emerald stud earrings, and a minimal amount of make-up, hoping that she would prove unattractive to the camera-men and camerawomen pointing their infernal contraptions at the contestants.

To her horror, when she was pouring the cake batter into the baking pans, a reporter walked right up to her, shoved a microphone under her nose and said, "You're Elise Gilbert, right, of San Francisco? Can you tell us why you chose this particular cake to prepare for the competition today?"

Elise painted on a smile as she bent to put the three pans in the oven. "It's an old family recipe. It was my great-grand-parents' wedding cake, and from what I hear great-grandma and great-grandpa were married for seventy years until he died. I guess you can call that lucky."

The reporter, a tall, dark-haired, blue-eyed hunk in his late twenties smiled at her. "What's this good-luck cake called?"

"The Ambrosia Cake," Elise told him.

"Food of the gods," the reporter said, getting so comfort-able with Elise she feared he might never move on. "What's in it?"

Elise could not stop what she was doing and chat, she had to continue working. Time was running out. So, she began combining the ingredients for the icing. As she worked, she smiled and tried to imagine she was in the kitchen of the Vineyard. "Well, my mother says you take one part love, two parts affection, combine them with time and patience and you'll get a good marriage. If you're talking about the sugar, the flour, the flavorings, well, those are very common things you can find in practically anyone's kitchen—flour, sugar, butter, vanilla and lemon flavorings. Crushed pineapple that's cooked down to a syrupy consistency and put between the layers of the cake, then a rich vanilla flavoring for the icing."

"Sounds delicious," said the reporter, forgetting himself and looking at Elise as if she were a desirable woman instead of a contestant in a food competition. He cleared his throat, recognizing his faux pas. "Good luck, Ms. Gilbert," he said, and moved on to the next contestant.

"Thank you," said Elise, flashing him a smile. She was glad to see him go.

As the reporter, Guy Hamilton, walked away he heard an insistent voice in his headset. "Guy, Guy, who was that girl? What do you know about her? She was fantastic, and she had you blushing, you dog!" The voice was female and it belonged to his producer, Tamryn Baylor.

"You heard what she said, Tamryn. Her name's Elise Gilbert and she's from San Francisco. I haven't heard any interesting buzz on her. She's not famous like Shoji Yamaguchi, whom I'm getting ready to speak with now."

"I like her," Tamryn said, her tone firm. "Get me more footage on her, just in case she does well so we can include them in the highlights. She's pretty, articulate and sweet. Plus, it doesn't hurt that she's the only African-American female in the competition. Why is it males dominate this field? Generally, women do most of the cooking in American homes. Do you think I can get Jeff to cook for me? No way!"

"Tamryn, you're rambling," Guy said dryly. "I'm turning you off now."

Back in her kitchen, Elise was whipping the white vanilla cream icing into frothy peaks. This done, humming, she stirred the crushed pineapple in the saucepan and turned off the heat, allowing it to cool. She tapped her foot. The timer on the counter said she had one hour and ten minutes left. The cakes needed forty minutes to bake. She could not frost a warm cake.

Bailey dropped by to cheer her on. Team members were not required to hang around while their teammates were cooking, but they weren't banned from the floor, either. They simply couldn't assist them in any way. There were spies looking on to insure the rules were adhered to.

Bailey had her long black hair in a bun, too, and wore black lipstick and had painted her nails black. "What's with the black?" Elise asked. Yesterday, Bailey had been ultra-feminine where her makeup and nails were concerned, wearing various shades of pink.

"I like the witch thing you and Daniel came up with. Practically everybody here has an angle, why not me? Do you think Shoji Yamaguchi looks that intense because he's constantly constipated? No, he looks intense because he wants people to *think* he's intense. And don't be fooled if you speak to him and he pretends not to understand English. He speaks perfect English."

"So, you'd like to be thought of as a witch?"

"I just want to be thought of," Bailey said. "I don't want to be invisible."

"You could never be invisible, Bailey Hitchcock, you fairly vibrate with personality. A person would have to be deaf and blind not to know you're in the room."

Bailey grinned and Elise noticed black lipstick on her teeth. She picked up a stainless-steel saucepan lid and held it up so that Bailey could see her reflection. "I think the black lipstick has to go," she said with a smile.

Bailey's eyes stretched in surprise and disgust. "I've got more than an hour before I'm in front of the cameras. Yes, I think I'll go dewitch myself."

Elise watched her friend hurry away. She hadn't wanted to mention the fact that the judges might have frowned on the black nail polish, even if Bailey had worn gloves when she whipped up the chocolate confections that were her specialty. Black nails on a cook simply didn't encourage appetizing thoughts. Presentation, after all, was a part of the competition. She didn't know why Bailey didn't think of that before she'd put on the black lipstick and nail polish, except that Bailey was probably as nervous as she was, but was hiding it better. She was glad Bailey had decided to remove it. If she'd gotten a lower score because of that, she'd never forgive herself.

Soon, the timer buzzed, and Elise removed the golden-brown cakes from the oven. She waited a few minutes before transferring them to the cooling racks. And with ten minutes to spare, she iced the cake and put yellow florets around the top and bottom edges of it, using a pastry bag filled with icing dyed a light yellow with food coloring.

The icing on the cake was vanilla cream, however the icing in the pastry bag that had been tinted yellow was pineapple-flavored. This done, she had to complete the final step of this part of the competition: pick up the cake and carefully walk across the big room and place the cake on a table adjacent to the judges' table. Her team's number was in the spot where the cake had to be placed.

She gingerly picked up the cake. As she turned and walked out of the open cubicle that was her kitchen space, she stepped into something slippery and almost dropped the cake. She got her balance in time and the cake didn't fall from her grasp. Standing perfectly still, she looked down. Setting the cake on a nearby counter, she bent and touched the liquid she'd stepped in. It had the consistency of cooking oil. She sniffed her fingers. It smelled like canola oil.

She looked around her. Everybody appeared to be too busy doing their own thing to have conspired to make her slip as she left her cubicle/kitchen. Surely it was just one of those things. Someone had been carrying canola oil and hadn't noticed the container was leaking. At any rate, no harm, no foul. She was fine. The cake was fine. She picked it up again, and continued across the room, walking with care so as not to slip on the oil left on the bottoms of her rubber-soled shoes.

She noticed that five other contestants had finished before she had. There were six spots left for the remaining contestants. She was not to engage the judges in conversation or even look in their direction and smile at them. That might be construed as fraternization, and that was forbidden. She made her way back across the room to tidy up the kitchen. They were also judged on neatness. They were to leave their work area spotless for the next teammate's use.

She washed the dishes and utensils and put everything away and left the kitchen exactly as she'd found it. Relieved to have the first part of the competition behind her, she went to get something to drink. If she were a serious drinker, she would have made it the bourbon that Franklyn's grandmother, Monique, enjoyed.

By the end of the day, eight of the teams had been eliminated. Out of four different categories, team eight won two. Elise came in first in her category. Daniel came in first in his category. Bailey squeaked by with a third place in the chocolate confections category, and Justin placed second in his. With their combined points, team eight earned the right to go on to the next level in the competition.

Later that evening, at dinner, Bailey was practically inconsolable she was so depressed over coming in third in her category. They'd all gone to their rooms for leisurely baths hoping that the hot water would relax them. All of them admitted that they had never been under this much pressure, not even during their final exams in culinary arts school.

"You don't have anything to feel bad about, Bailey," Daniel said quietly. He was in his early twenties, with dusky brown skin, and dark-brown soulful eyes. "You did your best. That's all you can do. We don't know from day to day whom we're going to be pitted against. Today, two others' skills were superior to yours. Tomorrow you may be the best among those you compete against. That's what makes this so stressful and exciting all at once. The unknown."

Bailey tried to smile but it came out as a grimace. "I had such high hopes."

"We're not out yet," Elise said, smiling at her. "We've got the second highest overall score, Bailey. We can still win this thing."

"Shoji Yamaguchi's team has the highest scores," Justin said cynically. "It would take a miracle to pull our butts out of the fire."

Elise raised her glass of white wine. "To miracles, then."

Everyone clinked glasses.

Before bed, Elise phoned Franklyn. She knew he was home by now, it was after eleven-thirty on Saturday night. Sure enough, he picked up on the second ring.

"Hey, baby," he said after she'd said hello to him.

Elise was so happy to hear his voice that tears immediately sprang in her eyes.

She supposed this was a form of stress release. Stress release, and missing the hell out of him. "We're still in the competition," she told him right away.

"I know," Franklyn said. "I had a big-screen TV put in the dining room so everybody could watch. We were cheering you on, baby. When they announced you'd taken first place in your category, everybody in the restaurant applauded and this was during the dinner rush."

Elise was momentarily stunned to silence. She clearly remembered asking Franklyn not to tell anyone the competition was being televised, and he'd set up a big-screen TV so that his staff and patrons could watch!

She couldn't do anything except laugh for the next minute or so. "I can't believe you did that. What if I'd fallen on my face?"

"Don't you know by now that you can never fall with me around? I won't let you," was all he said. "I had no doubt you'd do well."

"Obviously not!" Elise cried, still laughing. "Who else did you tell?"

"Just family," Franklyn said. "Mom phoned from Florida. She said to tell you that you did a wonderful job. They're making their way back home now, by the way. She and Dad are going to start construction on their house sometime in June."

Elise smiled warmly on her end. "We'll be married by then."

"Husband and wife," Franklyn intoned.

"The old ball and chain," countered Elise with a giggle.

"Jumpin' the broom," said Franklyn with affection.

"Hitched," Elise said, her tone husky.

"Oh, baby, the sound of your voice makes me want you so badly, I'm in pain," said Franklyn, the longing evident in his deep voice.

"Let's not start anything over the phone," Elise said. "It's not fair. I'll never be able to get to sleep tonight. You've already got me quivering. Don't say anything else except good-night. I love you."

"I love you, girl. But tomorrow night, all bets are off. It's going to be on!"

"Agreed," Elise said, her breath coming in short intervals. "Bye!"

Franklyn chuckled as he hung up the phone and turned off the bedside lamp. He had gotten hard just thinking about her. Elise, Elise, Elise.

In Phoenix, Elise lay on her back, staring at the ceiling. She couldn't wait to get home. She knew precisely what she wanted to do to Franklyn. He would be worn out when she was finally through with him. Then she'd let him rest, and do it all over again, only with more passion.

Sunday's round of competition began at nine in the morning. Team eight arrived, looking fresh from a good night's sleep and crisp in their white uniforms and chef's hats. Overnight, workers had been busy dismantling the unneeded extra eight cubicle/kitchens. Now there were only four, side by side.

Shoji Yamaguchi's team was to the right of Elise's team. The four of them stood erect, waiting for instructions from the designated judge who would come and set forth the final challenge for the teams.

Elise glanced at Shoji. He was her height with straight

black hair, slightly tanned skin and a thin moustache. Of average weight, he appeared to be in top physical condition.

He cast his dark eyes upon her and smiled. She smiled back.

Bailey caught them in the act and said, "Oh, my God," under her breath.

Hearing this, Elise asked, "What is it?"

"He smiled at you," Bailey said, concern written all over her face. "Shoji only smiles at someone he plans to eviscerate."

Elise laughed shortly. "Can't you people just treat this as another day in the kitchen and stop making it a life-or-death situation? You're starting to get on my nerves."

"I'm only telling you what I've heard," Bailey said in her defense.

The judge who was to get them started hadn't arrived yet, so Elise broke rank and walked over to Shoji Yamaguchi's kitchen. "May I have a word with you?" she asked when she was standing in front of him. He had most definitely heard her, yet he didn't utter a word. He looked through her. Elise smiled. If he was trying to intimidate her, he could keep this sorry effort. She'd lived with Derrick Scott for more than four years, she was beyond intimidation.

"Look, my teammate seems to believe that you only smiled at me because you consider me your competition and you plan to, in her words, eviscerate me. I know that's ridiculous, so I just came over to say, may the best team win."

She didn't wait for a reply, time was winding down, and the judge would most assuredly arrive soon to get them started. She stopped in her tracks, however, when she heard him say in perfectly enunciated English, "You have excellent balance."

Elise rounded on him, her eyes flashing fire. He was the

one who had oiled her floor, hoping she would slip and send her cake flying in the air. Was this how he'd won so many competitions, by cheating? And she bet he'd never been caught. No, she knew he'd never been caught because he continued to qualify for competitions around the world. Shoji Yamaguchi. He wasn't even *Japanese*. He looked like your average white boy from Hometown, USA.

Elise held her anger in check. She wouldn't jeopardize her team's chances by behaving aggressively toward the competition. She wouldn't give him the satisfaction. That could have been his plan from the beginning, to make her react.

She took a deep breath and gave him an angelic smile. Then she went and joined her teammates. To Bailey, she said, "Let's kick his ass!"

Bailey grinned. "Yes, let's."

A little while later, the judge, a portly gentleman with white hair and deep-brown eyes, delivered the challenge: "You will work together to create a centerpiece consisting of all four of your specialties. At the center will be the cake— however, working upward and outward there must also be evidence of the work of the chocolatier, the pulled sugar expert, and the sugar blower. From conception to finish, you have six hours. Your theme will be the opera. Choose any opera you like. Good luck."

To be fair, the teams had been given the theme beforehand, so they had planned the architecture of their centerpieces. They now had to make those plans a reality.

They had chosen the opera *Carmen* by Georges Bizet. Elise made a red velvet cake with white vanilla icing. Atop it, Bailey, the chocolatier, erected the figure of a dancing woman. With pulled sugar, dyed red, Daniel created a backdrop that looked like curtains descending upon a stage.

With blown sugar, Justin produced sparkling stars that made the stage, with the beautiful brown woman upon it, appear to be outside on a star-filled night. A night at the opera.

They worked well together, sometimes actually bumping hips in the tight confines of the kitchen, but their focus was on the work, on the ballet of four like minds behaving as one.

When they were finished, they stood looking at it sitting on the counter.

"It's gorgeous!" said Bailey.

"But is it delicious?" asked Justin worriedly.

"If we all followed the recipes to the letter, of course it's delicious," Daniel said with confidence. "What do you think, Elise?"

Elise measured her words because this felt like an important moment to her. She knew she had done her very best, and that's all she could conceivably require of herself. Her teammates had done their best. That should be enough. However she felt that wasn't what they wanted to hear, that their efforts had already made them winners.

"I think it's the best centerpiece here," she said, her voice strong with conviction. "Shall we put it in front of the judges and see what they think?"

That seemed to move her teammates to action. They could not stand there all day admiring their handiwork. They had beat the clock by thirty-seven minutes.

Each of the teams stood behind the table upon which their centerpieces sat.

The judges took their sweet time deliberating while the teams sweated under their uniforms and tall chef hats. Elise was so nervous she started to itch, but did not dare scratch. She hoped she wasn't popping out in hives under her uniform.

Finally, one of the judges, a woman with silver hair and pale-blue eyes, rose from her chair and cleared her throat. She smiled prettily, mindful of the cameras that were rolling. "On behalf of my fellow judges and myself, I'd like to congratulate every team that has participated in the competition this year. We have seen skill that has been unprecedented the years we have been judging these competitions. All of you deserve a round of applause." The audience, numbering in the thousands now, clapped loudly for the teams. The judge cleared her throat again and spoke into the microphone in her right hand. "It gives me great pleasure to award the bronze medal to team six."

Team six, consisting of chefs from the state of Georgia came forward and collected their medals along with checks for five thousand each.

Everyone waited with bated breath as the judge announced the next winning team. "The silver medal goes to team one."

Team one was Shoji Yamaguchi's team. He smiled for the cameras. The rest of his team looked very relieved and were practically jumping up and down with joy. They each had a check for ten thousand dollars in their hands, and a certificate for a brand-new double oven.

Elise's hopes for the double oven plummeted. That little cheater was getting her oven! She tried to maintain a pleasant expression, but it was hard to do so.

"Finally," said the judge, "the gold medal goes to the superb team from San Francisco, team eight!"

Elise felt weak in the knees. She grabbed hold of Daniel's arm for support. He immediately turned toward her and hugged her. Bailey yelled and did a cheerleader's split. Justin started laughing uncontrollably. They hugged each other before going forward and accepting their medals, plus their checks for twenty-five thousand apiece.

After the uproar had settled down, the judge again spoke.

"As we all know, you eat first with your eyes, so presentation was very important. However, the proof is in the pudding. Team eight not only produced the most beautiful centerpiece, but it tasted divine. That, plus the points they'd accumulated in yesterday's competition put them over the top. I present to you our 2006 champions, Bailey Hitchcock, Justin Goldsmith, Daniel Martinez and Elise Gilbert. Congratulations!"

Elise's greatest satisfaction was in knowing that Shoji Yamaguchi had not won again.

Chapter 10

Photo after photo was taken of the winning teams. Elise's team was flanked by the other two. Following the photo session, the television crew got the opportunity to interview them, and take footage. Elise was surprisingly at ease with it all. Apparently, participating in the competition had imbued her with new confidence. She was charming without having to think about it. And naturally articulate. She was amazed by the words coming out of her mouth.

When Guy Hamilton asked her if she had any parting words for his viewing audience, she said, "Remember, stressed spells *desserts* backwards. So, don't forget to have dessert, you'll be a lot less stressed."

"I love that girl," Tamryn Baylor nearly screamed into Guy's headset. "I'm coming down there." Tamryn was in the control room on the upper level of the ballroom, monitoring everything her crew was doing below. "Don't let her go anywhere before I get there."

Guy had been trying to concentrate on something else Elise had been saying while Tamryn was screeching in his ear. He loved working for Tamryn because she was fair, energetic and generous to a fault, but her voice in his ear was extremely irritating.

He tried to cover the fact that he hadn't heard Elise's closing statements word for word by saying, "Wonderful sentiments, Elise. Congratulations, again."

"Thank you, Guy," Elise said, perfectly happy to be finished with the interview.

She smiled and walked away, clasping her medal and her check to her chest. All she wanted to do now was go to her room and sit quietly with her thoughts for a few minutes. Her mind hadn't completely grasped what had happened. It would take time to digest everything.

People were milling around her. With the interviews winding down, the audience had already dispersed. She estimated that about three thousand people had attended the competition. Most of them had left the grand ballroom and left the resort entirely or were drifting about the lobby or the grounds. When she finally reached the lobby and the bank of elevators, someone called out her name.

She turned to find Shoji Yamaguchi coming toward her. He had that intense expression on his face that he always wore. It made him look sinister, the effect he was aiming for, she supposed.

She thought of not waiting for him to catch up to her. He wasn't someone she wanted to be alone with after what he'd done, and she didn't owe him any respect. He certainly hadn't shown her any.

Curiosity made her stay. Her expression remained neutral when he greeted her with, "Congratulations are in order, Miss Gilbert. The best team won." He offered her his hand to shake.

She didn't take it. Looking him straight in the eyes, she asked, "Why did you try to sabotage *me*, of all people? I'm a nobody. I didn't know you from Adam before I arrived in Phoenix."

He smiled, his mouth barely curving, but his eyes losing some of their coldness. "But don't you see? That's why I considered you my only competition. Everyone else was in awe of me. My reputation was enough. All I had to do was maintain my magnificent persona, and I had psychological control over the competition. Everyone except you. I overheard your teammates talking about you in the lounge before you arrived our first night here. Bailey Hitchcock referred to a cake you had made as an aphrodisiac. She said she could have died happy after eating it. I had never heard of you, some obscure baker from San Francisco, so I hedged my bets. I thought I'd get rid of you by making you drop your entry, and therefore get disqualified from the first round. Now, do you see that there was method behind my madness?"

"Frankly, no," Elise told him. "I still think it was sneaky, underhanded and damned childish. If you're such a good chef, why do you need to resort to dirty tricks like that? Grow up!"

Shoji threw his head back in laughter. Elise stared at him, sure that he was going to hurt himself because that was the most emotion she'd ever seen him display.

"Careful, don't injure something," she said. "Your stiff body's probably not used to hilarity."

Shoji laughed harder. "You know, if you had not just made yourself my dearest enemy, we could have been friends."

"Thank you, I have enough friends," Elise said, and left him standing there.

Shoji stood watching her walk away with a smile on his face.

"What a nut," Elise said under her breath as she stepped into the elevator that would take her upstairs. No apology whatsoever for his behavior, just a reason for it. His reason had been as twisted as he was.

In her room, she made sure the door was locked behind her then went and placed the medal and the check on the writing desk near the window. She peered down at the check a moment. It was the most money she'd ever earned in one lump sum. Being her parents' daughter, she was familiar with saving money. This was going toward her dream-bakery fund. One day she'd have enough for a down payment.

Turning away, she went to place a phone call to Franklyn's cell phone. It was Sunday afternoon, and he could be anywhere since he had the day off. He wasn't supposed to be at the airport to pick her up until 7:00 p.m., which meant there were more than three hours for him to kill before then.

She pulled off her chef's hat and placed it on the nightstand, kicked off her shoes, and stretched her legs out on the bed as she got comfortable.

"How does it feel to be a champ?" Franklyn asked, after recognizing her number.

"You know?"

"Of course, I was watching when your team won. Couldn't wait for you to phone to tell you how proud I am of you. You did it! Hey, why so quiet?"

Elise was busy taking the pins out of her hair. It fell down her back. "To tell you the truth, I'm kind of stunned. Plus, I just had a very weird conversation with another one of the contestants, a guy named Shoji Yamaguchi."

"Yeah, he's supposed to be the next superstar in the pastry world, but according to some restaurant owners I know, he's too ambitious to risk hiring him. He has a shorter shelf life than milk."

"*Ambitious* is putting it lightly." Elise told him about the cooking oil incident. And why she hadn't reported him.

"I can see why you were reluctant to say anything, you didn't want to spoil things for your fellow contestants or cast aspersions on the organizers of the competition. A scandal like that could ruin them. They would be blamed for not investigating their contestants closely enough. But his getting off scot-free doesn't sit well with me."

"I agree," Elise said. "But what can I do? Write an anonymous letter warning them to keep an eye on him in any future competitions?"

"No, no, that wouldn't work. They'd just think it was bitter grapes. I really don't know what can be done, sweetheart. It isn't fair but life isn't fair."

Elise bit her bottom lip, thinking. "So true." There didn't seem to be a solution to the problem. She had faith, though, that Shoji Yamaguchi, or whatever his name was, wouldn't get away with it indefinitely. There had to be justice in the universe.

"I'm going to try to put him out of my mind," she said. "I'm going to shower and dress for the airport. Definitely don't want to miss my flight this afternoon."

"You'd better not. I've got something special planned for you."

"What?" she asked, her tone seductive.

"I'm not telling."

"Okay, well I'm not telling you what I bought you from the resort's boutique."

"I hope it's something *you* wear, and I can take off you."

That's exactly what it was, a beautiful silk teddy. "What are you, psychic?"

Laughing, Franklyn said, "No, I've just got you in my head. Come on home, girl."

"You might have to take me in the parking lot," she said. "Because I can already taste you."

"We'd be arrested because of all the yelling," Franklyn said of their public coupling.

"You?" Elise asked innocently enough.

"No, you."

"You've got that right!" Elise told him with a laugh. "Let me go. See you soon. Love you."

"Love you," Franklyn said, his voice so sincere that Elise felt all warm inside.

After they rang off, she got up and began removing her uniform.

Before she could get all of the many buttons of the tunic undone, someone knocked.

Quickly rebuttoning her tunic, she called, "Just a minute!"

Remembering the check was exposed on the desk, she went and grabbed it and the medal and shoved both of them into her shoulder bag in the closet. This done, she went to peer through the peephole.

Bailey stood there grinning at her. "Open up, Gilbert, you didn't think you were leaving here today without us having a private celebration, did you? Justin and Daniel are with me and we've got champagne!"

Elise had swung the door open by the time she'd finished her sentence. Bailey strode in with a chilled bottle of champagne in one hand and two flutes in the other. Daniel and Justin already held their flutes at the ready for the champagne.

Bailey poured them all glasses of the bubbly. "To the best team I've ever partnered with," she toasted them. "An African-American, a Mexican-American, a Jewish-American, and a West-Texas American, ah, I mean, a Scottish-American, at least I think we're Scottish, who cares? Cheers!"

"Cheers," everyone else said in unison.

They sat around the room, either on the bed or in one of the three chairs.

"Well, it was hell, but it's over with," said Justin. "I can go back to my restaurant and see if my assistant chef has chased away all my regulars."

"I can go back to Dorie and await the birth of Daniel, junior," Daniel said, a beautiful smile on his face.

"With enough money for a very nice layette," Elise said.

"Layette?" said Daniel. "College fund, more likely. My son is going to be doctor."

"He'd be doing pretty well if he grew up to be just like his father," Elise told him.

"What is this, a mutual admiration society?" Bailey joked. "Okay, okay, Daniel is going to have a beautiful baby boy with Dorie. How could they not, look at his father! I want to hear your plans for the future, Miss Gilbert."

"I'm going to go back home, marry Franklyn and be very happy, thank you very much."

"Well, I'm not going back to the same old, same old," said Bailey. "I'm high as a kite right now, and all I can think about is, how can I use this win to go a step farther? If we play this right, we could write our own tickets. The publicity in the food industry is going to be significant. We'd be fools not to take advantage of it. Look for better positions. Do interviews whenever we're asked. Don't turn anything down, unless the offer is just too sleazy to accept.

You're gonna meet some freaky people, too, so watch out. All I'm saying is, don't just go back home. Go back home with a plan!"

"Of course I'm going to take advantage of everything that comes my way," Justin said. "But I really only did this to prove to myself that I could do it without throwing up."

"Me, too!" Elise cried, laughing.

They chatted about the industry for a few minutes more, then they promised to keep in touch, and Elise saw them to the door.

As soon as she shut the door behind them, the phone rang.

"Hello?"

"Elise Gilbert?" asked a female voice.

"Yes, it is."

"My name is Tamryn Baylor, I'm a producer for Food Network. I'd like to speak with you about an employment opportunity."

Elise was conflicted. With Bailey's speech about not turning down opportunities resounding in her ear, she felt she should at least hear Tamryn Baylor out. On the other hand, she had less than an hour to make it to the airport.

"Where are you, Ms. Baylor?"

"I'm downstairs in the lobby."

"My flight to San Francisco takes off in exactly fifty-five minutes. I have to be out of here in twenty minutes if I'm going to make it to the airport on time."

"No, problem," said Tamryn. "I'll drive you to the airport. We can talk on the way."

"Deal," said Elise. "I'll be down shortly. How will I know you?"

"I'll be the fine sister in the red suit," said Tamryn.

"You should be easy to spot, then," Elise returned easily.

* * *

Tamryn started talking the moment she and Elise got close enough to one another in the lobby to be heard. "Hey, Elise, you made good time."

Elise, wearing jeans, a comfortable chambray shirt and athletic shoes, smiled at the stylish African-American woman in the red power suit. She was tall and amply proportioned with an hourglass figure. Her short black hair was relaxed, wavy and combed straight back from her forehead. Light-brown eyes met Elise's with confidence.

"I've got a good reason not to want to be late," Elise said, feeling that she could be herself with Tamryn. They walked swiftly over to the reservation desk where Elise informed the clerk that she was checking out. She handed the woman her card key. In a couple of minutes, she was told that everything was set, and the clerk wished her a good evening. "Same to you," said Elise.

She and Tamryn then began walking swiftly toward the exit.

Tamryn adjusted her shoulder bag, her car keys already in her hand. "Which is?"

"Sorry?"

"Your good reason for not wanting to miss your plane."

Elise pushed the door open and held it for Tamryn. "The man I'm going to marry."

Tamryn instinctively glanced down at Elise's ring finger. As a woman who had owned three previous engagement rings, she could tell quality when she saw it. A two-carat flawless white diamond in a platinum setting was preferable to a less flawless 5-carat diamond in a yellow-gold setting. "He's got good taste," she told Elise. "In rings and in women."

Elise smiled at her. "Thank you."

Tamryn pointed to the red Mustang convertible in the parking lot. "That's me over there."

Elise saw a theme here. Red suit, red car.

"What I'd like to do," Tamryn said as she backed the Mustang out of its parking space, "is develop a show for women, about women, that isn't always telling them that in order to be happy, they've got to be a size zero like some actresses I know who could use a plate or two of collard greens and corn bread."

"I like the thought of that," said Elise encouragingly.

Tamryn smiled and sped out of the parking lot. Elise saw that not only did Tamryn like to wear the color red and drive sporty red cars, but she drove like the car was on fire and she was trying to put it out with the sheer force of the wind sweeping over it. She drove like a bat out of hell.

"Let me guess," Elise said as Tamryn sped past, and around, every car on the road. "You learned how to drive in New York City."

"How'd you guess?" Tamryn asked.

Elise didn't say it, but once you've been to New York City and seen the traffic, been in the car with a New York driver, you never forgot the experience. Besides, New York drivers had jokes about California drivers and vice versa. Each group thought their driving abilities were vastly superior.

"Just a wild guess," Elise said. "Your company is based in New York, after all."

"Yes, it is, but don't worry, if the show I'd like to develop around you is okayed, you can tape in San Francisco. We have a studio there. I don't mind commuting. I love to travel."

"At light speed," said Elise.

Tamryn laughed. "I tend to do things fast, that's just my personality. You're more laid-back, I like that. I want the show to be laid-back. I want women to feel an affinity for you. Like you're their sister-friend. And that thing you said about stressed is desserts spelled backwards, I'd like to keep that. We eat too much, drink too much, smoke too much, to relieve stress. And we're not enjoying ourselves while doing it. A great deal of guilt has to be dealt with afterwards. But you, my dear, are going to let women indulge in rich desserts in moderation and it's going to be a sensuous experience that they're not going to feel guilty about later on."

"You've really given this some thought," said Elise, impressed.

"Honey, the idea has been distracting me from my work ever since you said that desserts/stressed thing to Guy yesterday. I'm stoked. I think I can go pitch this idea with my eyes closed—and sell it!"

"The possibility is exciting, I admit. But how do you know I'd be any good as a show host? You've just seen me in the competition."

"Easy. We'll fly you to New York for a screen test. You're the talent. You need to put together a demonstration on how to make a certain dessert, and you'll be chatting throughout the process. That's all. Don't do anything elaborate. Speak from the heart, the gut. Be yourself. Be natural. At the same time, be fabulous. You get me?"

"When do you want to do it?"

"Next week, of course," Tamryn said with a laugh. "Told you I do everything fast. I will propose the show to my bosses on Monday. You will fly in on Thursday evening, we'll put you up in a hotel. Early Friday morning, we'll tape. Now, the decision will probably take longer. When it comes to money, which producing a show takes buckets of, the bosses like to balance this and weigh that. It's easier getting money from my Momma, and that woman can make the eagle scream on a dollar bill!"

"I suppose it wouldn't hurt to give it a shot, as long as you understand that, should they buy your idea, I definitely don't want to move to New York. I like your city, but my heart, as the song says, is in San Francisco."

"I understand," Tamryn assured her. "Just like my heart's in New York. *His* name is Jeff. What's yours?"

"Franklyn."

As Elise hurried down the gangway, she realized that this was a new experience for her. Being met at the airport by the man she loved. She'd seen all those wonderful scenes in movies where long-parted lovers had finally come back together and they would kiss upon meeting with such passion that it was tantamount to making love while standing up. Powerful scenes, those. But real life wasn't like the movies, was it?

Her heart was in her throat as her eyes searched the waiting area of the carrier she'd used. When she spotted him, he was standing, not sitting, and he was leaning against a building support. He saw her at the same time, and pushed away from the support.

Elise restrained herself from running toward him. She took all of him in. How the waist of his button-fly jeans fell a little below his bellybutton. She noted that his flat stomach was revealed as he raised his hand in a wave. He smiled, and her heart did a happy dance in her chest.

For his part, Franklyn got tunnel vision when he saw her. Her hair was wild about her face. Airplane hair, she would call it, and complain that she needed a mirror so that she could style it. He loved her hair wild and loose like that. When she smiled at him, all he could think about was tasting her again after nearly three days apart.

When they collided, because it certainly was not simply a coming together, their mouths sought succor one from the other. Elise had had the presence of mind to sling her shoulder bag's strap across her chest so that she would not have to worry about it slipping off her shoulder. Her dress bag and carry-on bag, both lightweight, went on the floor. If anybody grabbed them while she was kissing Franklyn, well, no great loss.

Right now, her mind was on one thing, trying not to faint from pleasure. His mouth was so sweet to her, his taste so addictive, that she dearly wanted to make this moment last forever. She felt his arm muscles as he held her fast against his chest. Knew when he started to get aroused, and it only excited her more.

Franklyn knew he had to gain control. They were in a public place, after all. He couldn't go around with a hard-on. Not him, it'd be too noticeable. He'd look like a pervert. So, he found the strength to break off the kiss.

He looked deeply into her eyes. "God, I missed you so much."

Elise kissed his chin, one of her favorite spots on his face. "I missed you, too, baby."

"But let's get a move on before this gets embarrassing." He briefly glanced at his crotch.

Elise blushed, smiled and said, "Good idea."

In the truck, as soon as Franklyn turned the key in the ignition, the sound of Amos Lee singing "I've Seen It All Before," accompanied only by his acoustic guitar, filled the cab. Elise had placed her bags on the back seat. Now, she moved close to Franklyn on the front seat and as soon as their skin touched, they were once again locked in a passionate embrace.

Her emotions were so intense, so close to the surface that she felt tears prick the backs of her eyes. If her love for him were an energy source, like electricity, then she would be able to light up San Francisco.

"Elise, you're driving me crazy here," Franklyn said between lip-locks. "I'm too big to have sex on the front seat of a truck, but hell if you're not gonna make me try if you don't stop right now."

Elise was up on her knees, straddling him, her mouth on his neck. His aftershave, a subtle Asian-inspired scent with a mixture of spices, assailed her nostrils. He smelled so good, she wanted not only to kiss him, but to lick him.

Franklyn sighed as if he had given up the fight, and kissed her mouth again, this time leaving her too weak with satisfaction to do anything except sit quietly like a good girl and let him buckle her seat belt. He smiled as he put the truck in Reverse.

"You're not the only one with self-control, you know," Elise said, letting him know that she'd stopped of her own free will.

"I know that," said Franklyn. "Otherwise we would be back there making love right now. But how much self-control do you have? I need to go by the restaurant for a minute before taking you home."

"Oh, okay, if you must," groaned Elise. She obviously didn't have that much self-control.

"It'll only take a minute," Franklyn promised, smiling.

A few minutes later, Franklyn was getting out of the truck with his keys jangling in his hand. "Come on, get out, stretch your legs."

Elise didn't care about stretching her legs, but she

wouldn't mind testing out that comfortable-looking couch in Franklyn's office. They hadn't put their imprint on it yet. "All right," she said, scooting across the seat to the driver's side where Franklyn helped her down.

The corner where the restaurant sat was well-lit. Cars moved swiftly past on Stockton Street. A breeze ruffled Elise's hair as she stood behind Franklyn. Soon, they were inside, and Franklyn turned to lock the door behind them.

Elise watched him do this. Finished, he clasped her hand in his. "This way."

He was taking her to the big dining room. She couldn't imagine what was in the dining room that was so important he couldn't wait until tomorrow morning to come and get it. They had Mondays off, and there would be plenty of time for a trip down here.

As they turned the corner leading into the dining room, the lights suddenly came on and what sounded like a roomful of people shouted, "Surprise!"

Elise jumped into Franklyn's arms. He easily lifted her, where she sat perched in his arms, looking around the room at all of her crazy friends and *relative*. Mariel was there with Paulo.

Franklyn set her feet back on the floor, and she was engulfed in the arms of first Lettie, then Mariel and practically all forty of the folks who'd cared enough to come show her some love.

Elise cried. Then Lettie started. Mariel joined in.

Franklyn, Kendrick and Paulo looked on as the three women formed a group hug.

"It's their way of letting out the built-up pressure," Kendrick said sagely.

"What's our way?" Franklyn joked, knowing full well Kendrick would say sex.

"Well, son, if you don't know the answer to that, I ain't gonna tell you."

"I'd like to know, too," said Paulo.

Shaking his head, Kendrick said, "You young men today are pitiful. Pitiful!"

Chapter 11

The party broke up early, at ten-thirty because several guests had to get up and go to work in the morning. Some stayed behind to help clean up, which didn't require much exertion since only drinks and hors d'oeuvres had been served.

Elise and Franklyn, Mariel and Paulo, and Lettie and Kendrick were finished in less than half an hour. The three couples said their good-nights on the walk in front of the restaurant, and went off in separate directions.

When Elise and Franklyn were in the truck on the way to the Victorian on Filbert Street, she said, "Thank you, it was very sweet of you to put together that impromptu surprise party for me."

"My pleasure," Franklyn said. "But I couldn't have pulled it off without Lettie and Mariel. Those two know how to get things organized, and quickly."

Elise laughed shortly. "Yeah, sweetie, it's called being a

woman. I'll have to do something nice for them real soon to thank them. You, I plan to thank as soon as we get to my place."

"It was kind of hard to concentrate on anything *else* tonight," Franklyn said. "I kept thinking that if I had been selfish and not gone through with the surprise party, you and I could have been on round three by now. Sorry, baby, I guess at heart I'm not as sensitive as I could be. I want you naked, 24/7."

The sound of his deep voice, in the relative silence of the truck, was music to Elise's ears. She reached over and grabbed his muscular thigh. Franklyn insisted on her wearing a seat belt at all times when the car was moving. She knew it was wise, considering the fact that San Francisco's traffic was heavy, even at this time of night.

Still, she longed to be closer to him.

"You don't hear me complaining, do you?" she asked in all seriousness. "I like feeling like a desirable woman. I love it when you look at me as if I'm something good to eat."

"You *are* good to eat." Franklyn's voice, so mellow, so full of desire, wrapped around her like a gentle yet sensuous spirit. He was turning her on with just his words, and if she had any modesty left where he was concerned she might be blushing to the tips of her ears right now. But she had none. She was his to manipulate sexually. And he was hers. Luckily she knew he would not abuse that trust. That's what made loving Franklyn such a high. She could let go of all inhibitions and not be afraid of future repercussions.

"Home!" Elise said, seeing the house only a block away. Her hand was on the door's handle.

"Baby, let me park," Franklyn said, laughing.

"Well, park already," Elise said urgently.

Franklyn pulled into the driveway of the house and cut the engine. The outside portico lights, on a timer, were on. He was a cautious man, and scanned the area around the house before saying, "All right, you can get out now."

Elise grabbed her purse, dress bag and overnight bag and got out of the car. Franklyn was right there with his hand on her elbow. He took the overnight bag and left her with the lighter dress bag that only held her uniform and a couple of changes of clothing.

Elise ran up the stairs. He walked behind her, smiling at her eagerness. By the time he reached the top step, she had unlocked her apartment door. He closed and locked the door behind them, turned, and Elise was in his arms.

She'd dropped her belongings onto the foyer table. Walking backward, with Franklyn moving forward, with a short pause to deposit the overnight bag next to her other things, she kissed him.

She had switched on the light in the foyer, but neglected to turn on lights as they moved through the apartment on the way to the bedroom. She bumped into the big bookcase in the living room. A couple of books fell off the top shelf, but the bookcase itself did not threaten an avalanche of books. They broke off the kiss long enough to pick up the books, Elise retrieving one, Franklyn the other.

"Have you always been such a bookworm?" he asked, bending to kiss her lips briefly.

"Ever since I learned to read. I was a shy child. Books were my companions." She pulled him roughly against her, keeping them on track, and steadily moving toward the bedroom. "You like books. Your place has a whole wall of books."

"I know. We're going to have to buy a new house for all of the books."

"Nah, just extra shelving," Elise said.

"That's that woman/organization thing again, huh?"

In the bedroom, Elise began unbuttoning Franklyn's denim shirt. "Enough already about books, and a woman's talent for organization." The sides of the shirt separated now, she splayed her hands over his chest, felt his heartbeat, teased his nipples. Looking deeply into his eyes, she said, "No more talking. Anyone who says another word in the next hour will be severely kissed."

"But…"

She cut off his sentence by putting her tongue in his mouth. Franklyn moaned and pressed her lower body into his. Elise raised her arms over her head signifying that she wanted him to remove her layered T-shirts. He pulled them over her head and tossed them onto the green leather chair. Then he bent his head and rained kisses on the side of her neck, enjoying the warmth and scent of her fragrant skin.

Adhering to her vow of silence, Elise held up a finger denoting she needed a little space so that she could back away and take off the rest of her clothing.

She stripped for him, slowly and sensuously. After unhooking the bronze-colored bra in back, she removed the silken article of clothing and let it fall to the floor. Now she kicked off her shoes, a pair of two-inch-heeled mules, and she was barefooted. Franklyn noted that she wore pink nail polish, the same color they had been polished the first time they'd met. For some reason, this increased his desire.

He waited with bated breath to see what she'd do next. She stood before him in a pair of low-rider jeans, her hands covering her nipples as if she were too innocent to allow him to see the evidence of her arousal.

She turned around and unzipped her jeans. Pulling them

down, she revealed a very brief pair of bikini panties. The jeans fell around her ankles and she stepped out of them.

Franklyn inhaled sharply. She was aware he was overly fond of her behind. His heartbeat sped up because he'd anticipated what she was going to do next. She was going to bend over to pick up her jeans. She did, and through the thin material of the panties he could see the outline of her buttocks, ripe for the squeezing. And the outline of the lips of her sex.

What did she think he was made of, steel?

He was no superhero; he was just a man.

She straightened up, dropped the jeans onto the chair, and turned to face him, a delectable and calculated smile on her lips and a dare in the depths of her dark eyes.

Franklyn broke his own record for the time it took him to get out of his clothing. He peeled everything off so swiftly that Elise was reminded of a comedic film she'd seen in which the guy's clothing had simply flown off him without any help at all. Franklyn's clothing was flying all over the room, landing on the dresser, atop the lamp on the nightstand, and on a blade of the ceiling fan.

She calmly removed her panties.

He blew air between his lips as if he were letting off steam, and picked her up. She wrapped her legs around him. Unfortunately, when she did that the tip of his hardened member touched the opening of her sex. Both of them grew tense with longing and once he'd climbed the steps and her bottom touched the bed, she spread her legs and he thrust deeply. She raised her hips to meet him, and he was firmly and completely inside her. Elise sighed with satisfaction. The sound only made him harder, made his need more urgent. She felt so good to him, he gathered her ever closer to him with his powerful arms. Elise trembled slightly and held on to him, one arm wrapped around his back, the other lower on his buttocks as she writhed beneath him.

All the while they kissed each other's throats, chins, sucked on bottom lips, exchanged deep kisses in which their tongues teased and tempted, but they refrained from speaking. Their communication was limited to touch, and they reveled in it.

Their intertwined limbs were golden-brown here, darker brown there. Muscles strained, grew tenser, until release was inevitable or death was imminent. They would most assuredly die happy.

Elise came first, crying out softly, groaning, then letting out a contented sigh.

Franklyn followed, louder, a roar muffled by his mouth pressed between her beautiful breasts. He fell on his side, spent. Elise lay on her side looking into his dear face. Her feminine center still quivered inside, sending delicious aftershocks throughout her body. They looked into each other's eyes.

"Do you realize what just happened?" Franklyn asked.

"Hold that thought," Elise said. "It's still happening for me." She closed her eyes. "No, not over yet. I'm having a ripple effect."

"Well, when you're finally done, would you get up and go pee? We forgot the condom. It might help, but I doubt it. If you're pregnant, you're pregnant," he said gently.

Elise didn't move. Nor did she panic. The thought of being pregnant with Franklyn's child only brought her a feeling of joy. Committed couples sometimes forgot to use a condom. It wasn't unusual. Why should she be concerned? They were both disease-free, and nine times out of ten, anyway, she was not going to wind up pregnant. Getting pregnant was harder than some people imagined, especially if you were a woman of a certain age. She was thirty. Her eggs, what was left of them, would probably require more chances to penetrate than a one-time accident.

"I'm thirty," she told him. "It's probably not that easy to get me pregnant."

"Yes, but I read somewhere that chances are that if a man has been avoiding sex for a few days, his sperm is more potent. I have not…you know…since you've been gone."

Elise smiled. He'd saved himself for her and had not even masturbated.

Considering how often the average adult male masturbated, that was admirable.

She sat up in bed. "Okay, I'll go pee."

He clasped her arm. "How would you feel if you *were* pregnant?"

She met his eyes. "Very happy. You?"

He smiled. "Very lucky."

He kissed her slowly and with deliberation. When they parted, Elise climbed out of bed and went to the bathroom. He watched her go, thinking of the future, wondering what their children would be like. He smiled. One thing was certain, they would have beautiful souls with Elise as their mother.

He got up to join her in the bathroom. A shower was in order.

Elise was dreaming. In the dream, she was fully aware that she was dreaming.

It was her and Franklyn's wedding day. She was wearing the dress she'd chosen, a beautiful cream-colored simple sleeveless Empire-waist dress that fell in soft folds to her ankles. But the venue had changed. The wedding wasn't taking place at the Vineyard, instead she and Franklyn were standing beneath a gazebo on the beach and the wind was at gale force. First her bouquet flew out of her grasp, then her dress began to fall apart piece by piece until she stood before everyone, embarrassed, in her white underwear and a pair of high-heeled pumps. She looked like a stripper.

What was worse, she was calling to Franklyn as if he were far away, but he was standing right next to her with his back turned. She recognized his broad back, and his carriage. Suddenly, the wind lifted her off her feet. She desperately grabbed hold of Franklyn's arm so that she would not fly away. That was when he turned and she saw his face. Derrick.

He threw his head back and laughed, a wild maniacal laugh that sent chills up her spine. Wake up, she told her dream self. Wake up, now!

Then she was lying in bed with Franklyn, here in her apartment. She opened her eyes and recognized her bedroom. She must have cried out in her sleep because Franklyn stirred beside her, reached over and turned on the lamp on the nightstand.

She screamed. It was Derrick in her bed looking concerned, speaking tenderly to her. "Elise, darling, what's the matter? You look as if you've seen a ghost."

He reached for her as if to comfort her, and she jumped from the bed and ran down the hall, screaming all the way.

He was in hot pursuit. "Elise, get a grip on yourself. You're going to disturb the neighbors if you keep up this racket!"

He was stronger than she was, and faster. He caught up to her in the kitchen. In the dimness of the moonlight coming through the window, he grabbed her and pulled her into his arms and shook her.

"Elise, wake up."

Elise opened her eyes. She was in bed but the covers had been thrown off her and she was naked. The arms around her in the dark belonged to Franklyn.

He held her close. "You were having a nightmare. You screamed in your sleep."

Elise shuddered. "Oh, God, it was so real."

Franklyn reached over and turned on the lamp. "That must have been some dream. Want to tell me about it?"

He pulled her into his embrace and covered them both with the bedclothes she'd kicked off during her nightmare. They lay looking into each other's eyes.

"I'm waiting," he said quietly.

She told him the entire dream, leaving out nothing.

"What did you eat tonight?" he joked when she was finished.

Elise's eyes narrowed. "Don't make fun of this, Franklyn. Dreams aren't always nonsense. This could mean something."

Smiling down at her, Franklyn said, "First of all, you stripped for me tonight just before we made love—hence the scene in your dream in which you thought you looked like a stripper. Secondly, it's perfectly normal for you to put Derrick's face on my body in a dream. You *were* married to him, after all. If you insist on analyzing it, there you have it, an analysis."

"There could be more to it," Elise insisted. She racked her brain. The dream had been very surreal. The wind, for example, had had supernatural qualities. Although it had been blowing at gale force, it had affected her alone. No one else in the dream had even looked ruffled by a gentle breeze. Of course it had been *her* dream, and when we dream we're always the star of the show. But what if something in her real life could affect her in such a way that it would ruin her wedding to Franklyn? Derrick in place of Franklyn in the ceremony would definitely spoil her wedding!

Then, it occurred to her why she'd had the nightmare. She had neglected to tell Franklyn about the proposal from Tamryn Baylor. How could she have forgotten that? Okay, in her defense, Franklyn had swept her from the airport to the surprise party at the Vineyard in a matter of minutes. Then, after the party, only one thing had been on her mind, making love to him. But what about afterwards? She had showered with him and gone to sleep in his arms. She could have told him in the shower. She could have told him while they were snuggling in bed, but it had completely slipped her mind. Why?

"I know why I had that particular dream," she told him.

"Go ahead," he said patiently.

"After I went back to my room following the award presentation, a producer from the Food Network phoned. She wanted to talk to me. I told her that I was getting ready to go home. She suggested driving me to the airport. On the way to the airport, she started telling me about a show for women that she thought I'd be ideal for. She wants me to fly to New York on Thursday and give a cooking lesson so that they can film me and see if I'd be any good on camera."

"That's exciting news, babe. I'm surprised you didn't blurt it out the moment we saw each other at the airport."

"That's what I like about you, Franklyn. You're not going to lie here and pretend you don't think it's odd that I haven't told you this before now."

"No, I'm not. I'm sure you had a good reason not to, though." His tone of voice told her he was ready to hear that reason.

"Even though I told her I would not consider doing the show…if she sells it, and that's a big if. Her bosses might not like the idea. Okay, back on track— Even though I told her I would not even consider doing the show if I had to leave San Francisco, I must subconsciously believe that doing it could somehow come between us." She sighed. Her eyes raked over his face. She loved every feature of his face, those golden-brown eyes, that thick dark moustache, his generous mouth, masculine nose, neat brows, square chin. Everything went together so nicely. "It completely slipped my mind, Franklyn. Don't you see? That must mean that I believe it could be a threat to our happiness. I must have been thinking, deep down, of telling Tamryn I've changed my mind and I'm not interested in even auditioning for the show."

Franklyn released her and sat up in bed. "And what? Be back at square one? You said that you're not going to avoid anything else in your life that you're afraid of doing." His eyes were determined. "Don't tell Tamryn Baylor you're not interested on my account, Elise, because I'm going to support you, no matter what. But if you decide to forego the audition, I don't ever want to hear you say, later on, that you regret it. Or have you wondering what might have been years from now when you're the mother of six and working at the restaurant with me. Because, forgive me, that's how I imagine us years from now, with a big family, and working together at the Vineyard. But I'm an adaptable guy. What means happiness to you might not be the same thing that means happiness to me. If you want to do the show, I say, give it your best shot.

"I want you to be happy. But don't pass on the opportunity because you think that's what I want you to do." He smiled, seeing from the confused expression in her eyes that he'd succeeded in not being very clear at all. "What I'm saying is, I will love you even if we don't agree on everything. Don't be afraid to do something contrary to what you may *think* I want you to do. Talk to me. Give me the chance to tell you exactly how I feel about a thing before making a drastic decision like not even showing up for the audition."

"Are my eyes crossed?" Elise said, laughing. "So, my darling, tell me in plain English exactly what you mean. Tell me how you would feel if I actually nailed the audition and they offered me a show?"

"I would be extremely proud of you on one hand, and I would miss you on the other. I've gotten used to seeing you practically every day, Elise, working in the same place. But as long as you were taping in San Francisco and I got to come home to you every night, I'd be a happy man."

"So I should go for it," she surmised.

"Yes, blow them away."

"Shoot for the moon!"

"Over San Francisco," Franklyn added. He pulled her into the crook of his arm. They were both nude. Their warm bodies fitted well together, her softness a balance to his hardness. "'Cause, damn if I'm going to be without you naked in my arms every single night for the rest of my life. You feel too good. Call me selfish."

Elise climbed on top of him. "A good man is hard to find."

Franklyn smiled. "Yes, but a hard man is good to find."

Elise groaned at his lascivious joke. "I saw that one coming a mile away."

"Don't be ridiculous. I'm not *that* big."

Elise leaned down and kissed his lips. He squeezed her buttocks which, coupled with the feel of his member growing hard between her legs, sent delicious sensual currents careening throughout her sex. She throbbed, wanting him so badly she was suddenly panting with need.

"Wait, sugar," said Franklyn. He reached behind him and grabbed a condom he'd earlier placed under his pillow. Elise watched in anticipation as he slipped it on.

Done, he took her hand and pulled her back atop him. Elise sat poised with the opening of her sex pressed against the tip of his penis. They intertwined their fingers. Franklyn was fully erect now, and Elise slowly lowered herself onto him, keeping her eyes locked with his. Her vaginal muscles accepted his hard length. She slowly raised and lowered herself on him, enjoying the intense pleasure the friction provided, but enjoying even more the look of utter love in Franklyn's eyes.

The next morning, the phone rang as Elise was placing soft scrambled eggs onto two plates. She placed the skillet back on the stove and picked up the cordless phone.

"Elise, what are you doing for lunch today?" asked Mariel.

"I have nothing planned. I was going to the bank at around ten. I can meet you somewhere. What's up?"

"I need a sounding board, and you're it," Mariel said, sounding exasperated.

"Does this have something to do with Paulo?"

"Intuitive, as always. It's been three months, you know."

"I was trying not to say anything on the subject, but isn't this a record for you?"

"Except for the engagement, yes," said Mariel.

"So?"

"What do you mean, so?" Mariel asked, playing dumb.

"You know exactly what I mean by so. We've been discussing the male sex since we started showing an interest in them. Do you love him, or don't you?"

"It's not that simple."

"Of course it's that simple. Don't tell me you don't know because you're not flaky, Mariel. Never have been, never will be. You know how you feel about Paulo. You may keep your feelings to yourself, and that's your prerogative if you don't want to tell me. But you do know whether you love him or not."

"Okay, I love him, all right!" Mariel snapped.

"Ouch!" Elise laughed.

"What's so funny?" Mariel asked, still testy.

"You are. I'm going to tell you something that perhaps you haven't given much thought to. You never loved Adam. All that year up to getting engaged to him, you kept saying, 'Maybe it's time for me to settle down,' as if you were on a schedule or something. No emotion whatsoever. Just doing what you thought you should be doing. It was at about the time that I married the D-word. Remember?"

"Are you saying that I was afraid you were leaving me behind?"

"Friends think that way. We're competitive in a weird kind of way. I was married. You wanted to be married, too. But love? I didn't notice that between you and Adam. I, fool that I am, fell for the D-word and look where that got me, used and discarded. Maybe your parents' track record isn't the only thing that caused you to think twice before getting involved with anyone special."

"Get over yourself," Mariel told her. "It isn't your fault I'm the way that I am. I'm smart enough to know I made the decision to be alone the rest of my life. I can make the decision not to be alone."

"Yes, you can," Elise wholeheartedly agreed.

Mariel sighed. "Hell, I don't need to see you for lunch. We've already talked this out over the phone. I know what I'm going to do."

"What?" Elise tried to sound as unemotional as possible but she was far from unconcerned. This could be a breakthrough for her cousin. Her best friend since they were children, Mariel's well-being meant the world to her.

"I'm going to Italy to meet Paulo's folks," said Mariel. "Are they in for a shock, or what?"

Elise screamed in Mariel's ear. When she could control herself again, she said, "Sorry. I'm excited for you, Mariel. This is you, taking a chance on love. He does know that if he breaks your heart, I'll have to hurt him, right?"

Mariel laughed this time. "Now, Elise, that's my job. Okay, enough about me. What's going on in your life, besides being crowned champion of the pastry world?"

Elise told her about the show idea Tamryn had pitched to her.

"Ooh, sounds like a winner to me. I'd watch. All my friends would watch. Especially if you're not going to skimp on the good stuff. We're so tired of diet this and diet that. Girl, give me some real butter and rich chocolate. I mean, I'm not going to pig out on it or anything, but the luxury of dessert is in the sinful richness of it. It's a reward. We need to treat ourselves sometimes. Give us credit for having some willpower. Let me know how the audition goes."

"Wait, when are you going to Italy?"

"He wants to go in the summer, so after your wedding."

"You know what that means, don't you? You're seriously thinking of going to Italy with him in the summer instead of right away?"

"No, what does that mean?" Mariel asked, being facetious because Elise knew she was aware of exactly what she meant.

"That you think your relationship with Paulo is going to

last that long," Elise stated the obvious. "You and Paulo. Mariel Santini. It has a nice ring to it. Has he given you a ring yet?"

"You're getting way ahead of yourself!" Mariel cried, sounding a little panicked.

"Okay, I'll try to stay calm," her cousin said, but not very convincingly.

"Okay, he did ask me if I liked children."

"What did you say?"

"That I love kids. You know I do. I've even babysat those two boogers your sister gave birth to. They came out of the *womb* bad."

Elise laughed. "They're just energetic."

"Energetic? The Energizer Bunny is energetic, they're possessed!"

"Oh, they weren't that bad when you went for the weekend, were they?" Elise asked.

"That's the last time Dasia invites me down for the weekend, and then she and Aaron disappear for the whole weekend and leave me alone with those two. One's nearly two and the other's nearly three, but hell if they couldn't give Chucky a run for his money. And then Dasia comes back and says she hopes I appreciated the opportunity to experience motherhood first-hand. I wanted to give her the *back* of my hand!"

Elise was laughing uproariously. "What did they do?"

"They ran me ragged all day long, then when we all finally went to bed, they in their room down the hall, and I in the guest room with the door open so I could hear them if they needed me, I was so exhausted I was in a deep sleep and the next thing I know they're both bouncing up and down on my bed like it's a trampoline. Apparently the little chimpanzees cannot be contained within the walls of their cribs. I know I secured the sides of their cribs; although why the oldest is still in a crib, I don't know. That boy is so smart, he can open every locked door in the house with his eyes closed. They're either bringing up a magician or a criminal mastermind."

Franklyn walked into the kitchen wearing a pair of jeans and nothing else. Elise gestured to the plates with the scrambled eggs, hash browns and sausages.

"Mariel," she mouthed.

Franklyn smiled at her, walked over to her and said into the receiver, "Good morning, Mariel."

"Good morning, yourself, gorgeous!" Mariel called. "So, you got some last night, huh?" she said to Elise. "I guess you're glowing this morning."

Franklyn kissed Elise's forehead, picked up a plate and took it to the kitchen table where Elise had put two place settings, a pitcher of orange juice and a carafe of fresh coffee.

"I'm feeling pretty good. And you?"

"Kinda glowing myself, cuz," Mariel said. "Hey, I'd better go. Call me when you get back from New York."

"Will do. Bye."

"Bye."

Elise hung up the phone and picked up her plate to join Franklyn at the table. She put the plate at its place setting, walked around the table to where Franklyn was sitting and sat on his lap. Franklyn had just taken a sip of orange juice and he tasted tangy when she kissed him good morning.

Chapter 12

"You can start whenever you're ready, Elise," Tamryn's voice said over the studio's sound system. Elise stood behind a work counter in the kitchen of the elaborate set usually used by a famous chef who hosted a show on the Food Network.

She thought she could smell the Cajun spices he was known for in the air.

All right, she told herself, get this over with and go home.

Yesterday, when she'd gotten to New York, she had been met at the airport by Tamryn's assistant, Jake Meyers, and taken directly to this very studio where she was instructed to give Jake a grocery list of items she would need for her demonstration, keeping in mind that she would have to make the recipe twice, once while taping, and once the previous night so that after she'd finished demonstrating the procedure on tape, she could whip out the finished product and show the viewing audience how it looked.

So, last night, she'd made chocolate mousse, using her own recipe, and refrigerated it in individual serving dishes. Now, she was to simply prepare the mousse again, chatting while she worked. As Tamryn had requested, she'd written up what she was going to do and had presented it to her when she'd seen her this afternoon.

"Hi, I'm Elise Gilbert, and I'm the pastry chef at the Vineyard, a Californian-French restaurant on Stockton Street here in San Francisco. It's a great time to be a woman in San Francisco. Three of the top jobs in the city are held by women. Joanne Hayes-White is our fire chief, Heather Fong is our police chief, and Kamala Harris is our district attorney. But with added responsibilities come added stress. That's where I come in. Ladies, I'm going to help you release that stress and Unwind at the end of the day. I know, you're saying, unwind by doing more work?" She paused. "The difference is, you get to indulge yourself at the end of this little task. When I told my cousin, Mariel, that I was going to audition for a cooking show strictly about desserts for the Food Network, she told me, 'Just make sure you don't skimp on the ingredients. In other words, no diet this, no diet that.' Ladies, you're savvy enough to handle your own diets, so I'm not going to offer advice on how to make skinny brownies. My recipes use *real* butter. Rich chocolate. Real cream. Nothing low-fat here. If that's what you're looking for, keep looking. What I want to propose is a weekly show during which you learn how to make something so sinfully delicious that it becomes your little mini-holiday from life. And at the end of the show, guess what? You get to eat your creations!

"Okay, let's get started. Today we're going to make chocolate mousse. It's simple to make, but it tastes as if you've spent all day in the kitchen."

The ingredients were neatly placed in clear glass bowls on the counter. She pointed to each in turn as she demonstrated the recipe. "First, you need to melt half a cup of semi-sweet chocolate morsels in a double boiler. This step will probably take longer than any other in the process. After you've melted the chocolate, separate three eggs. You're going to beat the egg yolks only slightly, add one teaspoon of vanilla and one half teaspoon of salt. Blend the egg yolk mixture into the melted chocolate."

After she'd done that, she said, "In a separate bowl, beat the egg whites into soft peaks and gradually add two heaping tablespoons of sugar. Once you've beaten the egg white/sugar mixture for a good thirty seconds, fold it into the chocolate mixture and blend well. Some people add the chopped pecans to the mixture, but I prefer mine on top. Your choice. Put them in now or wait until later to add them when you garnish the mousse with whipped topping and chocolate shavings. At any rate, after you've blended the mousse, spoon it into four dessert dishes and chill for an hour."

She walked over to the refrigerator, and removed the dessert dishes containing the chocolate mousse she'd prepared the night before. "And here is how it should look when you're finished."

She set the tray of four desserts on the counter and put whipped topping on each, sprinkled a few chopped pecans, and then a few chocolate shavings. She ended by sampling the rich, chocolate dessert, letting the spoon glide slowly over her tongue.

"Mmm, and that's it. You've just made chocolate mousse, ladies. Invite your girlfriends over to share it, or share it with that special guy. And remember, *stressed* is *desserts* spelled backwards. Don't skip dessert, you'll be a lot less stressed!"

After she'd finished, Elise stood there, wooden. She thought she'd done a terrible job. For one thing, she couldn't recall if she'd remembered to smile or not, her brain had been so intent on demonstrating the recipe correctly. And secondly, that thing with the spoon and her tongue. They probably thought that had been too sensuous.

She held her breath for what seemed like an eternity.

Then, the bright lights dimmed in the studio somewhat, and the next thing she knew she was surrounded by a phalanx of people applauding her.

Tamryn broke through the line of people to hug her. "Great job, Elise. The camera loves you."

"The camera loves her," said Jake, smiling at her. "I loved her. I wanted to be that spoon."

Everybody laughed good-naturedly.

"What he's trying to say, Elise, in his own ribald way, is that you have sex appeal, which isn't a bad thing in this business." Tamryn pulled her aside and handed her a copy of the tape. "Now, this will go to the big guys and, soon, I'll contact you with a nay or a yea. I'm hoping for a yea."

Elise finally let out a sigh of relief. "Okay. One take, is that all you need?"

"That's all we needed," Tamryn confirmed. "I know you were nervous, but once you started preparing the mousse, you were so natural that I don't think anyone else noticed."

"All right," Elise said, squeezing Tamryn's hand in parting. "I guess I'll get my things and head to the airport."

"Jake will drive you," Tamryn said.

Elise smiled at her. "Listen, Tamryn, I wanted to thank you for the opportunity. Even if the show isn't okayed, it was very nice to be considered for it."

"Don't thank me now, thank me later," Tamryn said. She

was wearing a creamy white skirt suit today with tan accessories. Elise was wearing a sleeveless royal blue dress with a scoop neck, and her hair cascaded down her back in thick waves.

Jake walked up to them. "Your flight leaves in an hour and fifteen minutes. We should leave soon. Afternoon traffic can be pure hell."

"I just need to get my things from the dressing room," Elise said.

Jake pulled her coat, shoulder bag, overnight bag and a shopping bag that held a few things she'd bought at Bergdorf's last evening from behind his back. "You mean these things? I went and got them after Tamryn pulled you aside for a private chat."

"I can see why you hired him," Elise said to Tamryn.

"That, and he makes a mean cup of joe," Tamryn said. She briefly hugged Elise. "Go, I'll phone you as soon as I know."

On the way to the airport in the black Lexus that belonged to the company, Elise sat up front with Jake. He'd been right about the traffic. They had to sit for a while. However, Jake was entertaining.

"I hope I didn't embarrass you with my spoon comment," he said once they were underway. "I didn't mean anything disrespectful. Sometimes my mouth gets ahead of my brain. Tamryn encourages us to speak our minds. She thinks it makes for a livelier workday." He glanced at her engagement ring. "I see you're spoken for. But if you weren't I would definitely, and respectfully, ask you out."

Elise smiled at him. He was in his late twenties, tall, in great shape, with dusky brown skin and deep-brown eyes. He wore his shiny dark-brown natural hair in dreadlocks, and he had beautiful lips. He licked them when he caught her eyes on them. He knew she wasn't immune to him even though she was wearing another man's ring. Elise was amazed at the number of times she'd been hit on since she'd started wearing her engagement ring. Men seemed to be drawn to a woman who was already taken. Could it be they longed for a brief affair with no strings attached? She'd heard of the phenomenon, but had never before experienced it firsthand.

"You're a good-looking guy, and if I were not engaged, I'd probably say yes if you asked me out," she told him. "But, I am."

"Can't blame a guy for trying," he said softly.

Franklyn picked her up at San Francisco International for the second time in less than a week, and she told him all about the audition as they drove to the restaurant. It was Friday, and Franklyn still had a few hours to work. Elise changed clothes in the employee's locker room, rolled up her sleeves and got a head start on tomorrow's apple tarts.

She loved the hustle and bustle of the kitchen, the noise, the smells, the happy chatter and even the occasional spats that broke out among the workers. Friday night was usually their busiest night. Couples routinely made reservations for romantic dinners on Friday or Saturday night, Friday being the most popular. Tonight was no different. Franklyn and Lettie were up to their ears in orders for extravagant dishes and not-so-gourmet dishes. Although Franklyn's menu featured meals that one could find at the fanciest French restaurants, he also offered lobster, steaks and roasted chicken because the American palate demanded good old stick-to-your-ribs food. Whatever the dish, he put his stamp on it, and made it a delectable culinary experience. Elise was watching him now as he put the finishing touches on a plate of coq au vin. Made with both cognac and red wine, it had a wonderful savory aroma and was requested quite often by the regular patrons who liked hearty meals.

Finished, Franklyn placed the plate underneath the warmer. The waiter who was serving the patron who'd ordered the coq au vin would pick it up in less than a minute. That was Franklyn's rule. No one who came to his restaurant was served a cold meal. Unless it was meant to be cold. He'd fired waitstaff for shirking their duties in that respect. He was wonderful to work with as long as everyone pulled their weight.

Elise would not be baking the apple tarts tonight. She'd made the crusts and the filling, put the filling in the crusts and set the six dozen tarts in the big fridge. The ovens were in use for dinner orders tonight. Tomorrow morning, she'd come in and bake the tarts. Tonight, she wasn't even supposed to be here. She had just not wanted to go home without Franklyn, and doing the tarts had given her an excuse to watch him work.

At ten, she went to steal a glance in the dining room to see how many stragglers they had to wait on to finish their meals. To her complete and utter surprise, she saw Derrick sitting at a table with an attractive African-American woman. They had their heads together in an intimate conversation.

She spun around and nearly collided with one of the waiters. "Sorry," she said, and walked farther into the kitchen. As far as she knew, this was the first time Derrick had been here. Or was it? She didn't usually work the dinner shift. She left at three in the afternoon. The Vineyard could be his favorite restaurant for all she knew. No one else who worked here would recognize him as her ex-husband.

The thought of Franklyn having prepared meals for Derrick strangely disturbed her.

Something else disturbed her even more. If Derrick was indeed a regular patron, then he knew she worked here. Her name and face were on the dessert menu. If a patron enjoyed a dessert he/she could request however many servings to take home with them in lovely pink bakery boxes. What if Derrick had been eating her double chocolate cake for months now? Eating it and smiling. The image of his eating anything she'd prepared with her two hands gave her a creepy feeling.

She suddenly wished she'd gone straight home from the airport, and not been here for these unsettling revelations.

"Hey, Elise," said Charles Whitman, a twenty-year-old college student who waited tables. "The guy at my table asked if he could meet you. He says your strawberry short-cake is the best he's ever had. Wants to tell you himself. When he asked, I told him he was in luck because you're not normally here at night, but you happened to be on the premises tonight. What should I tell him?"

You can tell him to go to hell, Elise thought. She couldn't believe her ears. Derrick had some nerve, asking to see her.

But Charles was such a happy-go-lucky type of guy that she managed a wan smile for his benefit. Plus, there was no way Derrick was going to leave here tonight thinking she'd hidden in the kitchen because she didn't have the guts to face him.

"Lead the way," she told Charles.

"Okay!" said Charles, hoping there would be a generous tip in it for him. He fairly walked on the balls of his feet all the way to Derrick's table where he introduced Elise and left.

Derrick smiled at Elise. "Chantal is a devotee of the Food Network. She was watching when your team won the gold medal in the pastry competition. When I told her that I knew you, she didn't believe me."

Chantal, a lovely, golden-brown-skinned doll with wide-spaced brown eyes, a button nose, a generous mouth and a heart-shaped face, smiled up at Elise with admiration.

"Hi, I'm Chantal," she said. She had the sort of voice that, if she ordered a pizza, the guy who took the order would ask to speak with her mother. Elise supposed some men found childlike voices on women sexy. But she checked herself after having that thought, because anyone with Derrick would probably irritate her just by their association with him.

Therefore, she smiled at Chantal, and said, "Hello, Chantal. I hope you enjoyed your meal tonight."

"Oh, it was scrumptious," Chantal said, smiling broadly. "I especially enjoyed the lobster and the strawberry short-cake. It was yummy."

Elise smiled as though she were humoring a child. "Thank you. Well, it was very nice meeting you. I hope you both enjoy the rest of your evening."

"Nice meeting you, too," Chantal said.

Elise looked at Derrick. "Mr. Scott." She turned and left.

Derrick hurried after her. He caught up with her and grabbed her by the arm. Elise immediately jerked her arm out of his hand and faced him.

"When Mariel told me you were engaged to be married, I didn't believe her. And then when I saw you on TV in the competition I went to the competition's Web site and there it was, your profile. It gave your background and where you worked. I called and made a reservation, using Chantal's name. Don't worry, she isn't anyone special. Just someone who amuses me."

Elise rolled her eyes. "Why are you telling me all of this? I don't care whom you date. And I can't imagine why you went to all of the trouble of looking me up on the Web site, and then coming here for dinner. What was the point?"

"The point was, I had to see you."

They were standing in the alcove between the kitchen and the dining room, a few feet away from the double doors that led into the kitchen. Elise expected somebody from the wait-staff to come through those doors at any second, and she didn't want to be seen conversing with Derrick.

"Okay, you've seen me. Now, go pay your check and get the hell out of here and don't come back," she said. "There are dozens of restaurants to choose from in this town. Eat elsewhere!"

Derrick laughed softly, his handsome face crinkling around the eyes. "You know, I don't think you've never been more beautiful, Elise. Apparently being in love suits you."

"Yes, it does. I'm happy, Derrick. Why don't you go some-where and be happy with Chantal?"

"I will," he said smugly. "As soon as you thank me for in-spiring you to greatness."

Elise wanted to ball up her fist and slam it into his jaw. "Thank you?"

"You're welcome," he said, pretending not to have noticed that's not how she'd meant the "thank you." "After all, if I hadn't treated you badly, you would have had no reason to rise above your lot in life. You would have had no one to hate enough to mentally say, 'kiss my ass' to while you worked toward your goals."

"You are one sick puppy!" Elise cried. "Arrogant and stupid, all at once, just like you've always been."

Elise was so upset, she didn't notice Lettie stick her head out the door, and duck right back in again. A few seconds later, Franklyn was coming through the doors removing his chef's hat and tossing it aside onto a nearby chair.

"Elise, what's going on?" he asked as he walked up to them.

Derrick, who was only an inch shorter than Franklyn, and nearly as powerfully built, did not shrink back at the sight of this stranger. He was, after all, only a cook, and *he* was a paying customer. The customer was always right.

"Nothing's going on here," he said, looking Franklyn in the eye. "I'm just catching up with my ex-wife. My date and I had dinner, and I saw her name on the dessert menu and wanted to say hello."

Franklyn looked at Elise for further elucidation, ignoring Derrick.

She didn't want to go into what Derrick had just said to her, thinking it would only end up in a fight. So, instead, she said, "You've said hello. Now, I have to go. Good night." She had no intention of introducing him to Franklyn. She didn't owe him any courtesy whatsoever.

But he would not let it go. "Hey, don't tell me that *this* is the guy that Mariel said you were engaged to." He stuck his hand out. "Congratulations, big guy!"

Franklyn grasped his hand in a firm grip, the hold getting tighter and tighter as he led Derrick across the room toward his table where he'd abandoned Chantal several minutes ago.

"Thank you, Mr. Scott, for your patronage. Now, I would appreciate it if you would pay your check and leave my establishment."

The dining room was empty of customers. Chantal sat watching the two men with an expression of wonder on her beautiful face. She was, however, still too far away to hear what the big guy was saying to Derrick because he was saying it in a very low voice.

"Listen, buddy, I don't know why you would come here expressly to upset Elise. It seems to me you've already done enough to hurt her. But know this—I will break you in half if you ever do anything to upset her again."

Franklyn let go of his hand then. Derrick shook it, and worked his fingers which had nearly gone to sleep due to poor circulation.

"I'm a lawyer, I don't scare easily," he told Franklyn confidently.

"I'm a chef, I own lots of big knives," Franklyn countered. "Get out."

"Okay, I'm going," Derrick said. "But you don't own all of San Francisco. If I see Elise on the street there is nothing you can do if I want to walk up to her and speak to her."

"Maybe you didn't hear me," Franklyn said menacingly, taking a step toward him.

Derrick jerked his head at Chantal. "Come on, babe. Let's blow this joint."

Chantal hastened to do his bidding. She looked back at Franklyn once, and smiled.

"Chantal!" Derrick bellowed.

He stopped to pay his check, and then they were gone.

Franklyn went back to the alcove where Elise was waiting.

"So, that's Derrick," he said. He was actually smiling at her.

Elise blew air between her lips and forced a smile, too. "He came to accept my thanks for making me into a better person," she told him. Then, she went on to recite what had transpired between her and Derrick. Franklyn already knew about Mariel's gloating to Derrick about how Elise was so much better off without him.

When she'd concluded her story, Franklyn laughed. "I guess he's the type who can't be happy if someone else appears to be more content than he is. Let's just hope he isn't a sociopath, and this incident satisfies him."

Later, as they walked hand in hand to his truck to head to her place, she asked, "Would it be okay if I stayed with you tonight? You have a VCR/DVD player, I only have a DVD unit. They gave me a tape of the audition."

"Why didn't you mention it earlier?" Franklyn wanted to know. "There's a VCR player in my office."

"I know that," said Elise. "But you know you. You would have had everybody back in your office watching it, and I would have been mortified. I only meant for you to see it. What if I was awful?"

"You're probably right. I would have wanted everybody to see it. But you couldn't have been awful. Tamryn Baylor said you did a great job, and from what you've told me about her, she doesn't seem to be the type who says something she doesn't mean."

"I trust your judgment," Elise said. "If you watch it and say it was good, I'll believe you. I just can't watch it."

Franklyn unlocked her door and helped her in. She leaned across the seat and unlocked his side. After he'd gotten in, he said, "Oh, you're gonna be one of those stars who can't watch herself."

Elise laughed. "I don't want to even hope I get the job so that I won't be too disappointed when Tamryn phones and tells me they're gonna pass on it."

"The answer's going to be yes," Franklyn said as he buckled up and started the engine.

Elise fastened her seat belt. "It doesn't matter, really. I went through with the audition. I'm satisfied."

"Yeah, but you'd be happier if they wanted you to do it, right?"

"Maybe a little," she hedged.

"Woman, please. You know you want it."

"Can we change the subject? I don't want to talk about it."

"All right. Let's talk about Derrick," Franklyn suggested.

The Friday night traffic was even worse than during the week. He drove with caution, and with abandon. Faint hearts were not advised to drive in San Francisco; they should take the bus.

"It was a shock seeing him there, in the place that's been a sanctuary for me," Elise said without hesitation. "It felt like Satan the Devil walking into a church. That's how I felt, violated. Thank God what I imagined when I first saw him—that the Vineyard might have been one of his favorite restaurants and he might have been coming there for ages without my knowledge—was wrong."

"His looking up your profile online disturbs me," Franklyn said, his voice grave. "Then to go through with his plans and actually come to the restaurant hoping to speak with you. He's trouble, Elise. I don't understand his motivation, but I know he's trouble. When I came out there and confronted him, he arched his back up like a junkyard dog. I ought to know, I've faced guys who behaved the way he did. They have ultimate confidence in their ability to defeat you. It might be one hell of a fight, but they know they'll be the victor."

"Oh, he's good at mind games," Elise said, remembering all the times Derrick had tried to control her with words, with actions, with threats. "But underneath he's a coward."

Franklyn agreed with her estimation of her ex-husband. Any man who debased a woman was a coward. Derrick Scott was a calculating coward, that was the difference. The kind who guarded his flank at all times, and went for the jugular given the chance. He'd do anything to win. Look how cold and calculating he'd been to have used a woman as innocent as Elise had been when she'd met him. Elise had been gullible to fall in love with Scott. But you couldn't fault someone that young for being taken in by the object of their affection. Love was blind in that respect. It was the manner in which he'd taken advantage of her innocence that was despicable.

"Coward or not," he said, "I want you to be careful from now on. He said that he was within his rights to approach you anywhere else he happened to see you. That tells me he's going to make sure he sees you again, and probably soon."

Elise shuddered at the thought. It had been months since she'd seen Derrick, spotting him at a friend's party on New Year's Eve of last year. She'd dropped in after the party at the Vineyard because her date had insisted he was not in the least tired and could party all night long. He'd ended up falling into a drunken sleep on her friend's couch. That was the last time she'd seen him. However, that night, Derrick had walked into the room shortly after she and her date had arrived and because of their unspoken agreement concerning not being in the same room at the same time, he'd turned around and left.

She couldn't understand why he'd go out of his way now to seek her out.

At Franklyn's place, which had more than twice as much space as her apartment, they immediately went and got in his shower together to wash away the grease and grime of the restaurant.

Anyone who works at a restaurant knows that food smells, no matter how wonderful originally, get in your skin, hair, clothing and soon turn into something noxious. So, they bathed.

Franklyn washed her hair, Elise's back to him, her head tipped slightly back, the tresses hanging halfway to her waist. Franklyn enjoyed the feel of the strong, thick, silken strands playing between his fingers. After he'd rinsed all of the shampoo out, he turned her around to face him. She looked so beautiful to him with her hair wet and wavy and as dark as a raven's wing. He bent and kissed her. She clung to him while the shower rained warm water down his back. She was mostly shielded from the spray, with droplets falling on her face in a mist. Her sooty eyelashes had tiny droplets on them. When they parted, she opened her eyes, and gazed at him dreamily.

"Baby, let's elope," she said.

Franklyn smiled down at her as he smoothed her hair behind both ears at once and cupped her face. "Where'd that come from?"

"I feel like dark forces are gathering to tear us apart. I can't explain why. But first I had a bad feeling about doing the audition, and now Derrick shows up. I just want to be your wife."

"Dark forces? You sound like a science-fiction novel. If dark forces are really gathering then we'll meet them head-on and fight them. We're not running away to Vegas to get married because you think that will somehow save us. We've made plans, and we're sticking to them. To hell with dark forces, and with Derrick, too. You deserve a beautiful wedding. We *will* be happy, and nobody's going to get in the way of that. Now, stop worrying about everything that comes down the pike. You're a survivor. Do you mean to tell me that after everything you've done to get over the experience you had with that man, you're going to let him affect your actions with just one reappearance?"

Elise was trembling with emotion. Franklyn had never raised his voice in anger to her, and yet, he had done it now. Perhaps his anger wasn't directed at her, but was as a result of his encounter with Derrick, but that simply proved her point: Derrick's little stunt tonight had negatively affected them. And she strongly believed he was just getting started.

Franklyn let out a long breath and pulled her into his arms. The hurt expression in her eyes was his undoing. How could he have spoken to her like that? He was deeply regretful. It must have been a real shock to the system to see her ex-husband out of the blue like that. Why couldn't he have been more sensitive? He just knew that from the moment he had come face-to-face with Derrick Scott, some beast, a long-dead aggressive tendency, had been reborn in him. He'd wanted to smash Scott's face tonight. He could still taste it, that blood lust.

He squeezed Elise tightly. "I'm sorry. That anger wasn't meant for you, but for your ex-husband. You're right, he got under my skin."

He grabbed a bath towel and wrapped her in it, helped her out of the tub, then grabbed one for himself and quickly dried off.

Elise wrapped and hooked the towel underneath her arms, then took another towel from the shelf to dry her hair with. She slowly walked into the adjacent bedroom, towel-drying her hair as she did so. She still had not said anything because she didn't think she could speak now without sounding hurt and resentful.

Anyone looking on might believe that Derrick's appearance tonight could only cause dissension if they allowed it to. They had to make a conscious decision to let him become a wedge between them. But you would have to know their individual histories, the very experiences that had shaped them. Insecurity. Sure, they had both risen above the insecurity that had plagued them in the past, but it was still there waiting somewhere in the recesses of their minds.

Franklyn was right, they would have to fight for their love, and not allow dark forces to ruin what they had. That meant the next time she saw Derrick, she would have to be ready for whatever he dished out. And she would be.

Elise was sitting on the bed, putting her somewhat dry hair into a single braid down her back when Franklyn, his towel tucked around his waist, sat down beside her.

"Forgive me?" he asked quietly.

Elise looked at him with moist eyes. "I know that wasn't you talking."

"Still, I hurt you. I can't forgive myself for that."

She finished braiding her hair, and with the towel still wrapped securely around her bosom, she moved over and pulled him into her arms. Franklyn laid his head on her chest, listening to the steady rhythm of her heart. She held him and tenderly kissed him behind his ear.

Chapter 13

"You're not transparent, you know," Franklyn said from his seat on the couch in his living room. Elise didn't budge. Elise had put the tape Tamryn had given her into the VCR and when it came on and her "video self" started talking, she couldn't believe her eyes or her ears. She'd never seen herself on TV before. Did everyone look this exposed? She could see the freckles across her nose. Blast high-definition TV!

She moved aside so that Franklyn could see. "I'm glad I didn't have an uninvited guest in my nose at the time. They would have gotten that, too," she complained.

Franklyn went and got her and pulled her onto his lap on the couch. "Will you please be quiet so I can hear what you're saying?"

A couple minutes later he noisily kissed her cheek. "You plugged the Vineyard."

"Of course." She smiled.

He watched intently. When the tape ended, he gazed up at her admiringly. "Let me see if I can taste that mousse you ate at the end."

Elise bent and kissed him. As the passion built, she twisted on his lap and without breaking their lip-lock, got on top and pushed him into a prone position on the couch.

They were sharing a pair of Franklyn's pajamas and both of them were naked underneath. Franklyn's big hands sought the round firmness of her buttocks. She moaned as he gently squeezed them, and pressed her lower body against his.

Franklyn unbuttoned her top and explored the silken heaviness of her breasts. Elise closed her eyes and arched her back, relishing the feel of his hands on her.

He sat up and buried his face between her breasts, then raised his head and looked her in the eyes. "You were so good to look at and listen to, all I wanted to do was come through the TV and ravish you."

"Yes, but you want to do that all the time anyway," Elise joked. "Those network executives don't want to ravish me. They want audiences to tune in to their show."

"They're going to call," Franklyn insisted.

He set her aside for a moment while he got to his feet, then he grasped her hand and led her down the hall to the bedroom.

On Saturday they went in to work together. They left early enough to swing by Elise's apartment to drop off the bags she'd brought back from the New York trip, and to put her bike in the bed of Franklyn's truck. She was going to need it when she left work at three in the afternoon.

The Saturday lunch crowd was steady, and the flow in the kitchen was brisk. Elise stayed busy baking her apple tarts and preparing three other dessert choices. Franklyn had few breaks, but he liked the pace, preferring not to have too many lulls in his day.

At three, Elise went and changed out of her uniform and into her street clothes—a pair of jeans, athletic shoes, and a denim shirt and jacket. The temperature in late March tended toward the fifties during the day and the forties at night. It was also overcast today.

She walked out of the employees' locker room, and saw Franklyn waiting for her in the hallway. He was on his way to his office for his two-hour break during which the assistant chef would assume his duties. They briefly kissed.

"Want to go dancing tonight?" he asked.

Elise smiled warmly. "I'm game if you are. You're the one who pulls the double shift."

Franklyn shrugged that off. "We'd better go dancing while we still can. We can sleep in tomorrow."

She tiptoed and kissed his cheek. "You're so sweet, trying to cheer me up because Tamryn hasn't phoned."

"That never occurred to me," he denied. "I just want to take my girl dancing, then take her home and make love to her."

"It's a date then. I'll be ready at the midnight hour."

They kissed again, more lingeringly since no one else was in the hallway.

Saturday afternoon, Derrick always went to his favorite barbershop in Oakland to get his haircut freshened up. His barber, Al Jenkins, a tall, barrel-chested man in his fifties had been cutting his hair for years, and loved to jabber while he worked.

Derrick was more introspective, and would have preferred that Al simply do his job and be quiet. However, today, Al had struck the right chord. "I saw my ex-wife in the grocery store the other day and, Lord, that woman looked better than she ever looked when she was with *me*," Al said. "She'd lost weight, gotten a new hairstyle, was wearing a short skirt that showed off her legs. She always had nice gams. Gotta give her that! But for a minute there, I entertained the thought of going over there and saying something to her, something wicked. She loved it when I was a bad boy. I caught myself just in time because as I stood there drooling over her, some dude walked up and she took his arm and sashayed off with him. I ask you, gentlemen, what possessed me even to give that woman a second glance?"

Al would often pose questions to his regulars in order to start debates that would go on and on. This time, Derrick had something to contribute.

"It's because, like in most marriages, there were good times as well as bad times. Maybe seeing your ex looking so attractive made you recall how good she was in bed."

"It's true, she was a tigress in bed," Al said. "I was the one who strayed. I have to admit, Derrick, you've got something there."

"I want to know why you strayed if she was so good in bed," another man asked, putting down the newspaper he'd been reading. "She must not have been *that* good."

Ten men, sitting around waiting for their turns in the chair, laughed. Ribbing your friends was a part of the barbershop's mystique.

"Oh, she was good all right," said Al. "I was just a dog. Always had to sniff round some other woman's goodies. Don't pretend you fools don't know what I'm talkin' 'bout."

More laughter.

"I ain't frontin'," Derrick said. "We've all got a little dog in us. Some of us control it better than others, that's all. I recently saw my ex-wife again, too, and I must say she was more beautiful than I'd ever seen her. And she's engaged to some jerk."

"Bet you were jealous," Al joked.

Derrick laughed. "Of course. You know that somewhere deep inside, we always think they still belong to us."

"I think you old dudes need to get a clue," a young blood spoke up. He looked like a straight-up hood, but everyone knew he owned a nightclub there in Oakland. His manner of dress was good for business since his clientele were of the hip-hop generation. Image was everything.

"You can't own a woman," he continued. "You can try, but in the long run she'll resent your ass and take you to the cleaners in the divorce. I say treat her like an equal. And get a prenuptial agreement."

"A prenuptial is a good idea," Derrick said. They knew he was an attorney, so his word was golden on the subject. He had been asleep on the job when he'd married Elise and had not made her sign one. Of course, back then, he didn't have anything to protect. Today, he wouldn't be that foolish.

"It seems to me," the young guy said to Derrick, "you should be glad she's engaged to somebody, jerk or not. Aren't you paying her alimony?"

"Paid," Derrick informed him. "She requested a certain amount, after which my debt would be paid in full. Believe it or not, she said she didn't want an extra penny from my trifling behind. I sent her the last payment over a year ago."

"She was *glad* to get rid of you!" Al said, his belly shaking with laughter.

Derrick smirked. "That was my plan all along, fellas. I wanted her to be happy to see me go." Now, he wondered if he'd made a huge mistake by divorcing Elise.

He hadn't seen her potential. Of course, he hadn't been a

total idiot. He'd realized she was attractive and had a kind heart. She was loyal to those she loved and was willing to work hard. All admirable. But those were not qualities he thought he wanted in a wife. After the divorce he'd dated several women he thought were more to his liking. They had been educated and accomplished. Thin and stylish. Eager to make a bundle of money. In less than two years he'd grown bored with that sort of woman, coming to the realization that none of them put him first. None of them were remotely loving. They looked good, but their hearts were like ice. Essentially, he had to admit that he missed Elise's warmth. Her down-to-earth personality. It was exhausting trying to communicate with women who were always showing him their best faces, unwilling to remove the mask long enough for him to get to know who they really were beneath the facade.

When he'd complained to his mother, in whom he did not often confide, that he was tired of women who only cared about his pedigree, she'd laughed at him and said, "First of all, Derrick, animals have pedigrees, people don't. And if you had wanted a woman who was a human being, you wouldn't have divorced Elise." He had gotten no sympathy from her. He had a sneaking suspicion that she was enjoying his predicament, and felt he was getting exactly what he deserved for divorcing Elise.

"If I wanted her back, I could get her," he announced to the room. "The guy she's engaged to owns a restaurant. It's a nice place, but he's no competition for me. He seems to be a decent man, but I have an advantage over him."

"Which is?" Al asked, skeptical. "You talk a lot of bull, Derrick, but we both know that if your ex-wife didn't try to milk you for every bit of alimony she could get out of you, she wanted to limit contact with you. And that means only one thing—the woman hates your guts. There's no way she'd ever go back to you!"

"You've got that right," the nightclub owner chimed in, enjoying a good laugh at Derrick's expense. "Man, you need to keep it real!"

But Derrick had made up his mind. He was going to woo Elise away from that fry cook!

"I *am* keeping it real," he told them with confidence. "And what's real is that I was the first man she'd ever loved. I know her like the back of my hand. I know what makes her tick."

There was a message from Tamryn waiting for Elise when she got home that afternoon.

"Elise, the execs can't get to your tape until Monday. I'm phoning because I don't want you to be on pins and needles all weekend. Enjoy your weekend, and know that I'll contact you on Monday with the verdict. Later!"

Elise was relieved to receive it. Now, she could postpone worrying about whether she was going to be phoned or not until Monday.

She listened to a second message on the machine. "Hey, girl, you must be back from New York by now. How was the trip?" Mariel.

Elise picked up the receiver in the kitchen where she had grabbed a bottle of water from the fridge and was drinking it while listening to her messages. She set the bottle on the counter, and dialed Mariel's cell phone number.

Mariel answered right away. "Elise!" she said, after seeing Elise's number on her phone's screen. "How did the audition go? Do you think you got it?"

"I'm ambivalent about it, but Franklyn says I aced it," Elise replied casually.

"You haven't heard anything yet?"

"Only a message from Tamryn saying they won't make a decision until Monday."

"Now you're going to wonder about it all weekend," Mariel lamented.

Someone knocked on the door.

"Can you hold a minute?" Elise asked. "Somebody's at the door."

"Sure," said Mariel.

Elise put the receiver on the counter and hurried through the living room to the door. She peered through the peephole. Mariel grinned at her.

"Good one, Mariel," Elise said after opening the door and jerking her cousin inside.

Laughing, Mariel put her cell phone in her purse and hugged Elise. "I was passing right by your place so I thought, why not stop?" She looked ready for spring in a multicolored midriff blouse, low-cut jeans and red sandals. She wore a short red leather jacket over the blouse, and her hair was a red-gold shade, not as fiery red as she normally wore it.

Releasing her, Elise smiled. "What's with the hair?"

Mariel preened. "Like it? I'm testing some less radical shades for when I go to Italy. I don't want to show up black, *and* with bright red hair. I may revert to my natural shade before long."

Her natural color was dark brown. Elise hadn't seen her hair that color since she was around seventeen and Elise, nineteen.

"I like it," Elise told her, walking through the living room to the kitchen where she put the cordless phone back on its base. "Can I get you something to drink?"

Mariel sat down at the kitchen table and put her purse in the chair next to her. "Some water would be nice."

Elise got another bottle of water from the refrigerator and handed it to Mariel. She sat across from her with her own bottle of water in front of her. "I'm glad you dropped by because I wanted to see your face when I told you about Derrick's appearance last night at the restaurant."

Mariel rewarded her with a bug-eyed expression. "What?"

"He brought a date to dinner last night. They were the last couple to leave. It seems they liked my strawberry short-cake."

Mariel worked her mouth like a fish out of water. It was obvious she was upset about the news, and would like to express that emotion, but couldn't find the words with which to do it. Elise took pity on her, and said, "I don't blame you. He would have come looking for me without your gloating. His girlfriend saw the competition on the Food Network, or maybe they were watching it together, I don't know. And from there, he got online and looked up my profile which listed my work experience along with the name of the res-taurant where I presently work. He enjoyed telling me how easy it was for him to find me."

"All those years you received alimony checks through your lawyer so that he wouldn't get your home address, and now he sneaks up on you," Mariel sympathized. "Honey, I'm sorry I ever opened my big mouth. He might not have even thought of looking you up if I hadn't told him how well you were doing without him. I messed with his pride, that's what I did. Men like him have to be the center of the universe, and I made sure he knew that you had succeeded in being happy in spite of what he'd done to you."

Elise told her about his ridiculous notion that she actually owed her success to his verbal abuse. "He thinks he's my in-spiration for every positive thing that I go for in life."

"Negative reinforcement," Mariel said. "I knew he was sick, but I didn't realize how sick!" She blew air between her lips. "From this point on, I really don't think anything he does will surprise me."

"Me, either," Elise said. "He literally blew my mind with that statement. But I'm telling you now, if he shows up again, and keeps hassling me and Franklyn, I'm going to get a restraining order. I'm not taking his crap."

Mariel drank some of her water. Setting the bottle on the table, she met Elise's eyes. "That's the only way to handle somebody like him."

They were silent for a minute or two. Then Elise asked, "What was it you came by to tell me?"

Mariel smiled at her cousin. "You do know me well."

Elise arched her brows in a silent suggestion for her to spill whatever she had to say.

Mariel didn't say anything. She simply showed Elise her left hand.

Elise screamed and got up to hug Mariel. However, Mariel was much more subdued than she ever imagined she would be when she finally got engaged to the man she loved. Elise grabbed her by the shoulders. "What is it?"

"Paulo's not a naturalized citizen," she said.

That was enough for Elise to pull her into her arms again for a sympathetic hug.

After a while, they parted and sat back down. Elise pulled her chair close and clasped Mariel's hand in hers for support as Mariel began talking. "Maybe I'm being paranoid. But he never told me that he wasn't a citizen until after he presented me with this rock."

Indeed, it had to be five carats at the least, and of good quality too.

"Now, I'm having these doubts," she continued. "Did he pursue me so aggressively because he needs to marry a citizen in order to make the process of his naturalization easier? You know, I was curious as to how he could own three coffee-houses around town and not be a naturalized citizen, but apparently foreigners buy American businesses all the time." Her eyes were moist. "I'm in love with him, Elise. It would kill me if he really didn't love me. I can't marry him if I'm not convinced he actually loves me. I won't do it."

"Obviously, this is all speculation on your part," Elise said softly. "He hasn't even hinted that marrying you would be a solution to his problem?"

"No, of course not."

"Maybe he told you he was seeking citizenship to have everything out in the open. And the way to get around the whole issue is to wait until he's a citizen before you marry him."

"But if I wait, he may think I don't trust him," Mariel pointed out.

"That's a hell of a test to put you through," Elise cried. She was outraged because this situation reeked of the predicament she'd been in with Derrick. He'd used the institution of marriage to manipulate her. If Paulo sought to marry Mariel only because he'd get citizenship that much quicker, then he was also using her.

His telling her only after giving her the ring was suspicious. Could he possibly be that naive that he hadn't anticipated Mariel's reaction to his news? He appeared much smarter than that to her.

Elise looked at Mariel. What man in his right mind wouldn't be attracted to her? She was not only lovely, but she was smart, a successful business owner, she had a great sense of humor and she was resilient. A fighter.

Paulo didn't know whom he was tangling with, if his intentions were indeed dishonorable. Mariel was capable of handling him.

What Elise worried about was Mariel's ability to bounce back from being hurt. She'd said she was in love with Paulo. She hadn't said that about Adam, and she'd been within two months of marrying him before backing out of the wedding.

"Then what are you going to do?" Elise asked. "If you don't want him to think you don't trust him, and he wants to get married before he's declared a citizen?"

"I don't know," Mariel honestly said.

Elise nodded. Sometimes there were no answers, easy or otherwise. Especially when the heart was involved. She felt bad for encouraging Mariel to go with her gut feelings and give Paulo a chance. But, then, she couldn't predict the future. Nor did she know what was going on in Paulo's head. Perhaps all of his actions were innocent.

"I'm here if you need me," was all she could say to Mariel.

"Ditto," said Mariel.

And they drank their water and sighed.

The last hour of work that night, Franklyn knew he wouldn't be doing much dancing on his bad leg. He hadn't been in this much pain in a long time. He should have known that something was amiss when the day proved to be overcast for the duration, and the air frosty. One without the other rarely bothered him, but when both occurred and the barometric pressure worked its mojo on him, too, he knew he was in for a world of hurt.

Nevertheless, he was not going to disappoint Elise. He showered in the bathroom in his office before leaving the Vineyard, and dressed in his favorite jeans, a soft cotton denim shirt, leather jacket and black motorcycle boots. The warm water of the shower had somewhat eased the pain in his leg, but nothing short of a pain pill was really going to do the trick. He hated taking the pain pills his doctor had prescribed. He only took them when he was in severe pain, taking Advil in place of them most of the time. The pills the doctor had prescribed made him drowsy.

He popped a couple of Advils before locking up and driving to Elise's place.

When he got out of the truck to climb the stairs, the chill of the night had managed to draw whatever heat the shower had provided from his leg. Now, he was in excruciating pain as he climbed the steps and knocked on Elise's door.

"Coming!" he heard her call.

A few seconds later, she was standing in the doorway looking beautiful and smelling heavenly.

She grinned and fell into his arms. They kissed. She threw her arms around his neck as she usually did, her body going limp in his arms. However, this time, her added weight was a burden and, even though he tried not to, he groaned softly when the pain hit him.

Elise pulled him inside and closed and locked the door.

He smiled for her benefit, but, as far as Elise was concerned, it was too late to put on an act because she'd already sensed he was in pain. Her mind was clicking along at a hundred miles an hour trying to figure out some way to get out of going dancing that would not insult Franklyn's intelligence, or his pride.

She was wearing jeans and a dressy blouse in deep purple with a golden chain belt around her waist. Her purple suede sandals had three-inch heels, but with Franklyn she could wear heels as high as she liked. It was the heels that gave her the idea.

She spun around. "I'll just get my coat."

When she was in the hallway and out of Franklyn's line of sight, she slipped on the hardwood floor and fell down with a satisfying thud. She cried out for added effect.

Luckily, she was sufficiently padded as far as butts went, and didn't hurt herself. By the time Franklyn arrived in the hallway, though, she made sure that her right ankle was twisted awkwardly beneath her left leg.

"Damn!" she said from the floor. "I think I've sprained my ankle."

Laughing, Franklyn bent to survey the damage. "That was quite a performance."

Elise looked up at him, confused. She grimaced and reached for him. "What do you mean, performance? I slipped on these slick soles and went flying, and you're laughing?" She sounded incredulous, even to her own ears.

Franklyn took her hand, finally, and pulled her to a standing position. She put her weight on her left leg since her right one was supposed to be injured. "Don't ever play poker, Elise, my darling, because you would give your hand away every time."

She smiled up at him. "I gave it a shot."

He touched her behind. "I hope you didn't bruise that beautiful bottom of yours."

"Better take a look to make sure," she said saucily.

Franklyn pulled her fully into his embrace. "I will, as soon as we come home from dancing all night."

Elise frowned at him. "What?"

He grinned. "Just kidding. My leg is killing me. There will be no dancing for me tonight, except between the sheets."

Elise smiled her pleasure. "Getting straight to the good part. You do know how to please a girl." With their arms about each other's waists they went to the bedroom.

* * *

Franklyn awoke with a hard-on. And no wonder. Elise, though she seemed to still be sleeping, was writhing seductively against him. Neither of them had on a stitch of clothing. Her warm, silken body wrapped itself around him. She moaned softly as if in the throes of passion. Franklyn didn't know what to do, wake her, or make love to her. He didn't want to make love to her without her knowledge, that felt like a violation to him, but his body was definitely voting for choice number two.

"Elise."

Her taut nipples were rubbing against his chest. Her groin pressing against his. He was so hard now that he was perilously close to an orgasm.

"Elise," he said, more forcefully.

Even though the room was dark, he knew when she opened her eyes. Her breathing changed. She let out a soft sigh. "Oh," she said as she realized the state his body was in. "I'm sorry. I was dreaming I was making love to you."

"I gathered as much," Franklyn said, his voice husky with unspent passion.

"Do you mind?" Elise asked as she climbed on top of him and reached over to turn on the light on his side of the bed.

"Mind?" Franklyn said with a short laugh. "Men dream of this moment."

Elise bent to kiss his mouth, then she proceeded to put the condom she'd retrieved from atop the nightstand onto his hardened penis. The dream was fresh in her mind.

In it, she'd been on top of Franklyn and he'd felt so good, she'd been crying out in pleasure. Even though she was awake, she was still experiencing a delicious spiking sensual throbbing in her vagina. As she placed his penis at the opening of her sex, she quivered with delight.

Franklyn grabbed her hips and as she lowered herself onto him, he slightly lifted his hips from the bed. When Elise was in her own special rhythm, he raised his hands from her hips, upward, past her waist to the voluptuous sweetness of her breasts. His mouth watered because he wanted to take her nipples in his mouth and suck them, but on his back like this that pleasure was denied him. He was content to watch Elise's face. She was wonderful to watch when she was near completion. Her skin glowed, her lips were pursed as though she were breathing through her mouth as she panted, sometimes softly, sometimes not so softly. He took great pleasure in knowing that she truly did enjoy herself in bed.

He felt her come, and deftly turned her over in bed so that he could be on top. He liked the feel of her quivering vaginal muscles around his shaft. She spread her legs wide, and lifted her hips to meet his thrusts. Their eyes met and held. This way they were witnesses to each other's most spiritually naked moments.

His orgasm was powerful. He wanted to shout, but instead muffled his shouts by burying his face between her breasts. She wrapped her arms around him, and he shuddered with release.

When he stopped shaking, he kissed her soft mouth. "Feel free to wake me like that anytime."

Elise just smiled and ran her hand over his hair, which was a bit damp with perspiration. He was hers in her dreams and her waking hours. How did she get so lucky?

Chapter 14

Sundays and Mondays, Elise and Franklyn's off days, were devoted not so much to relaxation but to handling the mundane affairs of life. They grocery-shopped, cleaned their houses, paid bills and made phone calls to friends and relatives.

On Monday afternoon, Elise was alone in her apartment running the vacuum cleaner across the short-napped carpet in her bedroom when she heard a loud noise downstairs. It had to be loud to be heard over the vacuum cleaner, so she assumed it wasn't simply someone knocking on Hilary's door downstairs.

She switched off the vacuum cleaner and listened. She wondered if it could be Hilary down there crashing about. But she doubted it. Hilary usually announced her imminent arrival days in advance.

Hilary was still in Tahiti as far as she knew. Her e-mail of a few days ago had said she planned to stay at least another month. When Elise had written back, she'd wanted to pry into Hilary's personal life because this was the first time Hilary had ever stayed in one place more than two weeks. She had been in Tahiti since November of 2005, nearly five months. What could be making her extend her stay?

After another loud crash, she got her baseball bat out of the hall closet and cautiously descended her back steps and walked around to the front of the rambling Victorian.

A taxi was parked at the curb, and two men were trans-ferring suitcases from trunk of the taxi to the front porch. One man was white, bulky and grizzled. He wore a faded gray T-shirt and a pair of well-worn jeans. Tan work boots were on his huge feet. The other man was dark-skinned, with long dark-brown hair with silver streaks in it. He was dressed in a khaki safari suit, a white cotton shirt with a mandarin collar, and brown sandals. He was of average height and average weight, and Elise noted that his brown eyes were remarkably friendly when he looked up and smiled at her.

"You must be Elise," he said in well-modulated English. His accent had a lovely lilt to it, as if he might be from Bombay, or some other part of India.

Elise had lowered her bat, and was casually leaning it against her right leg.

"Yes, I am. Who're you?" She glanced up at the open front door of the house. "What are you doing here?" She walked up onto the porch. He followed her.

"Hilary!" he called. "Elise is here, and she looks quite upset by the commotion."

Hilary yelled from within the house. "Coming, dearest. I've finally caught the little rascal."

Elise walked into the foyer. They had thrown open the

windows and opened the curtains to let fresh air and light into the closed-up house. Elise let in a cleaning woman once a month to dust, mop the floors and wash the windows. The last time had been less than a week ago, so the house did not smell stale, nor were there dust motes floating upon the air.

She looked around for Hilary, but did not see her. "Hilary, you almost gave me a heart attack. What was that noise?"

Hilary suddenly appeared at the top of the stairs. In her right hand, held aloft, was a white cockatoo. "That would be Tiki, here. As soon as I brought him inside, the door of his cage popped open and he flew out and knocked down two lamps before I could snag him." She grinned, which transformed her plain face to pretty.

She was wearing her customary jeans and khaki jacket over a short-sleeve white T-shirt. Sturdy brown Birkenstocks enclosed her slim feet.

Jeremy, who had the birdcage in his hand, went to her and together they put Tiki in his cage. Elise thought what a nice-looking couple they made. Hilary was only an inch or so shorter than Jeremy. She had graying dark-brown hair that she wore short and naturally curly. The edges were curling even tighter now due to the sweat trickling down her face. She must have had to run after Tiki.

The bird safely in its cage, she went to Elise and hugged her tightly. "Hello, dear. We sneaked up on you, didn't we? I have no excuse. With all of the travel arrangements and the wedding and everything, it simply slipped my mind."

She patted Elise on the back for good measure and let go of her.

Elise stared at her. "Did you say wedding?" She looked at Hilary, then at Jeremy.

"Yes," said Hilary, beaming. "Jeremy and I got married

two days ago. We decided to spend our honeymoon here, and then we'll be living in Tahiti."

Elise laughed shortly. Hilary, at fifty-five, had never been married. To be honest, Elise had thought she might be gay. She had plenty of women friends, but she'd never seen her with a man. "Hilary, that's wonderful!" And it was. She couldn't have been happier for her. Turning to Jeremy, she offered him her hand in congratulations. He gratefully shook it, a smile on his lips. "Thank you," he said.

Hilary draped her arm about Elise's shoulders. "Elise, I want to ask you a very important question. I don't want you to answer right away because what I'm asking is a huge responsibility."

She led Elise over to the bottom steps of the staircase where she sat down, and Elise sat beside her. They turned to look each other in the eyes.

Jeremy left the room with the birdcage.

"I know you love this house," Hilary began. "That's why I thought of you."

By the time she'd gotten out those words, Jeremy had returned. He casually leaned against a newel post next to Hilary, listening.

"Jeremy and I want to live in his house in Tahiti year-round. The weather is wonderful and we're both very productive there. Jeremy is a painter. A very successful painter, and his muse is his homeland."

"You are my muse now, darling," he corrected her.

Hilary gave him an indulgent smile, and returned her attention to Elise. "You know I'm rarely here in this house. I've only kept it because as the last of my line, it was my responsibility to see it was taken care of. Well, I think I can accomplish that by signing it over to you. You and Franklyn will fill it with beautiful children. A house this size needs to be lived in." She paused.

Elise was so shocked, she momentarily had no response to such a grand gesture.

"Hilary, this is incredibly generous of you. I don't know what to say."

"Don't say anything right now," Hilary suggested. "Talk to Franklyn about it. And honestly, Elise, this house can be a burden as well as a treasure. Property taxes are off the charts. It costs money to maintain it. I may not be doing you any favors."

She smiled and clasped Elise's hand in hers. "But you're the only person I want living in my family home. I know you'll cherish it. And it'll do our hearts good to know that a couple who is truly in love with each other is making this house their home."

Jeremy sat beside his wife on the wide step and pulled her close. "We waited years to find each other. I was obsessed with my art, and one day I looked up while strolling in the market and saw her standing a few feet away. My heart immediately recognized her as its mate."

"My heart was a little more stubborn," Hilary joked. "He was much too good-looking to be interested in me. And way too sophisticated. He spoke to me in three languages before he finally said something in English, and I could understand him."

Jeremy laughed. "She was just playing hard to get."

They moved the conversation to the kitchen where Hilary made tea and put butter cookies they'd picked up at a nearby bakery on a plate in the middle of the table.

An hour later, Elise left the lovebirds alone and climbed the stairs to her apartment where she phoned Franklyn and told him about Hilary's generosity.

"We could definitely have six children in a house like that," were his first words.

Elise laughed. She thought he'd been joking when he'd told her he imagined them with six children years from now. "And it's only two miles from the restaurant," Elise said, pointing out another advantage of owning the Victorian.

"With the money from the sale of my place, we could pay the property taxes for several years," Franklyn said, letting her enthusiasm affect him.

Realizing that Franklyn would probably do anything for her, including take on the responsibility of a house that might very well prove to be a burden in the end, Elise felt duty bound to offer a few dire warnings. "We need to think this out, Franklyn, before agreeing to do it. Can we project our financial status into the future? What if we should have a downturn in fortunes?"

"Baby, I'm doing well. I'm even thinking of opening a second restaurant somewhere else in the Bay Area. We can handle the property taxes and the upkeep on the house. I'm a good handyman, as well. You don't have to worry about my doing a Cliff Huxtable on you. I do know my stuff. This is a great opportunity. But you're right. We shouldn't make a snap decision."

Less than five minutes after Elise said goodbye to Franklyn, Tamryn phoned her. With the excitement of Hilary and Jeremy's surprise return from Tahiti, plus the offer of the house, Elise had forgotten that she was expecting Tamryn's call.

She was cleaning under the bed with a damp mop when the phone rang. She picked up the phone on the nightstand. "Hello?"

"Hi, Elise," Tamryn said. Elise immediately knew it was good news because from the sound of Tamryn's voice, she could barely contain her joy.

"Tamryn," Elise said a bit cautiously. The suspense was killing her, but she didn't want to rush her.

Tamryn breathed deeply on her end of the line, and with her exhalation, shouted, "You're the next 'big thing' on Food Network, honey chile!"

Elise screamed like a game show contestant who'd won a pile of money. "Oh, my God!"

She kept repeating that until Tamryn cut in with, "Elise, God knows you love Him, now stop that. Listen to me, we've got to move fast on this. I'm coming to San Francisco. This is my baby. I'll be bringing Jake, of course, because he's indispensable." She was thinking out loud. "They're offering you a contract for twenty-six shows to start with. We've got to test the market. There will be a media blitz. You will be photographed in and around the Bay Area. So, it's makeover time, sweetie. Not that you necessarily need a makeover, you're gorgeous the way you are, but we have an expert who knows how to play up your best features and downplay your worst. We don't want you too glamorous, but this is TV…" She breathed.

"The studio is in the SOMA area of the city. That's South of Market Street, right?"

"Uh-huh," Elise confirmed. "It's the heart of the art scene here in town."

"Yeah, well the company bought a warehouse in that area and converted it into a studio. It's huge. Yours will be the first show to tape there, actually. But we see a great future there in San Francisco. You know you all are known to have more restaurants per capita than any other American city?"

"I'd heard that," said Elise.

"Yes, and we plan to visit a few once the show gets started. Beginning with where you presently work. Think the owner will go for it?"

"I think I can talk him into it," Elise said. "I'm engaged to him."

Tamryn laughed. "Oh, that's your Franklyn. Wonderful. The viewers will eat up the romance angle. The show is for women, after all."

"Move soon," Elise said. "How soon are we talking?"

"Monday morning, a week from today," Tamryn told her. "I will courier the contract to you after we've discussed the terms."

"The terms?"

"Yes, the why and the wherefore, how much you will earn per episode. The terms of your servitude, sweetie. How much of yourself you're willing to part with."

Elise never thought of a contract in that way, but she supposed she *was* selling herself. She had to consider carefully every word on the contract before she signed her life away.

"Sounds like I'm going to need an attorney," she said.

"I would advise it," Tamryn said. "Now, how does ten thousand per episode sound to you?"

Elise had to bite her tongue to keep from exclaiming that ten thousand sounded wonderful to her. She realized that from now on she had to have a level head. She could not react with emotion. But her mind couldn't help calculating that ten thousand per episode equaled two hundred and sixty thousand dollars!

She had brain freeze for a few long seconds. She cleared her throat. "That sounds very promising."

Tamryn laughed softly. "That's my girl. Make me negotiate. Twelve thousand."

Elise didn't want to appear greedy, so she said, "All right."

"Whew!" came Tamryn's reply. "I thought you were going to make me sweat."

Elise had read somewhere that some popular TV stars made upwards of one hundred thousand per episode of their sitcoms. However, she was new at this, and twelve thousand was a very fair amount for an unknown, in her opinion. "If the show is successful we get to renegotiate my next contract, right?"

"That's the routine," Tamryn told her.

"Excellent. What else should we discuss about the contract?"

"Within a certain amount of time, you must submit to me twenty-six show ideas, that is, the desserts you will prepare for each show, and the script for each. We do not expect you to follow it to the letter, of course. It will be a guideline for us. Also, you must agree to a certain amount of publicity for the show. Local morning news programs during which you will discuss the show. Magazine and newspaper interviews. And we also want you to be thinking about doing a cookbook as a tie-in for the show."

Elise liked the sound of that. She had been experimenting with recipes for years and had a stack of them in a box on a shelf in her kitchen. "It would be nice," she suggested, "if we could have each recipe I do on the show in the book, week by week."

"I like that," Tamryn returned. "Do you have any ideas what we should call the show? We've been tossing around a few ideas: *Eat it!*, to imply that you shouldn't deny yourself dessert. *Real Women Eat Cake*, to convey the same sentiment. What do you think?"

"I like *Real Women Eat Cake*," Elise said. "But I was thinking that simply calling it *Just Desserts* would say it all. The show is only about desserts and when someone says 'She got her just desserts,' it means she got just what she deserved, and women deserve rich, delicious desserts."

"You've got your thinking cap on!" Tamryn said, excitedly. "We'll call it *Just Desserts*."

They hammered out the rest of the details, then Tamryn left her with this advice, "Your life is getting ready to change forever, Elise. People you don't know are going to start walking up to you on the street and requesting your autograph. So, try your best to hang on to those things that keep you real."

"Thanks, Tamryn. I will," Elise promised. "Thank you for everything. If not for you, this wouldn't be happening."

"Wait to thank me after the ratings start coming in," Tamryn joked.

Saturday, May sixth. Elise kept her and Franklyn's wedding date firmly in mind as the month of April became a whirlwind of activity. Her schedule was jam-packed.

She left at six every morning and went down to the Vineyard to prepare the desserts for the day. She was picked up at the restaurant at one o'clock and driven to the studio by Jake. From one-thirty until nine at night, they diligently worked to refine show ideas.

By mid-April Elise had put together the scripts for the twenty-six shows they had requested in the contract. She was given an assistant who did all the grocery shopping so she'd have one less task to do.

They started filming the shows soon afterward. Tamryn wanted to go with a live audience but that idea was vetoed by the executives who said that meant more money, since the studio did not have adequate seating or bathroom facilities for an audience. If the show did well then they would think about adding an audience.

The afternoon they were to film the first show, Elise was

sitting in her dressing room before the mirror at the vanity, applying her makeup. Her hair and makeup had been over-hauled by an expert. She drew the line at letting them cut her hair, but it was now very manageable due to the treatments she'd gotten, and it was a blue-black color with thick glossy waves that cascaded down her back. It wasn't wild anymore the way Franklyn preferred it.

She peered at her face. Before, she'd worn nothing but lipstick and a little mascara, but the makeup artist had shown her how to apply all sorts of products that were supposed to enhance her beauty. The result looked natural, although her skin felt as though it had an inch of gook on it. She didn't like that feeling, and would be glad to wash it off after the taping.

Someone knocked on her door.

"Come in!" she called.

Jake strode in carrying a bouquet of yellow roses. Elise wondered whom they could be from. Franklyn had already sent her a dozen long-stemmed red roses, her favorites.

"You've got an admirer," Jake said as he placed the flowers, in a clear crystal vase, on the corner of the vanity table next to the roses Franklyn had sent her.

Elise, dressed in a bathrobe, stood up and went to read the card. "Thanks, Jake."

He smiled at her. "Anytime. You've got about ten minutes before you're needed on the set. I'll come get you a couple of minutes before time."

"All right," Elise said absently, her eyes on the small card in her hand. *Remember the cable car on Hyde Street?* the message read. Elise dropped the card as if it were on fire. She held her breath, a reflex caused by fear and panic. Her legs felt weak. She managed to grab hold of the arm of the chair she'd been sitting in before Jake had come into the room with the flowers, and she lowered herself into it.

She looked around the room for affirmation that she was indeed in a dressing room in a studio. This felt like a dream. No, a nightmare.

For more than two weeks, she had given Derrick no thought whatsoever. She'd been too busy working on the show and putting the final touches on her wedding plans to give him any consideration.

But now he'd intruded on her life once again.

Her mind went back to that day. She'd been twenty-one and fresh out of culinary arts school. Back then, it was to her advantage to take the cable car whose route ran past the hotel where she was working. She caught it on Hyde Street. Unfortunately, it was also the cable car that Derrick took every day. That's how they'd met.

She was getting on the cable car and he was getting off and they ran into each other, literally. He apologized, smiling at her, and he was gone. The next day when she got on, he stayed on the cable car and struck up a conversation with her. That went on for several days until he asked her out. She was reluctant to accept at first, but was won over by his charm.

On their tenth, or thereabouts, cable ride together they got off together and went to dinner. When they got back on a few hours later, they kissed for the first time. And it was a passionate kiss. The most passionate Elise had ever experienced. That kiss made her fall in love with him. She was taken in by the length of time it had taken him to kiss her. She thought he respected her. Cared about her. However, that had just been a part of his plan to get her to trust him, to have unflagging faith in him.

She got out of her chair and picked up the card. He had

put his number below his message. Her first impulse, after seeing the phone number, was to call him and cuss him out. But she didn't want to hear his voice. Not right now when she was getting ready to go before the cameras.

She put the card into her purse, and removed her bathrobe. Underneath was a casual outfit of a sheer long-sleeve turquoise blouse with a camisole of the same color, blue jeans and sandals in sky blue. She also wore a long turquoise necklace and matching drop earrings. She had been given a budget for her wardrobe and the admonition to keep it casual but feminine. She did her own shopping.

Standing in front of a full-length mirror, she painted a smile on her face. "To hell with you, Derrick."

A knock came to the door. Jake.

She walked over and opened the door. "I'm ready," she said.

Jake grinned. "Blue is your color."

"Thank you," Elise said as she began walking down the hallway to the set with Jake. He still made it known he was attracted to her, but out respect for her relationship with Franklyn, he had not made any overtures. She appreciated that.

On the set, the director, Hank Zimmer, a tall, slim bespectacled forty-year-old with dark, curly hair he wore shorn close to his scalp, called, "All right, everybody, our meal ticket has arrived."

Everyone on the set laughed.

Elise laughed, too, which set the mood for the next three hours. They were going to tape three shows that day. She would be required to change clothing between tapings. It took an average of an hour to do the taping of each show which was only about twenty-five minutes of material because they had to allot time for commercials within the thirty-minute time frame.

By the time she was getting ready to tape the third show, Elise had relaxed and gotten into the rhythm. She was wearing a V-neck sweater over jeans this time. The sweater was a deep shade of pink, and it brought out the red undertones in her skin.

She was preparing fudge brownies. "Here's an easy tip to make your brownies nice and moist," she said as she stirred the batter in a white ceramic mixing bowl. "Melt your chocolate on low heat in the microwave along with your butter. Stir them together and add to your sugar/egg/vanilla mixture while still warm from the microwave. Slowly add the flour/baking powder/salt that you've sifted together. Mix well, and add your chopped nuts last. You should gently fold in the nuts. When you've baked the brownies in a 350-degree oven for about 35 minutes, there will be a nice crunchy chocolate sheen on top, and your brownies will be moist and delicious."

She bent and reached into the oven, producing the pan of brownies she'd earlier made and set aside. "And they should look like this." She placed the pan on the counter and began cutting the brownies into squares. They easily came out of the pan. She held up one between her forefinger and thumb and gently squeezed to demonstrate to the viewing audience how moist the brownies were. Then, as always, she sampled it. She didn't have to pretend it was delicious. It practically melted in her mouth, and the ratio of chocolate to vanilla to nuts was nearly perfect.

"Mmm," she said, smiling. "This one was for all of you brownie lovers out there. What better comfort food is there? Enjoy them with milk, or a scoop of vanilla ice cream. But, enjoy them! And remember, *stressed* is just *desserts* spelled backwards. So, don't pass on dessert. You'll be less stressed."

"And, cut!" yelled Hank. He grinned. "I love saying that."

The crew descended on Elise, or rather, on her brownies. The pan was empty in no time. The bright lights in the studio dimmed somewhat and Elise felt someone's hand on her arm. It was Jake. "Way to go, Elise. Tamryn wants to see you in her office before you leave. Just page me when you're ready to go home."

Elise smiled up at him. "Okay, thanks."

Tamryn invited her to have a seat. Elise sat down and crossed her legs. Tamryn's color scheme was red and white. Red leather couch and chairs, white shelving and desk. Elise was getting a sneaking suspicion that her boss had pledged Alpha Kappa Alpha sorority.

"How did it go?" Tamryn asked about the tapings.

Elise smiled. "Better than I imagined. I actually felt comfortable going into the third show."

"Good," Tamryn said, "because we're already getting requests from the local media for interviews both on television and in the print media. I only want you to do what you feel comfortable doing."

"I will do anything as long as it's tasteful," Elise told her. She wanted to be a team player.

"I'm glad to hear that. You'll start tomorrow morning. The television station wants you there at seven-thirty. A quick in and out. You won't have to cook. They already have your profile. They'll ask you a few questions about what audiences can look for from the show. And they might ask about your upcoming wedding. It's the sort of show that gets off on that sort of thing. Then tomorrow afternoon when you arrive here for taping, there will be a newspaper reporter waiting to inter-

view you. Something short. A few photos and you'll be done."
She smiled. "I'll try my best not to put too much on your plate
but while we're trying to launch the show these things will
be necessary."

"I understand," Elise assured her.

Tamryn rose. "Okay, let's get out of here. It's been a long
day."

"I second that," Elise said as she rose, too, and dialed
Jake's number thereby paging him as he'd asked her to. "I just
want to get home and sit in the tub."

"You?" Tamryn said. "Sit in the tub and let Jeff rub my
feet. Too bad he's in New York and I'm here!"

Elise sighed sympathetically as they left Tamryn's office.
"One more day, and you'll be back in his arms."

"I'm counting the hours," Tamryn told her with a tired sigh
of her own.

When Elise met Jake in her dressing room, he was already
gathering her roses in his arms to carry to the car. "You don't
have to worry about the yellow ones," she said. "I'm not
taking those home with me."

"But they'll wither and die faster if you don't take them
home and take care of them."

"They're from my ex-husband," Elise said. No need to be
secretive about it. If Derrick went into overdrive with his
craziness, she would have to take Jake into her confidence
anyway in order to help fend off Derrick's advances. She
wished she could have predicted he would send flowers to the
studio. With Jake informed, he could have held off telling her
about them until after the taping and she wouldn't have been
freaked out prior to taping. But, all's well that ends well.
She'd gotten through the taping without having a nervous
breakdown.

She looked Jake in the eyes. "He knows I'm engaged, and yet he won't leave me alone. I don't want any contact with him. If he comes here, please don't let him in."

"I'll need his name and a description," Jake said. He took his job seriously, and would do everything in his power to protect her.

"His name is Derrick Scott and he's thirty-five, six-two, around a hundred and ninety pounds and he's a lawyer, so expect him to be in an expensive suit. He's slick. Watch out for his tricks."

Jake held the door open for her. "Don't worry, he won't get past security."

Derrick was tying his tie in front of the TV. He had to be at work at nine, but he liked to check the local news before heading out. He couldn't believe his good luck when the host of the entertainment segment of the show introduced Elise. She was beautiful in a brown sweater that was almost the same shade of brown as her eyes, and a pair of cream colored dress slacks. Her hair was in a curly tousled style that made her look very sexy. "Elise is the host of a new cooking show on the Food Network that's taped right here in San Francisco. Elise is one of the 2006 winners of a national pastry competition and, from what I hear, a wonderful pastry chef. Elise, tell us what the show's focus will be."

Derrick sat down as Elise began to speak. He felt a little light-headed, and could have kicked himself for letting her affect him like that. What was wrong with him? Before his run-in with her evil cousin, he had not given her a passing thought. Okay, he had thought about her on occasion, but only to assure himself that she must be miserable without him. Her poor heart broken still, after four years. He'd

really been deluding himself. He knew that now. She wasn't
pining for him. She was well rid of him, and that's what
rankled the most. How could she forget about him so thoroughly? She'd professed love for him. You didn't stop
loving somebody just because you divorced him. He was
not so easily forgotten. That's what had compelled him to
get in touch with her, to assure himself that she hadn't
really forgotten him. He was not invisible. She was going
to see him for what he was: her first love. She owed him
that much respect.

Thankfully Chantal had seen an announcement for her
new show on Food Network's Web site and had told him
about it. It had taken him less than half an hour to find out
where the studio was, and he'd spontaneously sent flowers.
He'd written his number on the card, but she hadn't even
phoned to thank him. That ungrateful bitch!

He watched her as if he were hypnotized. Why hadn't he
noticed how beautiful she was when they'd been together? It
must be because she was one of those women who got more
beautiful as she aged. He'd let her go before she'd ripened.

He'd zoned out while he'd been staring at Elise and found
that, after he managed to focus again, they were wrapping up
the segment.

"Be sure to watch Elise when her show, *Just Desserts,* pre-
mieres on Saturday, May thirteenth at 8:00 p.m. on the Food
Network. Elise, thank you for joining us this morning."

"It was my pleasure," Elise said with a warm smile.

Derrick frowned. She looked so sweet and innocent. But
he knew her for what she really was, a conniving user. She'd
married him and then taken him to the cleaners just like his
mother had done to his father. Alimony. She hadn't deserved
a cent from him, but the judge had been sympathetic to her

because she was attractive. She'd flashed those big brown eyes, and the judge had been eating out of her hands.

Since Elise was no longer on the screen he got up, went into the bathroom and took a Xanax. The doctor told him not to miss a dose but he only took them when he was feeling tightly wound up. And he was, after watching her charm her way into the hearts of the poor, defenseless San Franciscans who'd been watching her shameless display.

It was Friday night, and Elise got out of the studio at eight instead of nine tonight. She had Jake drop her off at the Vineyard where she went and waited in Franklyn's office until the restaurant closed. He found her asleep on the couch when he walked in at eleven. Everyone else had gone home, and he'd come to get her so that they could go home, too.

She was sleeping so peacefully, he loathed having to wake her. He put a hand on her shoulder and gently shook her. "Elise, baby, wake up."

Elise mumbled in her sleep, and slowly opened her eyes. She smiled. "Hi."

"Hi, yourself," Franklyn said as he sat beside her on the couch. "Had a hard day?"

She told him about both interviews, the television one and the newspaper one. Plus, they'd taped two shows, and Tamryn had given her several more media appointments for next week. "Thank God, it's Friday!"

Franklyn bent and placed a kiss on her forehead. "You don't have to come in in the morning. Get some rest."

Coming to work at the Vineyard in the mornings on Saturday felt like a holiday to her. She could leave at three in the afternoon, and go home and sleep. "You're sweet, but I love coming here with you in the mornings. I get to watch you work."

Franklyn smiled tiredly. He suppressed a yawn. "Yeah, I'm sexy as hell."

Elise laughed softly. "Yes, you are."

Franklyn got up and pulled her to her feet. "Enough of that talk. Let's go home and shower, then you can talk sexy to me. Right now, I smell offensive even to myself."

Later, as he pulled into traffic, a black Subaru Trooper, followed. The driver of the Subaru stayed a couple cars behind him, but did not lose sight of the Ford Truck. When Franklyn parked in the driveway of the Victorian, the driver of the Subaru parked on the street about a block down. He turned off his headlights and watched as Elise and Franklyn walked around the side of the house. They disappeared from view, but he assumed there was a side entrance to the house. In a few minutes he would get out and go check his theory. But not now. He wanted them well inside and engaged in whatever activity they were going inside to engage in before he went snooping.

He'd noticed that the big guy favored his right leg. Maybe he had an old injury.

He liked knowing his enemy's weaknesses, it gave him an advantage. In a fight, it was wise to concentrate your energies on your enemy's weaknesses. A good boxer, which he was, knew that.

He smiled as he settled down to wait. This was going to be fun.

Chapter 15

Two weeks before the wedding, Hilary and Jeremy invited Elise and Franklyn down for dinner so that they could finalize the transfer of ownership of the house.

Hilary and Elise were in the kitchen where Hilary was checking on the cioppino, a fish stew featuring Dungeness crab. In season from mid-November to June the creamy and chewy Dungeness crab was a favorite in San Francisco. Hilary's mother had made the stew often, so she thought it fitting to prepare it in honor of the new owners of the house.

Elise leaned against a counter as they talked about the many changes that had taken place in their lives. "If somebody had told me a year ago I'd be engaged and about to debut in a TV show, I would have looked at them like they were crazy."

Hilary laughed. She closed the lid of the Dutch oven and placed the spoon in its holder on the stove. "Yes, when I left here nearly six months ago you were still pining for Franklyn. Trying to get up the nerve to say something to him. You were pitiful."

"Hilary!"

"You know it's true. I was tempted to go over to the Vineyard, hog-tie him, bring him back here and make the two of you talk to each other. Remember when I went to the restaurant for lunch and went into the kitchen to see you? That was when I knew your feelings were reciprocated. I practically melted when he looked at you. I tell you, that look almost made me want to try my hand at writing romance novels. Luckily, I was able to resist!"

"There are some good romance novels out there," Elise said.

"Oh, I know there are," Hilary said. "Some of my best friends are romance novelists. I just didn't want to write about something I would never experience."

"Now, look at you!" Elise's happiness for her landlady was reflected in her eyes.

Hilary blushed and sat down at the kitchen table. Elise sat across from her. "Love changes everything. I was such a prude. Before Jeremy, the men I dated were erudite types who quoted British poets and drank tea with their pinkies extended. They were so full of themselves, it was ridiculous. I thought that was the type of man who would complement me. I was wrong. They bored me. You see, I wanted to think of myself as an intellectual who wrote mysteries to keep my old brain from fogging over. But the fact is, I wrote mysteries because I craved adventure. And I didn't just want to write about adventure, I wanted to experience it. Jeremy opened up a whole new world for me. I feel as if a filmy layer has been peeled from my eyes and I can finally see clearly."

"I know what you mean," Elise said. "We erect such

limited lives for ourselves when, really, the possibilities are endless. You can have both, be an intellectual and a lusty dame who enjoys making love to her husband."

Hilary blushed even brighter. She placed her hands on her cheeks and met Elise's eyes across the table. "Yes, that's it, exactly. I can have both worlds and enjoy both of them. Jeremy is so sensual, and I'm not just talking about the sex, which is good, believe me. I'm referring to how he appreciates the physical world, its beauty. He is aware. He's present. Half the time we simply glide through life, not paying attention to its beauty, its mysteries. Jeremy tries to pay attention to every moment. He lives in the moment. But he also cares about the past. He's trying to make certain that his people's contributions are not forgotten. He owns an art museum in which the artwork of his people is displayed, reflecting the past, the present, and the future. Young artists come there to learn. Older artists come there to mentor the young. It's a wonderful concept, Elise."

She grasped Elise's hand. "That's what gave me the idea of offering you and Franklyn the house. If I had ever had a daughter, Elise, I would have wanted her to be someone like you. Someone with a warm heart who cares about others and proves it all the time. In a way, you've been my family since you came to live here. That time I had the flu, who took care of me? You did. When I had that breast cancer scare, you talked me into getting the biopsy. And getting it sooner rather than later. I wanted to ignore it. It's really easy to pretend something doesn't exist when it scares the crap out of you. That's human nature. But you made me get it done, and then when I found out the lump was benign, I felt as if I'd been given a second chance. And how many times have we stayed up late just gabbing? I would have writer's block, and you would have those nightmares about Derrick. You're not still having them, are you?"

"Not so much anymore. Now, he's just making an ass of himself."

Hilary's brows nearly met in a frown. "You mean he's contacted you?"

Elise got her up-to-date on the Derrick situation. "He's been sending flowers and candy and anything else that crosses his mind to the studio. And I think he's following me. There's a black SUV that I see everywhere I go. I even broke down and phoned his mother and she told me that more than likely he's off his medication."

"Medication?!"

"He's on anti-psychotic medication, but his mother says he can be hardheaded. Sometimes he goes off it, or takes it only occasionally. She found that out last year when she got a call from a hospital saying he'd been admitted. Apparently, he ran his car into an embankment on purpose because he was suffering from side effects of withdrawal from Xanax. They can be loss of reality and heightened awareness of noise and bright lights. Anyway, the cars' lights upset him and the noise from their horns blaring when he slowed down to a snail's pace irritated him; so he irrationally thought running his car into an embankment would stop all of the unwanted stimuli. It did. It also got him a concussion, a short stay in the hospital and put back on Xanax for the duration."

"I know you're sympathetic because he has a mental illness, Elise, but if he's stalking you, you need to go to the police."

"His mother promised she would handle it," Elise said, not sounding very convinced. "If she can't, then I'll have to get a restraining order."

"Good girl," Hilary said, patting her hand.

Franklyn and Jeremy were in the library, also drinking wine and talking. They did not have the advantage of years of friendship upon which to base easy conversation.

They both thought themselves worlds apart in temperament and experience. To Franklyn it appeared as if Jeremy, who was an artist, would not know what made the common man, which he saw himself as, get up in the morning.

To Jeremy, Franklyn appeared to be a man who put his faith in the physical. He was at least five inches taller than he, and looked as if he could break him in half if he had a mind to. He imagined Franklyn spent a great deal of time working to hone his body to perfection, and paid little attention to fine-tuning his intellect.

They were both wrong.

"May I ask you something personal?" Jeremy asked after they had been talking for several minutes, but saying nothing.

Franklyn's left brow rose a fraction of an inch. "Of course," he said warily.

Jeremy leaned forward. He was sitting in a chair across from the couch upon which Franklyn sat. He met Franklyn's eyes. "How did you resist Elise for practically four years? Hilary says you two danced around each other for that long. How did you manage that? I would have exploded if I had not walked up to Hilary the very first day we met and told her how beautiful I thought she was. My heart couldn't take it."

Franklyn laughed shortly. "Jeremy, I was frustrated all the time. I wanted to sweep her off her feet. On the other hand, I couldn't say anything because she worked for me, and I didn't want her to think I was only interested in sex, and if she didn't come through her job could be at risk."

"Ah, yes," Jeremy said, understanding where Franklyn was coming from. "Things are much simpler where I'm from.

A man states his case, and the woman says yes to his proposal or no based on whether or not he would be a good provider, husband and father to her children."

"But the final say is left up to the woman," Franklyn pointed out.

"Yes."

"Then we're not so different. Elise had to come to the point where she decided I was good enough for her. I was willing to wait for her to come to that conclusion because I already knew *I* wanted *her.*"

Jeremy, smiling and shaking his head, said, "No, we are not so different. Do you like soccer?"

"No, American football."

"The players are little girls," Jeremy said. "They wear padding."

"They need padding," Franklyn countered. "They crash into each other with the force of Mack trucks. Soccer players wear shorts and don't even have sense enough to wear helmets."

"The goalie does."

"Yes, I forgot. He might get hit in the head with the ball. In American football, you might get hit in the head with a linebacker."

Jeremy laughed. "All right, we're never going to agree on football. How about Easy Rawlins?"

"You read Walter Mosley's novels?"

"I have all of them."

"So do I. Which is your favorite?"

"Devil in a Blue Dress," Jeremy said, not having to consider his answer.

"Yeah, Easy has to find the missing Daphne Monet."

"What's yours?" Jeremy asked.

"*Black Betty,*" Franklyn replied.

"In which Easy has to track down Elizabeth Eady, a missing housekeeper who he later finds out is the girl he had a crush on when he was a boy," Jeremy volunteered.

"Who else do you read?" Franklyn wanted to know.

"I like Dean Koontz's books and Steven Barnes's. He writes..."

"Speculative fiction," Franklyn answered for him. "I really enjoyed his books in which he proposed a world in which black people were the slaveholders in history instead of the other way around."

"Yes," said Jeremy. "One does wonder how the world would have turned out if brown people held the power."

They talked on until the ladies called them in to dinner.

Later, after their meal, Hilary's attorney dropped by as scheduled and brought the signed and notarized papers to them. The house was officially Elise's and Franklyn's however Hilary and Jeremy were staying until after the wedding. Elise and Franklyn wouldn't move in until they returned from their honeymoon in Maui where they were going to make a 3:00 a.m. hike up 10,023-foot Haleakala to watch the sunrise. Then they would drive over to the island's southwest coast to watch humpback whales. That is, if they left their hotel room.

Elise ran up the steps of City Hall on Van Ness Avenue. It was a Monday morning, so she didn't have to work at the Vineyard today, and she didn't have to be at the studio until later in the afternoon.

City Hall's huge rotunda, topped by a gold-and-black copper dome, could be seen throughout the city. Elise had to admit it was imposing. And judging from the number of people around her, it was an extremely busy place. She went inside and was once again awed by the grand staircase and its ornate wrought-iron banisters. The place must have cost millions upon millions to construct. Everything about it bespoke wealth and elegance.

She hurried upstairs. Mariel had said she would meet her on the landing. She'd better, because Elise had no idea which room she was supposed to go to, nor exactly why she was there in the first place. Mariel had just phoned her and asked her to get down to City Hall, and she'd come. You did that for your best friend and your cousin.

Breathing hard after her sprint, Elise saw Mariel near one of the neoclassical sculptured guardians. Mariel was going to need a guardian angel if this little trip down here wasn't of the utmost importance.

"There you are," Mariel said, a touch of impatience in her tone. She took Elise by the arm and they began to walk down the long corridor, passing door after door.

"Paulo called and said it was a matter of life and death that I get down here," she said worriedly. She glanced down at a slip of paper. "I wrote down the room number. It's somewhere around here." She paused in her steps. "Oh, Elise, I'm a nervous wreck after meeting this man. Not only did I fall in love with him, now I find myself running around like a crazy person to please him. He calls and says it's a matter of life and death. I can't bear to face that alone, so I call you, and now I'm here outside of this door wondering why in the hell I'm letting him lead me around by the nose. Is any man worth the hassle?"

Elise smiled at her cousin, then read what was on the door they were standing in front of: Department of Citizenship and Naturalization.

Elise tipped her head in the direction of the door. Mariel

hadn't even taken the time to read what it said. Mariel's eyes scanned the words. Then she started silently crying.

Elise went into her shoulder bag for tissues. Handing them to her cousin, she reached out and turned the doorknob. "Let's go in, shall we?"

When they entered, Paulo was standing with about ten other foreign-born men and women. They had their right hands raised, and a gentleman in a robe, whom Elise guessed was a judge, was reciting the oath that was the preamble to their becoming citizens of the United States of America.

She and Mariel stood in the back, Mariel dabbing at her eyes. Paulo saw them and smiled. He looked very handsome in a dark-blue suit.

When they were finished reciting the oath word for word, the gentleman pronounced that they were now citizens of the United States. There were cheers, and loved ones rushed forward to offer hugs and kisses and heartfelt congratulations.

Paulo scooped Mariel up in his arms and kissed her. Mariel was still crying.

"I didn't know what was going on," she said, her voice trembling with emotion. "I thought you were being deported or something equally horrible."

Paulo smiled. "No, my love. I'm sorry I was so cryptic but I wanted it to be a surprise. I have hoped for this day for so long. Now, we can plan our wedding with nothing to stand in our way."

"But, Paulo, nothing stood in our way before you became a citizen," Mariel said.

Paulo shook his head in the negative. He smiled sadly. "I would never ask you to go ahead with the ceremony until I was a citizen. That way, you would know that I love you for you and for no other reason."

Elise was grinning like an idiot. What Mariel had feared had never occurred to Paulo. Wanting to get out of there to give them their privacy, Elise said, "I'm going now." She gave them pecks on their cheeks. "Congratulations, Paulo."

"Thank you, Elise," Paulo said. "And thank you for coming with Mariel."

"No problem." She hightailed it out of there, smiling all the way.

Paulo pulled Mariel into his arms. "I know you, Mariel Gilbert. It's hard for you to allow your heart to trust any man." He looked deeply into her eyes. "But I fell in love with you the moment you opened your mouth to speak. I knew then that angels do exist."

Then he kissed her long, and with all the passion his Italian ancestors had bestowed upon him. Mariel melted in his arms.

They kissed for so long that another recent citizen, a gentleman from India, walked up to them, tapped Paulo on the shoulder, and said, "You know, you can apply for a marriage license right next door."

"Oh, no, keep that thing away from me!" Elise screamed, and meant it. *That thing* was the much-padded crotch of the male stripper that Mariel had hired to entertain at Elise's bachelorette party. He was gyrating right in front of her.

"Come here, honey," Mariel said to the dancer, a ten-dollar bill in her hand. He bumped-and-ground his way over to her and she slipped the money into the waistband of his ever-so-brief briefs.

The back room of the bar where the party was being held was filled with Elise's women friends, and they were behaving as though they never got a chance to let their hair down. They drank too much, shouted lewd suggestions to the stripper about how to shake his booty, got up and danced with him, and kept stuffing money down the front of his "uniform."

Elise and Lettie were sharing a table with four other women.

"These broads are worse than the guys at strip clubs," Lettie said, laughing. "I hope we have enough designated drivers here tonight 'cause, Lord knows, a lot of them aren't gonna be able to drive."

Mariel got onstage and tapped the microphone a couple times to get everybody's attention. "Okay, ladies, our illustrious guest of honor, Miss Elise Gilbert, soon to be Mrs. Franklyn Bryant, is going to get up and sing for you."

Elise got up and yelled, "Elise doesn't sing!"

"You don't need any talent to sing this," Mariel said. "Hit it!" And she pointed to a woman standing on the left side of the stage who must have pressed the button connected to the bar's sound system, because "Crazy" by Patsy Cline could be heard loud and clear throughout the room. "Come on up, Elise. Now, every woman who is getting married is slightly crazy and this should be our theme song." And Mariel started singing. Elise laughed and hurried onto the small stage. She and Mariel, their arms about each other's waists, crooned the song loudly, if completely out of tune. They sounded like hound dogs howling.

Everyone applauded when they finished. Then Mariel said into the microphone, "I can tell by the clock on the wall that it's almost 3:00 a.m., ladies. I guess it's time we blew this joint and went home."

Elise took the microphone. "Thanks for coming. I love you all! Get home safely!"

More applause and raucous shouts of, "We love you, too, Elise!"

The women filed out of the room, groups heading to cars together, a few who lived in the neighborhood walking home in pairs or threesomes.

Elise and Mariel had come together. Lettie, with a friend who lived in her neighborhood in Oakland. Lettie hugged Elise at the door and grabbed the hand of her friend, who had had too much to drink to get to the car under her own power.

"See you on Tuesday. I'm going to sleep all day Sunday, and *think* about getting up on Monday."

She left, pulling her friend behind her.

Elise held her hand out for Mariel's car keys. "I'd better drive. You had three drinks. I only had one."

Mariel didn't argue. She smiled at Elise and leaned on her as they left the bar.

Outside, the air was chilly. They hurried to the Toyota Camry in the dark parking lot. There was only one streetlight for every two blocks, and the bar's proprietor hadn't shelled out the money for extra lights in his parking lot.

Mariel walked to the passenger side, and waited for Elise to unlock the car. Elise had put the key in the lock when a man ran out of the shadows and grabbed her from behind, his arms around her torso, imprisoning her arms at her sides. She screamed. Mariel ran around to the driver's side and swung her heavy shoulder bag at the man's head.

The man put Elise between him and Mariel. "Stop it, Mariel! I just want to talk to Elise!"

Elise tore loose from his grip and moved away from him, next to Mariel. "Derrick! Are you crazy, grabbing me like that? Why are you even here? Are you still following me?"

"Yes, I followed you here," he admitted breathlessly. "It was the only way I could get the chance to speak to you. You won't call me. You return my gifts unopened. You've turned my own mother against me."

"I didn't do that," Elise denied.

"You told her I was stalking you."

"You *are* stalking me! You're stalking me right this minute!"

"Well, I'm not going to follow you anymore. I'm back on my meds, and now I don't know why I was obsessed with you. There's nothing special about you. I must have been temporarily insane."

"You were," Mariel piped in. "And you still are if you think we're buying this."

"As a matter of fact," Elise said, "I prefer it when you say there's nothing special about me. Good. I'm glad you're back to your old, derisive self. And I hope I won't see you again until, well…ever!"

"Fine," said Derrick a bit petulantly. "Go on and have a perfect life with your fry cook. You two are made for each other."

"Thank you, we will!" said Elise, turning to go. She watched him as he moved away, back in the direction he'd come, into the shadows. His black SUV must be parked where she couldn't see it.

Before she could get the key into the lock, however, he returned, running and leaped onto her lower body, wrapping his arms around her legs, pleading with her. "It was all lies, Elise. I have to have you. Please don't marry that big fry cook. Give *me* another chance!"

Elise panicked and kneed him in the face. His nose spewed blood. She ran when he cried out in pain and released her. "Get in the car!" she yelled to Mariel who was coming to pummel Derrick with her shoulder bag again. Mariel changed directions and ran around to her side of the car. Elise jumped behind the wheel of the Camry, closed and locked her door so that Derrick wouldn't be able to open it and get at her, and then reached over and unlocked Mariel's side.

Both women in the car now, Elise threw the car in Reverse, saw Derrick on his knees beside the car, so she knew she wouldn't run him over, and backed out of the parking lot, all the way out. She didn't stop and put the car in Drive until she hit the main drag. Then, she burned rubber.

"My God, he's totally off the deep end," Mariel said. Normally she would be making fun of Derrick, but this was scary stuff. He was seriously deranged. "We've got to call somebody tonight."

Elise was concerned that Derrick might be following them. "Keep an eye out, will you? He drives a black mid-size SUV, tinted windows."

"Where are you going? You can't drop me off at my place and take the car back to yours. I'm not letting you out of my sight until I know he's locked up."

"I'm going to the nearest police station," Elise told her, sounding calmer than she felt. This was awful. What had she ever done to Derrick to make him behave like this?

"He's mentally ill, Mariel. I guess he's not on his medication as he said he was."

"That's an understatement." Mariel yawned. "It's too late to be going through this. All I want to do is go home and go to bed, but first we've got to go press charges against a lunatic. What if they don't believe us? We have no proof that he accosted you."

"Oh, I think we have proof now," Elise said, looking in the rearview mirror.

A black SUV was right behind them, its bright lights on.

It was rapidly closing in on them. Elise sped up. The police station was only about half a mile down the road. And even if he tried something dangerous, like rear-ending them, there were other cars on the road, someone would be a witness to his recklessness. She hoped. Sometimes people didn't want to get involved when they witnessed crimes, especially when the perpetrator was a madman.

"Mariel, buckle up! What do you have, a death wish?"

In her excitement, Mariel had forgotten to fasten her seat belt. She did it now. Her hands trembled. "Elise, I'm so sorry I ever spoke to that fool at the Christmas party. I brought this down on you. Me and my pride. I just couldn't let well enough alone. I wanted to make him suffer, if only a little, for everything he did to you."

"Honey, will you calm down, and help me watch what he's doing? The police station is right up there on the left. If there's traffic coming from the opposite direction I'm going to have to wait for it before I turn into the parking lot."

"He must have guessed where you're headed," Mariel told her, looking behind them. "He's slowed down."

Elise slowed down to make her turn. There were three cars in the opposite lane, all close behind one another. She would have to wait for all three to pass before she could turn. Quickly, she executed the turn and was safely in the parking lot of the police station. Incredibly, the black SUV turned in right behind her.

She pulled in front of the well-lit building but did not put the car in Park. Her foot was on the brake pedal. "What is he thinking?" she wondered aloud.

"Is he thinking at all?" Mariel worried. "The fool followed you to the police. Maybe he has a gun. Maybe he's thinking at this point that he has nothing to lose.

Maybe he's going to shoot us if we try to get out of the car and run inside."

Elise was so tense, she was grasping the steering wheel in a steel vise. Her hands didn't shake only because she was holding on to the steering wheel too tightly. Her legs were trembling, though. Her insides quivered.

"Mariel, call 911 on your cell phone."

Mariel did what she'd been told. When a dispatcher answered, she said, "We're sitting in a silver Toyota Camry in front of the police station on Vallejo Street. Please, you've got to send someone outside to help us. There's a crazy man in a black SUV right behind us, and we're too scared to get out and run inside!"

"All right, Miss. Stay calm," said the female dispatcher. "I'm patching you in to the Vallejo Street operator."

A few seconds later, the Vallejo Street dispatcher came on the line. "Police department. How can I help you."

Mariel hurriedly told her what she'd already told the first dispatcher. "You can look out your window and see both cars parked at your front steps!"

"Hold, please," said the dispatcher.

"She's got me on Hold," Mariel told Elise.

Elise's eyes were trained on Derrick's SUV behind them. He had turned off his lights, and was idling. He had not moved forward or backward. She couldn't imagine what he hoped to accomplish by terrorizing her and Mariel like this, except to get arrested for his trouble. He definitely wasn't thinking straight. Of course, being on medication, he might get off by using the insanity defense after he killed them.

Well, she wasn't going out quietly. If she saw him getting out of his car with a gun, she was going to back over him and not stop until she felt the thump of the car running over his body. She could plead self-defense.

The dispatcher came back on the line. "Some officers are coming out to neutralize the situation. I want you to get down as low as you can in your car and wait until a police officer comes to get you. Do you understand?"

"Yes," Mariel replied.

"And I'm staying on the line, so don't hang up," the dispatcher further instructed.

"Okay, let me tell my cousin what you said." Mariel related the instructions to Elise.

"All right," said Elise. "I'll be cool."

They crouched down on the car seats as low as they could. Mariel was practically underneath the dashboard. Elise leaned across the front bucket seats, the divider pressed into her shoulder. Mariel grasped her hand tightly. "If we get out of this alive I'm going to find his momma and slap her. I thought she was supposed to get him some help."

"I'm sure she did her best. She always tried to steer him in the right direction. She even cut him off financially when he was in his first year of law school so that he'd learn to take care of himself."

"Yeah, and he got *you* to take care of him. You thought he'd listen to a woman who cut him off? He doesn't respect her opinion! He probably told her anything to placate her, then went on with his plans to get you back, the sicko!"

"Shh," said Elise. "Let's be quiet. We might be able to hear what's going on outside."

"I hate this," Mariel whispered. "I've got to pee."

Chapter 16

Derrick didn't know what to do next. He sat behind the wheel and watched Elise's car. His nose had stopped bleeding. He still felt some pain, but not much.

He had an overwhelming impulse to get out of the car and walk up to her door, pull her out of the Camry, and shake her until she went limp as a rag doll. What had possessed her to knee him in the face? He had not threatened her. He had not had a weapon of any kind. Why was she so frightened of him? She'd kneed him and run as if he were a serial killer with an ax.

Now, he supposed, she thought that pulling into the parking lot of a police station would make him go away. She'd probably phoned the police en route. He dealt with the police all the time. He'd visited this very precinct on several occasions and knew a handful of the officers assigned to this station on a first-name basis.

Let her think she was safe. He would wait here until the

officers came out to question him, and then he would dazzle
her with his legal mind. He'd have them arrest her for assault.
Where was the proof that he'd done anything to warrant her
attack on him? Her cousin would, of course, lie for her. But
the facts spoke for themselves. He had blood down the front
of his shirt. His nose was swelling as he patiently sat there. And
she didn't have a scratch on her. Who would the evidence
support?

He could say they attacked *him* in the parking lot of the bar.

"Sir! Please step out of the vehicle!"

The booming male voice, muffled because Derrick had his
windows up, nonetheless made him jump. He'd been so intent
on watching Elise's car, that he hadn't noticed the four police
officers approaching from behind.

He slowly opened the door and stepped down from the cab
of the SUV. He was wearing a white shirt, so he knew the
bloodstains were noticeable as he turned to face the officers,
three men and a woman.

He kept his hands at his side and moved away from the
open door of the car.

"Raise your hands, please."

He lifted his arms above his head.

"Okay, now, move farther away from the car, and lie facedown on the pavement."

"Officer…" he began, wanting to explain that this was a
misunderstanding, and he wasn't the bad guy here. But he
knew the routine, and followed instructions.

Two of the officers rushed forward. One to farther spread
his legs while he lay on the pavement, the other to cautiously
peer inside the SUV with his weapon drawn.

Seeing no one else inside the car, the second officer yelled,
"Just him, Sarge."

The man he'd called Sarge said, "Okay, Wilson, handcuff him, then get him on his feet."

Wilson none too gently cuffed him, then helped him to his feet. He noticed that the other two officers were helping Elise and Mariel out of the Camry. The women, fine actresses, were behaving as if they were distraught. Profusely thanking the officers for rescuing them from a fate worse than death, he guessed. He smiled.

The sergeant waited until the two women were escorted over to where the suspect stood handcuffed. He sighed. He was a man of average height with a broad chest, powerful thighs and a flat belly. His buzz-cut hair was iron-gray, and he didn't look like he took crap from anybody.

"Okay," he said, looking at the two women. "Who are you? And why was he following you?" He didn't sound at all convinced yet that what they'd said about being followed was true.

Elise spoke for both of them. "I'm Elise Gilbert and this is my cousin, Mariel Gilbert. We were leaving a party when he grabbed me in the parking lot. Mariel started hitting him in the head with her purse. He let go of me and said he just wanted to talk to me. You see, he's my ex-husband, and ever since he found out I was remarrying he's been following me, sending me things. I asked him to stop, but he wouldn't."

"What's your name, sir?" asked the sergeant.

"Derrick Scott."

"Mr. Scott, do you have any ID on you?"

"My wallet is in the back pocket of my jeans."

"Wilson, get it, and hand it to me."

Once the sergeant had the wallet, he opened it and perused Derrick's driver's license. He peered up at Derrick. "You're that hotshot lawyer who got Benton Wentworth cleared of molestation charges."

Derrick wasn't sure how to respond to that. He was fairly sure that bragging about it wouldn't be a good idea though. "Just defending my client, sir."

Sarge's lips compressed somewhat. Sometimes it was a struggle to remain unbiased when dealing with lawyers. He reminded himself to focus on the problem at hand, and not let his personal feelings inform his judgment.

"Is Ms. Gilbert your ex-wife?"

"Yes, she is."

"Why were you following her?"

"I wanted to ask her why she kneed me in the face, and took off as if I was going to throttle her. I didn't raise a hand to her."

"That's how you got the blood on your shirt? She kneed you?"

"Yes, sir."

"Is she a karate expert, Mr. Scott?"

"Not that I know of, sir."

"Then how did your nose get low enough for her to knee it? Were you, perhaps, holding her around her waist? Were you on your knees in front of her? How does a woman who can't be more than five-six or five-seven knee a man of your height in the nose?"

"I did put my arms around her legs, sir. Only to keep her there so I could talk to her. It was then that she kneed me and ran."

The sergeant regarded Elise. "To the best of your knowledge, is that what happened, Ms. Gilbert?"

"Yes, I kneed him, and we ran, Mariel and I. I drove to the nearest police station because he was following us and I didn't know what he would do next."

Sarge nodded. "I see. The other Miss Gilbert. Do you corroborate that what your cousin has said is true?"

"Yes, sir, I do!" Mariel spoke up.

The officer blew air between his lips. "Then, Mr. Scott, you're under arrest for accosting Ms. Gilbert. Shall we go inside and get the paperwork started? I'm sure you'd like to phone your lawyer."

"But, but…" Derrick cried. He didn't know where his legal mind had gone. While in his car he had been prepared to send those two wenches up the river. But once the sergeant had started interrogating him, he could not think of anything except to relate the events as they had happened. To his way of thinking, he had not done anything wrong.

"But I didn't touch her!" he finally got out.

"By your own admission, Mr. Scott, you said you held Miss Gilbert around her legs in order to prevent her from leaving so you could talk to her. You held her against her will, therefore you accosted her. Let's get this over with as soon as possible, shall we? The sun will be up before we're finished processing you and you get to see a jail cell."

He turned to Elise and Mariel. "Ladies, would you follow me, please?"

Elise and Mariel, both clutching their shoulder bags, were happy to.

Franklyn and Paulo arrived at the Vallejo Street station at around 4:00 a.m. Elise had phoned Franklyn to explain what had happened, and he phoned Paulo. He went and picked up Paulo because there was Mariel's Camry to consider. Paulo could drive her home, and he would take Elise home.

When he and Paulo walked into the big open room where cubicles made up individual offices, he looked around for Elise. His brows creased in irritation. All he wanted was five minutes alone with Derrick Scott.

Finally, he saw her and Mariel sitting in front of a large desk in a corner. A female officer was typing behind the desk. "There they are," he said to Paulo.

Paulo murmured something like, "I will kill him!" under his breath as he hurried to embrace Mariel who looked up and saw them when they were halfway there, and reached over to tap Elise on the shoulder.

Relief flooded Elise when her eyes met Franklyn's across the room. She was on her feet and in his embrace in a split second, and he held her so tightly she could barely breathe, but she didn't need to breathe. He was there!

"Are you all right?" he asked, looking her dear face over as if he could spot any minute changes that her experience had wrought.

"I'm a little shaken up, but I'm fine," she assured him.

To the side, Paulo was whispering endearments in Italian into Mariel's ear as he held her securely. She didn't understand half of what he was saying, but his voice and his presence soothed her. He kissed her face repeatedly.

"Where is he?" Franklyn asked menacingly.

"They took him in the back somewhere," Elise said. "I don't think we're going to see him anymore tonight. We were told we could leave after the officer is finished taking our statements."

"Okay, well, let's get that over with."

He escorted her back to the desk where the officer, a petite brunette, held up two pieces of paper. "If you would both sign these, you can go."

Elise and Mariel quickly read the statements, signed them, thanked the officer, and left with Franklyn and Paulo.

The couples said their good-nights and hurried to their cars.

In the Ford truck, Elise went into Franklyn's arms. "Just hold me for a minute longer."

"Baby, I don't know what I'd do if anything happened to you," Franklyn breathed, kissing her hair, her face, the side of her neck.

"I'm fine, I'm fine."

"You're not fine, you're trembling."

"Residual shock, I guess," she said softly. "He really scared me tonight. He was not behaving rationally. It was as if he couldn't think the way he used to. As if he was not grasping reality."

"After this, you can't rely on his mother to bring him under control. You've got to let the authorities handle it."

"I know," Elise said, resigned to the fact. The only reason she'd phoned Derrick's mother, Vivian, was because she respected her. She knew Vivian had been trying to reach Derrick for years. Vivian had also confided in her about Derrick's father and his mental illness. It seemed Derrick was following in his father's footsteps. Even though there was no love lost between her and Derrick, she did not wish upon him the fate his father had been handed.

In the end, Stephen Scott had committed suicide.

Franklyn kissed her forehead. "Fasten your seat belt. I'm taking you home and putting you to bed."

Derrick didn't enjoy his mother's visit the next day. She arrived impeccably dressed, smelling of expensive perfume and told him that she was getting ready to commit him for his own good. Not only had she threatened to send him to a loony bin, but she had intercepted his attorney and told him that if he got Derrick out on bail, she was going to see him disbarred, because her son needed professional psychiatric help and he wasn't going to get it unless he was forced to get it.

Cowed by her wealth and ultimately charmed by her love for her son, the attorney, who up until that moment had been a cutthroat snake in the grass, slunk away with his tail between his legs and an odd smile on his face.

Derrick was sorry he'd asked his attorney to phone her.

Ever efficient, she got him released into her custody and had two armed guards, really his cousins, RayRay and Leland, drive him to a minimum-security mental-health facility in Oakland. The doctor had ordered anti-psychotic drugs, administered intravenously, and for a full twenty-four hours he'd been floating. The second day, they started him on pills which he slipped underneath his tongue and pretended to swallow. Once he was alone, he flushed them.

By the sixth day, and he was certain it was the sixth day because he marked it off on the calendar they so generously provided him, he escaped by pretending to be asleep when the orderly, an overweight guy by the name of Timmy, brought him his dinner and he got the drop on him, threatened to skewer him with his dinner fork, and forced him to lie facedown on the lumpy bed while he stuffed napkins in his mouth and tied his hands behind his back with strips ripped from the bed sheet.

He then tied Timmy's legs together, took his keys and slipped out of the room.

After that it was a cinch leaving the facility because, as the sign said outside, it was a minimum-security mental-health facility. He only encountered one security guard on his way out and he gave him a hearty, "How ya doin'?"

To which the guard replied, "Fine, how're you?"

"Doin' better all the time," Derrick said jauntily. Then he

walked through the front entrance of the facility and breathed the fresh air of freedom.

He hoped Timmy wouldn't choke on those napkins he'd stuffed in his mouth before somebody found him.

The night before Franklyn and Elise's wedding, a few family and friends attended a rehearsal dinner at the Vineyard. Afterward, Franklyn drove Elise home. At the door of her apartment, she barred him from entering.

Franklyn laughed. "I can't come in to kiss you good-night?"

Elise smiled at him. She had already told him that she wasn't going to make love with him again until after they were married. He hadn't looked too pleased when she'd told him, and he didn't look pleased now.

She tiptoed and gently kissed him on the lips. "Tomorrow night, at the hotel in Maui, we will make love in our marriage bed, and it will be sweet. So sweet that this little period of abstinence will seem like nothing to you."

Franklyn smiled ruefully. "You're wrong. I regret every moment I can't spend with you."

"That's really good," Elise teased. "And normally my underwear would just fall off by itself when you say things like that to me. But not tonight."

Franklyn gave her a look of consternation. He looked so handsome in his dress shirt of royal-blue silk and black dress slacks that she wanted to invite him in and rip them off him. She wasn't particularly happy to forego a night of passionate sex, either. But she'd promised herself she would stick to the tradition, just for the fun of it.

"All right," he said at last. "One more kiss good-night."

Elise sighed with longing. "Okay." But, she thought desperately, nothing that's going to drive me crazy, please, baby. Don't you know I want you just as much as you want me? He did not get her telepathic plea, however, because when he bent his head and met her mouth it was obvious that this was going to be a kiss to write home about.

He did not immediately target her lips, but planted a warm kiss on that spot just below her bottom lip. She tilted her head back a tad, and that's when he took her lower lip between his and sucked it. Now he kissed her full on the lips, turning his head so that their noses did not collide. Meanwhile, he'd pulled her into his warm embrace and her chest met his hard pectorals. She could not help running her hand over his chest, over his stomach, around to his back, and soon their lower bodies were pressed together and she could feel his erection. Her nipples grew hard and her vaginal walls wetter than they already were. She wanted him so badly, she felt weak.

Franklyn slowly broke off the kiss, pulling away from her by degrees. She would think, okay, that's it, he's going to leave me now. But, no, he wasn't finished and she breathed easier knowing this feeling would last a little longer.

When he did release her, she was breathless and weak-kneed. Her lips looked a bit plumper, her eyes were dreamy, and her color high. Franklyn turned and walked into the door. He'd forgotten to open it.

He laughed shortly, placed his hand on the doorknob and turned to face her. "Are you sure?"

She sadly shook her head in the affirmative. "It's just one night."

He smiled at her, and left.

Elise stood with her back pressed to the locked door. "Another minute, and I would have caved in." She fanned her face with both hands and went to get ready for bed.

The phone rang as she was getting under the covers.

"Hello?"

"Are you alone?" asked Mariel tauntingly.

Elise laughed. "Yes, I am."

"Are you sure Franklyn's not under the covers right this minute thinking about doing wicked things to you?"

"Why, is that what you're up to?"

There was a pause and Paulo said, "Hi, Elise!"

"Hi, Paulo."

Mariel got back on the line. "I just wanted to say good-night, cuz. Tomorrow's your big day, and I'm so thrilled for you. Also, I expect you to bug me like this the night before my wedding."

"Don't worry, I will," Elise said. "Good night. And let that poor man get some rest."

"He can rest when he's old and gray. I'm going to keep him busy until then."

Laughing, Elise said, "'Night, girl."

"G'night!"

She thought she heard Mariel giggle delightedly before she hung up.

Elise snuggled deeper in bed, switched off the light and closed her eyes. Tomorrow night at this time, she would be lying in bed with Franklyn and they would be husband and wife. She already felt like his wife, but tomorrow it would be legal in the eyes of God *and* man. She smiled, recalling the first time she'd met him. He had looked at her with intense interest after he'd looked up from his work on the computer.

She had heard several rumors about him from friends in the food industry. One was that he was no-nonsense and ran a tight ship. The other was that he was devastatingly hand-some, but, sadly, apparently gay, even though he didn't display any effeminate characteristics. How had that ridiculous rumor gotten started? She had never found out.

They knew that he was over thirty and never married. So what? Of course, they didn't know the real reason he was still single, because Franklyn had never told anyone until he confessed it to her. She'd never told him about the gay rumors. Maybe she'd tell him someday when they were old and had about twenty grandkids. He'd get a big laugh out of it.

She'd known he wasn't gay five minutes after being in the same room with him.

No gay male had ever looked at her with such open lust before. Yes, she knew he was attracted to her, and still she took the job. She was attracted to him, too, and the only way to make certain she would be near him to see where the attraction would lead them was to become his employee.

Now, after over four years of constantly craving him, he was hers.

She was too excited to sleep.

She closed her eyes, anyway, and willed herself to sleep. She wanted to be a beautiful bride for Franklyn tomorrow at two o'clock.

Chapter 17

A nurse found Timmy when she went to Derrick's room to administer his nightly meds. Poor Timmy was a mental basket case but otherwise unharmed. Once the nurse got the wad of wet napkins out of his mouth, he was able to tell her what had happened.

She alerted her supervisor, who then called *her* supervisor and so on until finally someone rang Phillip Newsome, the owner of the facility. "No, don't phone his mother or the police just yet," he advised. "Make a thorough search of the building and the grounds. If we haven't located him by tomorrow morning, we'll phone his mother and the authorities then."

Saturday morning, Derrick emerged from his apartment after a good night's rest.

When he'd walked out of the facility last night, he had gotten a cab and had the driver take him to his apartment house in the Russian Hill area where he told the man to wait while he ran upstairs for his money. The driver had been reluctant, but what was he going to do, wrestle him to the ground and beat his fee out of him? Derrick found the extra key he kept in a crack in the terra-cotta planter adjacent to his apartment door, went inside, got money and paid the driver. He certainly didn't want the guy calling the police about an unpaid fare. If he were ever arrested again, he planned on making it for a felony, not a misdemeanor.

By 8:00 a.m. he was parked across the street from Elise's place in a rented Chevy.

He'd had no qualms about using his credit cards. In fact, he'd gone by his bank to withdraw three hundred dollars before coming here. He didn't care if the authorities traced him through his credit card purchases. He had only one thing left to do before he got on a plane to Acapulco, Mexico. The successful execution of that task depended on his paying close attention to Elise's movements today.

He bit into a chocolate-covered donut, chewed, swallowed and took a big gulp of black coffee. He was subsisting on sugar and caffeine, the drugs of choice of so many of his colleagues. He didn't give Crenshaw, Davis and Benson much consideration. He'd worked hard to make partner and they'd practically made him beg for the privilege. They wouldn't have any trouble replacing him. There were many hungry lawyers in California, about one for every five citizens, he guessed. They would, however, have trouble replacing the five-hundred-thousand dollars he'd embezzled.

It had been so easy to do. As the grunt in the office, he often worked later than anyone else. And Myron Green, who ran the accounting department, also worked late. He would stroll into old Myron's office when they were working late and strike up a conversation. Sometimes he would bring coffee. Myron loved a good latte. One night he slipped a colorless, tasteless sedative into Myron's coffee, and went back to his office. A few minutes later, he'd gone into Myron's office and found Myron asleep at his desk with the program on his computer still open. He gently moved Myron aside and studied the program at his leisure. A quick study, he'd soon learned how to transfer some of those columns of cash over to an anonymous account in Mexico that he'd set up.

He couldn't pull his trick too many times without getting caught. So far, he'd only been able to sock away a little over half a million. He'd hoped to be able to put Myron to sleep a few more times, but that wasn't to be. Because of Elise, he needed to disappear. Once his mother found out he'd flown the coop, she would have detectives on his case. He already had a date before the judge to answer to the charges Elise had filed against him. He didn't predict he'd get any jail time, but still, his career would be ruined once the firm found out about his obsessive behavior. They got nervous if you showed any signs of being mentally unbalanced. He might be a liability.

So, the five-hundred grand was going to help him start over in Mexico. He needed a vacation anyway. A lifelong vacation. And if his plans worked out, no one would be looking for him. Not his mother, not the police, nor the firm once they figured out that Myron hadn't had anything to do with the missing funds.

The beauty of his plan was, he got to ruin Elise's life at the same time as he started his life afresh! He loved it. He shoved more of the donut into his mouth and chewed thoughtfully.

* * *

Franklyn strode into the kitchen at the Vineyard. Today, none of his people were working here. Mariel, Laura and their crew were busy putting the final touches on the sit-down meal they would serve in the big dining room following the wedding ceremony. The dining room could accommodate three hundred people. The number of guests invited to their wedding was only one hundred and fifty. Besides the tables set up in the room, there was a dais, a dance floor and a bandstand. The ceremony itself would take place on the dance floor, after which the band would entertain the guests with a repertoire consisting of various types of music.

"Has anyone seen Elise?" Franklyn asked.

It was nearly one-thirty. Elise was supposed to have arrived by one-fifteen. She had planned to bring her wedding dress and put it on in the office. They were planning on going straight to the airport from the reception, so Franklyn had already put his suitcases in the office. Elise would be brought to the restaurant by a hired car. She would store her bags in the hired Lincoln Town Car and carry her dress bag with her wedding dress and a change of clothing with her into the restaurant.

"No, she hasn't been in here," Mariel said, concerned. She turned the water off at the double sink where she was rinsing out a huge stainless-steel bowl. "Maybe you ought to phone her. It's not like her to be late. There could be a problem with the limo service."

"Right," Franklyn said, and turned to leave. When he was through the swinging doors, he pulled out his cell phone and dialed Elise's cell phone number. She answered after the third ring.

"Hey, I'm in the car, on the way. The driver's new and he got a little lost."

Franklyn had been cool as ice up until his discovery that Elise was late. For some reason, he had thought Derrick Scott might have somehow gotten himself released from that mental-health hospital where his mother had told Elise he was enjoying an extended stay. He was relieved to find out Elise was late because of simple human error.

"What's your ETA?"

"I should be there by one forty-five," she said. "So, make yourself scarce. Go to the dining room, not your office. We're not supposed to see each other before the wedding."

Franklyn laughed. "What? No lovin' last night, and now I can't kiss you before the wedding?"

"Stop messin' with me, Franklyn, and do as I say!"

"We're not even married yet, and you're ordering me around."

Elise laughed. "I'm not playin' with you, boy. Don't let me see you when I get there."

"Yes, ma'am," Franklyn said. "I love you."

"I love you," Elise returned with a sigh of longing.

He closed the phone and went to the dining room where his parents, his brother and his date, his sister and her husband, and his grandmother and her date were among the guests.

Elise's parents, her sisters and their husbands and children were also near the front where his family was seated.

As soon as he walked through the door, Jason, his best man, called out, "Franklyn, it's about time. Where have you been? The reverend was getting nervous."

Franklyn joined Jason and the minister—a tall, white-haired African-American gentleman who reminded Franklyn of the late great Ossie Davis, on the dance floor.

"I wanted to make sure there have been no changes in the program since last night," Reverend Erving said. "You haven't decided to write your own vows?"

"No, Reverend," Franklyn said. "We want you to do it exactly as you did last night."

"Have you got the ring?"

Franklyn looked at Jason. He'd given Jason the ring a few minutes ago.

Jason feigned ignorance and desperately patted his pockets.

Seeing the panicked expression on Franklyn's face, he took pity on him and pulled the ring from his inside coat pocket. "Don't have a stroke, bro. I've got it."

"No jokes today, man," Franklyn warned. "I'm already keyed up."

"Elise isn't here yet?"

"The driver was late. She's on her way."

Jason gave his shoulder a reassuring squeeze. "Then calm down. Everything's going to be perfect."

A few minutes later, the Town Car pulled up to the Vineyard and Elise ran into the restaurant, her dress bag flying behind her. When she got to the office, she dialed her sister, Dasia's cell phone number.

Dasia answered immediately. Seeing Elise's name on the phone's display, she cried, "Elise! My goodness, we expected you to phone fifteen minutes ago! We're on the way."

Dasia hung up, and said to her mother and sister, "Let's go, Elise is in the office."

The three women hurried from the room. They had to help a bride get into her dress and do her hair and makeup in under fifteen minutes. A daunting mission for lesser mortals, but a piece of cake for the Gilbert women.

Elise had removed her street clothes by the time her mother and sisters arrived, and she met them at the door in her bra and panties. Nedra started tossing out orders.

"Elise, put on your hose, then sit down in this chair." She pulled Franklyn's desk chair around in front of the full-length mirror attached to the back of the door.

Elise hurried to get into her stockings that would be held up by garters.

"Dasia, you stand in front of Elise and apply her makeup while I put her hair up. Chassie, you get the dress out of the bag and fluff it out. Unbutton all the darned buttons down the back so Elise will be ready to step into it when we're done with her hair and makeup!"

The women worked as a team. Years of cooking together, sewing together and getting ready for church together had prepared them for this day.

Twenty minutes later, Elise stood before the mirror and smiled. Dasia's makeup had been applied with a delicate touch and she actually looked like a blushing bride, instead of Bridezilla. Her mother had arranged her long, curly hair into a sophisticated style that was sexy as well.

"Darling, you look beautiful," Nedra cried, her eyes watering. "Now, I've seen all three of my girls look like princesses on their wedding day!"

Elise had tears in her eyes as she regarded her mother and sisters. "I love you all so much. Thanks for being here for me. I couldn't have done it without you."

"Girl, go on out there and marry that big, handsome man," Dasia told her with aplomb. "We can cry later."

"Yeah," Chassie agreed. "You've already kept him waiting five minutes over time."

Elise hadn't realized it was so late. She hurried to the

door, the dress not getting in the way because it didn't have a train and its hem came above her ankles.

Her mother and sisters followed.

Payton was waiting at the entrance of the dining room for Elise to put in an appearance.

When she turned the corner, he stopped her in her tracks. Taking her by the shoulders, he peered into her face. "Slow down, daughter. He's still gonna be there when you get there."

Elise took a deep breath and smiled at her father.

"Let me savor this moment," he said. He paused for a full thirty seconds before continuing. "You are a formidable woman, Elise Gilbert. Don't you ever let anyone tell you otherwise. I wish for you true happiness and lots of time with Franklyn to enjoy it."

"Thanks, Daddy."

He kissed her forehead. "Now, let's go."

She took his arm and they slowly walked down the aisle. Behind them, Mariel with Paulo as her escort, followed. It was a very simple ceremony with Mariel acting as Elise's maid of honor and Jason acting as Franklyn's best man.

As Elise accompanied her father down the aisle, she smiled at the people she loved. Her mother and sisters with their husbands and children. Franklyn's parents with his grandmother and his sister and her husband, and Sara Minton who had come with Jason, though he had told them they weren't really dating each other. They were just friends.

Lettie and Kendrick Burrows and several other people she worked with here at the Vineyard smiled as she passed. Hilary and Jeremy blew her kisses. Bailey, sitting beside her husband, Garrison, gave her a thumbs-up. Tamryn was there with her husband, Jeff, along with a few others from the show, including Jake, looking dapper in a suit with his dreadlocks gleaming, accompanied by an equally attractive sister, also wearing dreadlocks, and Hank Zimmer, her director, with his wife, Jane.

She had vowed that she would not look at Franklyn right away as she and her father walked down the aisle because if she did, her eyes would have been riveted on him all the way and she would not have experienced the pleasure of seeing the faces and smiles of her friends and family. She had been right, because the moment she looked up and saw Franklyn's eyes on her, she was drawn to him and could not look away. He was so handsome in his dark-blue suit and white shirt by Sean John. Masculine and daring all at once.

He smiled and her heart flip-flopped. She smiled back, thinking that she couldn't wait to kiss him and feel that well-manicured moustache tickle her upper lip.

Why were his eyes moist?

Franklyn had to swallow hard when he spotted Elise. She had kept the dress a secret, saying it was bad luck for the groom to see the bride in her dress. For someone who regularly declared she wasn't superstitious she had a lot of things she thought were bad luck. He was glad, now, that he had gone along with her little idiosyncrasies. She literally took his breath away. He didn't think he'd ever seen her looking more beautiful with clothes on. He still preferred her naked. But this moment definitely would be etched in his memory forever. Her red-brown skin glowed. The dress, sleeveless and showing just enough cleavage, enhanced her naturally voluptuous curves. He looked down. She was wearing sandals. He loved it when she showed toe cleavage.

Her sexy hair was what he loved the most. It was up in a flirty style that he knew he was going to have fun playing in later. Underneath the refined lady walking toward him was his wild woman.

He thought about how long they had waited. He thought of all the times he'd watched her as they worked together in the kitchen. All the times he'd wondered what she did when she left work, and whom she was doing it with.

He felt like the luckiest man alive. It choked him up, this emotion. His eyes grew misty, but he fought the sudden urge to shed tears because once he got started he'd probably bawl all afternoon, and he didn't want that to be the primary image he took away from their wedding day.

So he smiled at her, and when she stepped onto the dance floor and took his hand, he bent his head and kissed her.

Elise saw that Franklyn was about to kiss her, and she knew that it was a wedding faux pas. You kissed the bride *after* the ceremony. But she thought, what the heck? We don't have to follow every tradition. I'm not superstitious!

They kissed deeply, and only came up for air when the guests burst into laughter.

Reverend Erving tapped Franklyn on the shoulder. "Son, you're supposed to kiss the bride *after* the ceremony."

Both the bride and the groom looked sheepish, and then the reverend commenced with the vows. After the vows, they kissed again, and the band promptly began to play "So Amazing" by Luther Vandross.

Following much pandemonium during which they were congratulated, some order was brought to the chaos when Mariel took the microphone from the band's lead singer and announced, "If you will return to your assigned tables, your meals will be served shortly."

The guests returned to their tables while the bride and groom and their families and closest friends posed for pictures on the dance floor. The photographer and his assistant were taking still photos and video images of the wedding party simultaneously.

Elise and Franklyn posed with his family. Then they posed with her family along with Mariel and Paulo. Later they combined the families and also had photos taken with friends like Hilary and Jeremy, Lettie and Kendrick, and Bailey and Garrison Hitchcock. Elise wanted a complete record of their special day.

Two hours later, the bride and groom sneaked off and went to the office to change into casual clothing for their ride to the airport. Alone in the office, Franklyn pulled Elise into his arms. They breathed a collective sigh. It had been a long day, or all of the excitement had made it seem so.

"Well, we did it," he said.

"Made an honest man out of you," Elise joked.

"Rescued me from a life of barhopping and one-night stands."

"No more of that for you. Just quiet nights at home with me and the six children."

Franklyn grinned. "I can't wait."

They kissed then, and quickly changed clothes whereupon they tried to steal away without their family and friends being the wiser, but when they reached the entrance to the restaurant, Jason was acting as a lookout and shouted, "Here they come!"

At least twenty guests rained birdseed on them as they sprinted to the car. The driver was already behind the wheel of the luxurious Town Car with tinted windows.

Franklyn opened the back door for Elise, and got in after her. There was plenty of room for them to stow their bags on the floor. Laughing, kissing, holding each other, they didn't even bother to say anything to the driver because he already had his instructions: Straight to San Francisco International Airport.

After a rather passionate kiss, Elise sat back on the seat and just breathed. She looked at her husband, who was looking at her with nothing but lust in his expression. She might have gone overboard last night when she'd made him go home. He was going to be doubly energetic when they got to their hotel room in Maui.

"You're going to make love to me until I faint from exhaustion, aren't you?"

"That's my plan," Franklyn confirmed. He ran his hand down her silken leg. She was wearing a short skirt with no hose underneath, and a dressy white blouse tucked into the waistband. Her long legs enticed him. The warmth of her skin, the shape of her thighs.

Elise placed a leg across his hard-muscled thigh. "No."

Franklyn's eyes raked over her mouth, then he raised his gaze to her eyes. "You don't even know what I'm thinking."

"You're thinking that if we're real quiet, we can make love in the back of this limo. It's going to take us a good half hour to get to the airport."

"Okay, so you *did* know what I was thinking."

She laughed softly and leaned over to gently kiss his mouth. "It's a short flight, sweetie. We'll be there before you know it."

She knocked on the tinted divider, trying to get the driver's attention. "Hey, Mike, how much longer before we get to the airport?"

The driver pulled back the divider only a couple of inches, then he locked it in place. Elise peered at him, or what she could see of his brown skin. Brown skin! The driver who had picked her up had been a white guy.

"What happened to the other driver?" she asked the new guy.

"Oh, I knocked him out," the driver commented nonchalantly.

Elise went tense with fear. "That's Derrick," she whispered to Franklyn.

"What!" Franklyn shouted, and began pounding on the divider. "What the hell are you doing here, Scott?"

Derrick laughed. "I'm driving you and your bride to your final destination. So, just relax and enjoy the ride."

"You're supposed to be locked up!" Elise cried.

"And you were supposed to love me instead of him. Get used to disappointment."

While Elise was screaming at Scott, Franklyn was looking around the back seat to see if there was anything he could use as a weapon. There was nothing in his bags, but maybe Elise had hairspray or some other propellant that they could distract Scott with long enough for him to hit him. Hit him hard enough so that he wouldn't be able to get up again.

"Your mother said you were being medicated and you wouldn't be a threat to anyone ever again."

"That's my mother, always trying to neuter me."

"She wanted to help you. You need help, Derrick. This isn't you. What do you want, to end up killing yourself like your father did?"

"I have no intentions of killing myself. You, on the other hand, I am going to enjoy getting rid of."

"Why? What did I ever do to you? What has Franklyn done to make you want him dead?"

Derrick couldn't think with her incessant talking. "Just shut up!" he yelled.

Elise sat back on the seat.

Franklyn pulled her close and whispered, "The doors aren't locked. When he stops at a light, you're going to get out and run."

"We're both going to get out and run," Elise corrected him.

"Yeah," Franklyn agreed.

They were too quiet for Derrick's comfort. "What's going on back there? Thinking of maybe jumping me, fry cook? You're big enough to do it. But I'd be careful if I were you, I have a little equalizer." He held up an automatic pistol so they could see it. "Bought it years ago for protection. The city's a dangerous place."

Franklyn saw an intersection up ahead. The light was green now, but they would never make it through unless Derrick tried to run it, and he wouldn't do that because he didn't want to attract attention to himself. "Keep him talking," he whispered to Elise.

"You don't have to go through with this, Derrick. You can pull over and get out and walk away from the car. If you do that, we won't report what you've done so far. But think about what you're doing. If you hurt either of us, you're never going to see the light of day again. You'll grow old in prison."

"Not if I don't get caught. Do you know how many people get away with murder every year, Elise? I do. Hundreds are tried and their lawyers make sure they don't spend a night in jail. I know. I defend them."

"I don't care about those people," Elise said, relentless. "You're talking about two human lives, Derrick. You've never killed before. What makes you think it will be so easy? It will haunt you for the rest of your life. It doesn't matter if you get away with it or not. My face will follow you for the rest of your life. I will haunt your dreams and your waking hours. I promise you that."

Derrick laughed. "You're good, Elise. And I feel you, really I do. Maybe I won't kill you. Maybe I'll kill the fry cook and make you watch so the image will stay with you for the rest of your life. Yeah, that's a plan!"

He had to slow down. A van in front of him was going under the speed limit. If it would just speed up, he could make the light and not get stuck at this intersection. Damn, he was going to have to stop. He reluctantly put his foot on the brakes.

Suddenly, Franklyn whispered harshly to Elise, "Now!" He didn't wait for her to react, he threw open her door and pushed her out of the car. Elise fell to the blacktop, skinning her knees and abrading the palms of her hands. She desperately looked up at Franklyn to see if he would be able to get out before Derrick sped away.

But Derrick was on to them and hit the accelerator, swerving around the slow-moving van and tearing out into the intersection in spite of the red light. Elise watched, horrified, as the back door that Franklyn had pushed her out of shut of its own accord as Derrick flew around a curve and disappeared.

She scrambled to her feet and started yelling at the top of her lungs, "Help! Somebody help me! Please!"

The heel of one of her sandals was broken. She ignored it. "Help! Somebody! Call the police! Please!"

Cars drove past her. Then, an elderly woman in a battered Buick stopped and yelled out of her window, "Get in, honey, I'll phone the police for you."

Elise said a silent prayer to the maker of the cell phone. Everybody used them these days, even little old ladies in beat-up Buicks.

A few miles away, Derrick was hitting the steering wheel

with the gun. "Damn it to hell! She wasn't supposed to get away."

"Don't worry about her, Scott," Franklyn said, his tone calm under the circumstances. "You've still got me."

Derrick put the gun back on the seat, and paid closer attention to his driving. It wouldn't do for him to get pulled over by a cop. A few more miles and he'd be at his destination. He took a deep breath and slowly released it. "Yeah, you're right. The fun ain't over yet."

Franklyn sat back on the seat, strangely at peace. Elise was no longer in danger. He had only himself to get out of this predicament if he were able to. If not, then he would try his best to take Scott with him. It wasn't a question of whether or not he would fight for his life. He would. The question was, would he win?

After crossing the Bay Bridge, Derrick sped on until he came to a secluded spot overlooking a bluff. The Pacific Ocean crashed below. He used to come here to think in his happier days. Sometimes he would contemplate life and wonder if his mother would miss him if he fell over the cliff. It was over fifty feet to the rocks below. Nobody could survive that fall. And a car, going over, would explode in a ball of fire.

He parked the limo several feet away from the edge. "Okay, we're going to get out of the car, slowly," he told Franklyn. "Don't try anything heroic. I'd have to shoot you and I really don't want to have to do that."

He got out first, quickly, and held the gun on Franklyn until he also got out of the car. Taking a leather jacket from across his free arm, he tossed it to Franklyn. "Put that on. It might be a little tight across the chest on you, but it'll do."

Franklyn put on the jacket.

Derrick inched back. "Now, get behind the wheel."

Franklyn paused. "Why would I do that?"

Derrick shot the ground next to Franklyn's feet. "Do it!"

Franklyn slid behind the wheel, but left one foot on the ground so that Derrick could not shut the door. He saw that Derrick had left the car in Neutral.

"You son of a bitch," Derrick yelled, impatient. He angrily drew back to hit Franklyn on the head with the butt of the gun, and Franklyn grabbed the hand in which he held the gun and twisted his wrist, breaking it. Derrick howled in pain and dropped the gun. Franklyn threw the car into Drive and hit the accelerator. Derrick, who was half way inside the car, tried to grab the steering wheel with his injured hand and was unable to. He fell sideways onto the front seat, the car lurched toward the cliff. Once the heavy front end tipped over the precipice, the rest of the car followed.

Two men screamed.

A jogger, standing a hundred feet away, saw the car go off the cliff and went to investigate. When he got to the cliff's edge, the car was on fire.

Nobody could have survived the impact.

Therefore, he was awestruck when he saw a lone man clinging to the rock face. He was even more shocked when the man began to climb it.

The jogger, having on him only a fanny pack with his house keys and a small bottle of water, could offer no assistance to the climber. He would have to simply stand there and watch him until he reached the point where he could reach down and offer him a hand up. It took the climber several minutes to get to that point.

The jogger lay flat on his belly and reached down to the climber. The guy grasped his hand and pulled himself up the rest of the way.

Once he was safe, the climber lay on his back and looked up at the heavens.

"Would you believe," he said between breaths, "that I just got married today?"

Dear Reader

I hope you enjoyed CONSTANT CRAVING. It was interesting doing research on the food industry and I hope I got it right. I'm sure I will be hearing from someone who actually works as a chef if I did *not* get it right!

I was at a book signing recently and someone walked up to me and asked me what kind of books I write. I could have said I write romance novels, but what I truly believe I write are feel-good books. Romances are supposed to end with a happily ever after. Readers expect that. But my goal is to make you feel good about yourself.

I've always thought a good book should do that.

Look for the final book in the Bryant Winery Trilogy, ONE FINE DAY, in June 2007.

Wishing you continued blessings,

Janice Sims

Post Office Box 811

Mascotte, Florida 34753-0811

Or go to www.JaniceSims.com

07/18/2021